SONG
OF
SAMPO
LAKE

OTHER BOOKS BY WILLIAM DURBIN

WINTERING

THE BROKEN BLADE

SONG
OF
SAMPO
LAKE

WILLIAM DURBIN

WENDY
LAMB
BOOKS

Published by
Wendy Lamb Books
an imprint of
Random House Children's Books
a division of Random House, Inc.
1540 Broadway
New York, New York 10036

Visit us on the Web! www.randomhouse.com/kids
Educators and librarians, for a variety of teaching tools, visit us at
www.randomhouse.com/teachers

Library of Congress Cataloging-in-Publication Data
Durbin, William.
Song of Sampo Lake / William Durbin.
p.   cm.
Summary: In 1900, as a family of Finnish immigrants begins farming on the
edge of a Minnesota lake, Matti works as a store clerk, teaches English, and
works on the homestead, striving to get out of his older brother's shadow
and earn their father's respect.
ISBN 0-385-32731-5 (trade)—ISBN 0-385-90055-4 (lib. binding)
[1. Frontier and pioneer life—Minnesota—Fiction. 2. Finnish
Americans—Fiction. 3. Family life—Minnesota—Fiction.
4. Immigrants—Fiction. 5. Minnesota—Fiction.] I. Title.
PZ7.D9323 So 2002
[Fic]—dc21   2001008617

The text of this book is set in 10.75-point Lacko-Regular.

Book design by Kenny Holcomb

Printed in the United States of America

October 2002

10 9 8 7 6 5 4 3 2 1

BVG

To Wendy,
who proves her <u>sisu</u> daily

Chapter 1

The Soudan Mine—Soudan, Minnesota
March 1900

Matti tried to pull back. Too late. The sledgehammer grazed the drill rod, and a spark flashed.

Father jerked his hand back from the end of the drill, barely avoiding the hammer. "Take it easy there, Matti. Keep your mind on your work."

"Sorry, I—"

"Just watch that hammer," Father said. His dark eyes shined in the candlelight as he turned the drill rod in the hole and leaned his face away from the end. "Ready?"

Matti nodded and took a deep breath. He was lucky that he hadn't broken Father's wrist. Matti hoisted his hammer waist high and swung again. He hit the drill square, cutting away a fraction of an inch of rock. The iron ore was so hard that it took an hour to bore a hole deep enough for a single stick of dynamite.

"That's it," Father said. "Show us your *sisu*." Though Matti was exhausted from his ten-hour shift, he smiled. *Sisu* was a Finnish word that meant strength, courage, and stubbornness all wrapped into one. It was Father's answer for every challenge in life.

"I wonder how Timo's doing," Father mused as Matti pounded on the drill. For the last few shifts Matti's older brother, Timo, had been working in a different part of the mine with Uncle Wilho. Though Father would never say it out loud, Matti knew he meant that if Timo were working with him the drilling would be going a lot faster. Matti couldn't help that Timo was bigger and stronger than he was. If the mine captain here in Minnesota knew Matti was only fifteen, he never would have hired him.

At eighteen Timo was grown up. A great talker like Father and an athlete, Timo had won many prizes at school back in Finland. Matti's little sisters Anna and Kari were twins whom everyone called "cute" and "darling." That left Matti stuck in between.

Matti focused his gray eyes on the end of the rod. The steel rang out a sharp note each time the hammer fell. Though he had been working in the iron mine all winter, Matti still couldn't get used to the smell of spent powder that always hung in the air. The taste burned in the back of his throat, and his head ached.

In the weak light of their candle, puffs of reddish gray dust trickled from the blast hole.

"Time to switch?" Father asked.

As the steel rang, Father recited his favorite lines from the *Kalevala*. In his school days Father had memorized long sections of the Finnish epic poem. Though Father had the broad shoulders and thick chest of a blacksmith and could swing an eight-pound hammer with one hand, he also had a voice with a mellow, musical lilt. Speaking to the rhythm of his hammer, Father told the tale of his favorite Finnish hero:

> *Then the aged Väinämöinen*
> *Spoke aloud his songs of magic*
> *And a flower-crowned birch grew upward,*
> *With its leaves all green and golden*
> *And its summit arched to heaven . . .*

As they worked, Father went on to tell of the quest for the Sampo, a magic mill that poured out equal portions of gold and grain and salt. He had shared this poem so many times that Matti knew the words by heart. Yet there was something in the ancient song that helped him forget the dust and the dark of the mine.

When it was Matti's turn to drive the steel again, he thought back to a story that Mother had read to the twins in Finland the Christmas before last. It was a new translation of a book about a tight-fisted Englishman who hated to spend even half a penny. He growled "Bah! Humbug" at everyone, and he loved darkness because it was cheap. The longer Matti worked underground, the more he thought that the mine owners had a lot in common with that old candle-saving skinflint Ebenezer Scrooge.

Matti listened to the drill echo in the red-shadowed cold. Each day Matti was more convinced that it had been a mistake to come to America. When his family left Kuopio, Finland, everyone believed that the trip would be the answer to their prayers. They'd heard that America was a grand and golden place, filled with vast tracts of untilled land waiting to be farmed. Matti never would have imagined himself working in the bone-chilling night of a mine. Though Father's wages as a tenant farmer back in Finland had been low, at least he and Matti and Timo had worked under the freedom of the open sky.

Underground there was only a single season of dark and dust and cold. During the deep winter Matti could go a whole week without ever seeing the sun. He rode the mine cage into the bowels of the earth before dawn, and he didn't come up until after sunset. After spending his days drilling in red dust and candle smoke, he walked home under a sky lit by the flickering bits of blue-white stars. With every step he wished they had never left home.

Matti would never forget the day his father decided to move to America. They had just finished delivering the landlord's share of their potato crop on the afternoon that Uncle Wilho's letter arrived from Minnesota. At first Father read silently. Then his brown eyes flashed. "One hundred sixty acres are free to anyone willing to start a homestead. Just think! A whole quarter section, while we're struggling to survive on twelve rented acres!" He waved his arms as he always did when he got excited. "Wilho says that if I go to Minnesota first and work with him in the mine I can save enough money to send for the rest of the family."

"I'll not be made an America Widow, Leo Ojala," Mother said. "America Widow" was the name given to Finnish women who were waiting for their husbands to mail them steamship passage. One woman in their village had been waiting three years for word from her husband.

"But what if that pig Bobrikov drafts Timo into the Russian army while we're sitting on our hands?" Father said.

4

Bobrikov was the governor general of Finland who had been appointed by the Russian czar, Nicholas II. Though many people in Kuopio tolerated Russia's influence over their country, Father was convinced that young men would soon be shipped off to fight in foreign wars. "Give them enough time," he said, "and we'll all be speaking Russian."

Mother shook her head. "As much as I'd like my own farm, I don't care if Nikolai Bobrikov drafts us all into the army and declares Russian the official language of the Christian world. If this family moves we are moving as one."

Now, in the mine, the steady rhythm of Matti's hammer reminded him of the engine that had pushed their ship across the ocean. Most of the passengers were young men. To them the voyage was a week-long party, and they danced to an accordion and sang and gambled. Timo and Father joined in the fun, but Matti decided to hold his celebrating for their journey's end.

The ship reached New York harbor on a gray morning. Matti stood on the deck with the other passengers and searched the horizon for the golden shores of America they'd all been praising in their songs. Suddenly the fog lifted in a breeze, and the Statue of Liberty rose like a sea-stained goddess. Everyone pointed, waved, and hugged one another. A hundred fathers lifted their children high and called out in a dozen languages, "There it is, my son, my daughter, my child." Father balanced the twins on his shoulders and shouted, "That is a sight you must never forget, Timo." Matti kept his eyes fixed on the statue, but he thought, Why couldn't Father call my name for once? Would it cost so much to say, "What do you think of America, Matti?"

"Matti . . ." Now, in the mine, it took Matti a moment to realize that Father was talking to him. "Matti, it's time to charge the blast holes."

"Sorry." Matti's fingers were stiff as he set down the

drill rod and carried over the dynamite. "Should I check with the shift boss?"

Father nodded. He picked up the sack of blasting caps and the roll of fuse that he stored away from the dynamite for safety's sake. Then he opened his jackknife. "I'll trim the fuses while you're gone." Since Father didn't speak English, it was Matti's job to let the foreman know that they were ready to blast the ore loose. Before Matti started down the drift with his candle set in the wire rim of his helmet, he lit a second one for Father. As he walked between the tram rails he heard a mule bray.

The Soudan mine was deep and cold. Matti licked his lips and tasted salt, for they were working in the depths of an ancient seabed. The salty taste reminded Matti of the time he had traveled by train to the coast of Finland as a small boy. The Savo railroad had just opened, and Aunt Hilda and Uncle Wilho had come with his family. One afternoon as they walked along the beach, Wilho told him, "A boy like you would be perfect shark bait. You'd be nothing more than a biscuit to a big one." Aunt Hilda said, "Stop," but Wilho clapped his hands together to show an imaginary shark's mouth. "One bite is all it would take," he said, his white hair blowing back in the wind and his eyes alive with mischief.

Matti said, "And you'd better watch out for the whales, Uncle. They love to swallow storytellers."

As hard as the work was in the mine, at least Matti had Uncle Wilho nearby to cheer him up. Whether they were riding down the shaft in the cage, working as partners on the same contract, or cleaning up in the washhouse known as the dry, Wilho always livened things up. Most of the miners, like Matti's father, stuck close to their own national group, but Wilho loved to swap lunch pails and trade stories with the other men. "If the mules down here can understand Slovenian and Swedish and English," he said, "I surely can learn a few words from the other fellows." Wilho embraced American ways; he had even changed the spelling of his name from the Finnish Vilho to Wilho.

Matti got the all-clear from the foreman and walked back to Father. Dynamite made Matti nervous. He had heard too many stories of a "hot" fuse setting off a premature blast or a man's bootlace catching on a rail and tripping him as he headed for safety. Everyone's worst fear, other than a cave-in, was an accidental explosion. One mistake could be fatal.

After Father touched off his fuses, he and Matti hurried back to the main shaft for shelter. They crouched and listened. The first deafening crack of dynamite brought a rush of air. The rock underfoot trembled as the charges fired in perfect sequence. Father and Matti both counted on their fingers to make sure each stick exploded. Their candles flickered, and Matti coughed in the thick red dust cloud that rolled out of the drift. "The next crew should have easy loading now," Father said.

Matti and Father rode to the surface with a half dozen other miners. When the cage clattered to a stop, Uncle Wilho was waiting under the headframe. "Hey there, *Kapteeni*," Wilho called. Matti waved. Wilho called him *Kapteeni*, Finnish for captain, because when Matti was little, Wilho had carved him a small boat that he loved to sail on a pond near his house in Kuopio.

"Where's Timo?" Father asked.

"He went on ahead to the dry," Wilho said. "Time for a little cleanup, eh, fellows?" Wilho took off his helmet as they walked. Steam rose from his white head, and he wiped his ore-stained cheeks with the back of his hand. Like Matti, Wilho was slender with light blond hair and so tall that his friends called him the stork. When strangers noticed Matti's and Wilho's lanky frames and dimpled smiles, they sometimes mistook the two of them for father and son.

After the men stepped inside and took off their mining clothes, they washed at a long sink. Wilho whistled the whole time he lathered up his arms and chest, but Father grumbled, "This is a poor excuse for a bath."

"Get ready for the sauna lecture," Timo said.

Father ignored him. "When I get my homestead the first thing I'll build is a sauna, so I can take a proper bath."

"Even before you plant your potatoes?" Wilho splashed water on his face.

"My potato patch will have to wait," Father said.

Matti and Timo both grinned. Father believed that the heat of a sauna could mend both body and spirit, and his favorite saying was "If a sick person can't be cured by tar, whiskey, or sauna, then they will die."

The late-winter sun was low in the sky as they descended the long wooden steps that led from the mine to the town of Soudan. Anna and Kari ran up the street to greet them. They were skinny little blue-eyed blondes with an overload of energy and very different personalities. Anna tended to be careful like Mother, while Kari followed Father's lead. Uncle Wilho always warned her: "Look before you leap, little lady," but it did no good. From the time she was a toddler, Kari had tested hot stove lids with her fingers and splashed through puddles in her Sunday dress.

"How's my naughty little niece?" Wilho said as Kari held out her hand to carry his lunch pail. Anna took Father's.

"I'm not naughty," Kari said.

"Then how did you get that frosting on your cheek?"

"He caught you." Anna laughed along with Matti and Timo. "She snitched some of Aunt Hilda's cake."

"I think we can keep it a secret"—Wilho knelt down to wipe Kari's cheek with his handkerchief—"as long as you've saved a piece for me."

"So how are your English lessons going?" Matti asked the girls, practicing his own English as he carefully pronounced each word.

But before the girls could reply, Father said, "Talk so a man can understand you."

"There're no Finn bosses in that mine for good reason." Wilho pointed his finger back up the hill. "If a man wants to fit in he's got to learn how to do things the American way."

"The only place I want to be boss is on my own farm," Father said. "And as soon as I save up enough money to homestead I'll be done with that mine and its American ways for good. I'll not give up talking Finn for no man."

Father turned to Timo. "How did you do today?"

While Father and Timo talked, Matti looked out on the town of Soudan. The mining company had forbidden businesses here, out of fear that too many saloons would open, so all the stores and shops were in nearby Tower. Soudan was known as the city of houses. Except for a handful of spacious homes that were reserved for the foremen and timekeepers, the miners' houses were gray boxes scattered across a treeless hillside.

When Uncle Wilho had first written a letter about his life in America, Matti imagined a village like Kuopio with sturdy timber homes set above a blue lake. But Soudan had been built without a plan. The houses in the mining location were propped on wooden posts that tilted and heaved when the frost left the ground. Most were owned by the mine and rented to the workers. Even if Uncle Wilho piled hay around the outside of his home to keep out the cold during the winter, once spring came the floors bulged up in the middle and the doors and windows jammed. To add to the ramshackle mood, cows and horses wandered the streets, pigpens crowded the backyards, and garbage was piled high in the alleys.

"Welcome to America's golden shores," Matti whispered to himself as his ore-stained boots crunched on the frozen wooden sidewalk.

"What's that?" Father said, too busy listening to Timo to hear Matti.

"He's just thinking out loud," Wilho said, putting his arm around Matti's shoulders. "If we can hang on just a little longer, we'll be on our homesteads before you know it."

Chapter 2

For supper Aunt Hilda prepared Matti and Wilho's favorite meal, *kalakukko*, a special rye-crust pie filled with pork and fish. Mother tended to serve simple dinners of soup and bread, but Aunt Hilda loved to cook fancy meals. Mother and Hilda were identical twins like Matti's sisters. They were both slender with fair hair and blue eyes, but Mother was shy and deliberate, while Hilda was an outgoing amateur opera singer and actress.

"Cut me a piece of pie quick, Hildy," Wilho said as the family took their seats around the table, "before that Matti gets his hands into it." Matti laughed.

"Hush and be nice." Aunt Hilda smiled.

While Anna and Kari were still saying grace, Wilho took his fork and pretended to reach for the pie.

"Wilho!" Hilda said. "Set a good example for the youngsters." Anna and Kari giggled.

As Mother poured the coffee, Timo asked Father, "Do you think I should take that job on the raise crew?"

"Does the raise crew lift heavy things?" Kari asked.

"No," Timo said. "They cut chutes straight up through solid rock. The foreman says he needs big strong fellows. That's why he asked me." Timo held up his arm and flexed it. Show-off, Matti thought. Timo was tall like Uncle Wilho, and bull-strong and stubborn like Father.

"Isn't that dangerous?" Mother asked.

"You can't beat the wages," Timo said. "We'd be able to put more money toward our homestead."

Matti wondered if Timo should tell Mother the truth. Though the raise crew was paid well, the job was so dangerous that the bosses had trouble convincing men to sign on. The worst part was climbing up the ladders in the dust and dark after a blast, not knowing if all the rocks had been dislodged.

"If we could get out of that mine sooner, it might be worth it," Father said.

"I'd be willing to work with him at first," Wilho offered, "to show him the ropes."

"But you haven't been on that crew for a whole year," Hilda said.

"If they want strong fellows," Wilho said, flexing his skinny biceps and making the girls giggle, "I'm the man for the job."

As winter drew on, it seemed as if Matti had barely washed off the red iron dust from one shift when it was time to go underground again. Matti missed Kuopio more every day. This time of year back home a skating rink was cleared on a bay of Lake Kallavesi. Music played from a bandstand, and Matti and his good friends Paavo and Juha skated by moonlight or by torchlight. A bonfire was lit for warming chilled feet. Sleigh bells echoed up and down the shore. At least now Matti could look forward to the end of his days in the mine. Wilho and Timo had been working on the raise crew for a month. Their increased salaries meant that both families would be homesteading by summer.

At dinner one night Wilho said, "It's finally going to happen, isn't it?" He gave Hilda a hug.

"Wilho's been ready for a year," Hilda said. "He teases me about not wanting to leave my house behind to go and live in the woods. Last spring I said, 'Let's wait till summer.' Yet when summer arrived, I decided that we needed to save up for one more winter."

Though Wilho waited quietly for the day when he would have his farm, on each shift Father told Matti how he would build his sauna, plow his own patch of dirt, and be free of greedy landlords and Russian rulers. As he swung his hammer, Father said, "Take that, Mr. Bobrikov," and "Take that, Mr. Czar."

In the middle of a dull morning, Father waved for Matti to stop working. "Listen."

"I don't hear anything."

"That's what I mean."

The power drills in the newer workings near Timo and Wilho's crew had gone silent. Just then they heard a shout.

"Timo," Father breathed, grabbing the candle from the wall and starting down the drift. Matti jogged after Father and clambered up a manway ladder.

The site of the rockfall was dust and confusion. A dozen miners shouted in Finnish and Slovenian and English. Father yelled, "Timo!"

"Over here," Timo called. His next words turned Matti's heart cold: "It's Wilho."

Through the settling dust Matti saw Timo kneeling with men scrambling to uncover Wilho's legs. Wilho moaned weakly as Father and Matti helped toss the smaller rocks aside. Father whispered, "Good Lord."

A three-foot-long slab of rock angled across Wilho's back. A man wedged a lining bar under one end of the slab and pried, but Wilho let out a terrible groan.

"No, no," Father cried out in Finnish, "if you lift one side, it presses down the other."

Father motioned with his hand to show how the rock was tipping. Matti did his best to translate Father's warning into English. Father showed the other men how to lift straight up as Matti translated. Father said, "*Yksi, kaksi, kolme,*" and Matti repeated, "One, two, three."

The miners heaved with all their strength. Matti's arms trembled as the edge of the slab cut into his fingers, but he managed to help lift the rock clear.

Father and Timo eased Wilho onto his back. The brim of his helmet was crumpled, and a thin trickle of blood ran from the corner of his mouth.

Chapter 3

It was the day of Wilho's funeral.

Matti felt numb. Since Wilho's accident, Matti had been wishing he could turn back time and wake up on a still morning in Finland. If only Aunt Hilda and Uncle Wilho were living next door like they used to. If only he could sit down at his grandmother's long, dark table and taste her fresh *viili,* yogurt. If only he could look out her window on the pine-covered hillside of Puijo and its tower. If only he could see the blue waterway of Kallavesi, the granite church, and the shining new town hall.

The bitter weather and the bright light of Soudan made things even more unreal. It was cold enough in Minnesota to freeze spit in midair, yet Matti was continually amazed at the light. Winters in Finland were one long gray twilight, but here the midday air was bright and blue. The sun sparkled off the snowbanks and the windows, and the wind whirled up rainbows of snowflakes.

But what good was sunshine when Wilho was dead? When Matti spent all his waking hours underground? Matti's shift at the mine the day after Wilho's death left him shaking inside. He didn't want to go back, but it was keep working or starve.

At breakfast that day Mother urged everyone to quit. "Isn't losing Wilho enough?" she pleaded.

"You know there're no other jobs, Helmi," Father said.

"I'd rather have my boys begging in the streets than dead."

"I'm sorry," was all Father said as he picked up his lunch pail and led Matti and Timo out the door.

Matti sometimes wondered how Mother and Father had ever decided to get married when they were such opposites. This morning he had secretly wished that Mother could convince Father to stay home.

When they climbed into the miners' cage, every creak of the machinery made Matti hold his breath. A bell sounded and the cage dropped down. The cold smell of rusting steel and cable grease blew in with the wind that rushed through the open door. The light of a candle in an upper drift blurred past. If a cable snapped they would plunge a thousand feet, a more merciful end than Wilho had suffered.

The bell rang a second time, and the cage stopped. Matti's legs felt wobbly. As the miners started down the drift toward their work sites, a mule snorted on the tracks behind them. Matti was so startled that he dropped his lunch pail. Timo started to tease him, then stopped and touched Matti's shoulder. "Take care."

The dim light recalled the frost-rimmed reflections that had glowed in the train windows on the first evening they arrived in Soudan. The snowbanks were piled so high on both sides of the tracks that it seemed as if they had ridden past America and gone all the way to Lapland.

As much as Matti missed Uncle Wilho, he worried more about Aunt Hilda. She blamed herself for Wilho's accident instead of pointing to the unsafe conditions in the mine. "We had plenty saved for our homestead," she said over and over, "but it was never enough for me."

"Hildy," Mother said, "it wasn't your fault."

"No, it's true."

"Accidents just happen."

"I was greedy, Helmi," she said. "I was so afraid we'd have to do without. I might just as well have dropped those rocks on top of poor Wilho myself."

Matti had never seen Mother fail to calm his aunt. He could tell that it hurt Mother when Hilda refused to listen.

By the time of the funeral it had "warmed up" to fifteen below zero. The church bell tolled as a hearse pulled by two black horses carried Wilho's coffin from the house to the Finnish Lutheran church. Since Matti was a pallbearer, the undertaker had issued him a pair of black gloves and a mourner's scarf. Aunt Hilda wore a black dress and veil. Wilho's words, *We'll be there before you know it,* echoed in Matti's head. Who would have thought that Wilho's "there" would be a plain wooden coffin in a cold wooden church?

Through the service Matti studied the nickel plate on Wilho's coffin that read "At Rest." Between the hymns and prayers Matti listened to the mine at work: The engine house reeled in cable as the ore was lifted, the crusher rumbled and clanged, and the steam shovel dumped ore on the stockpile.

As the minister read a Bible verse, Matti stared at Wilho's waxen face, which was marred by only the smallest of bruises. Suddenly his uncle's white hair began to tremble. For a moment Matti thought his eyes were playing tricks on him. Then he saw Wilho's folded hands were moving. Was Wilho about to pull off his all-time greatest joke by sitting up in his coffin and saying, "How's that for a fine trick, eh, Matti?"

Matti was ready to shout when he noticed that the windows and the floor were shaking, too. They had blasted up at the mine. Though it lasted only a few seconds, everyone in the church felt the vibration. The minister paused to cough and wipe his brow. Aunt Hilda turned ghost white. Timo shut his eyes and drew a deep breath.

As the congregation tilted their heads to look up the hill, Matti was furious. Couldn't United States Steel stop blasting their precious ore long enough to let a funeral happen in peace? No! Never!

The next morning Matti was glad to see that Aunt Hilda finally seemed more like herself. "How's my Matti?" she said when he walked into the kitchen and gave her a hug. She set down the coffeepot. "I've decided to move back to Finland."

The whole family sat silent.

Then Mother said, "It's too soon, Hildy. You should think it over. At least wait until—"

"My mind is made up. The insurance payment from the mine along with our savings will leave me more than enough to be done with this godforsaken town forever."

Matti sank into a chair and stared at his aunt. Not only had he lost Wilho, but now Hilda also. His duty was to help his family with their homestead dreams, yet one part of him wished that he could get on a ship with Hilda and never come back.

Chapter 4

A month later Matti was walking up the street when he heard a scream coming from Aunt Hilda's back door: "Go away! Go away!"

Matti ran behind the house to find a horse standing with his head over the kitchen table, switching his tail back and forth. Kari yelled, "Go away!" while Anna waved a dish towel in the horse's face and squealed, "Shoo, horse. Shoo."

Just as Matti was about to grab the horse by the mane, Hilda stepped through the opposite doorway and burst out laughing.

"I'm sorry, Aunt Hilda," Anna said. "We opened the door and that big horse just shoved his nose in behind us, and—"

"It's all right, girls. When the bugs get bad, these poor animals try to find shelter wherever they can."

Matti laughed, too, mostly because he was so glad to see Aunt Hilda smiling for a change. Hilda continued to laugh as Matti pushed the kitchen table to one side and struggled to turn the horse around. The animal wanted to go anywhere but out the door. The girls looked ready to cry.

"It's not your fault." Hilda gave them a hug.

Matti slapped the horse on the rump and sent it scampering. There was a pasture at the edge of town for livestock, but a few stray animals were always wandering around town. Matti couldn't blame the horse for trying to hide. The bugs had been terrible since the first rains, when the weather had turned from winter to summer with no pause for spring.

"I certainly hope the men come to shovel up that mess soon," Hilda said, wrinkling her nose at the smell from the alley. "You'd think they would clean up the garbage more than once a year."

Matti nodded. Only a week ago the snow had vanished. The roads became mudholes and a stench rose from the outhouses and alleys, where slop pails had been dumped all winter. Flies swarmed and clouds of mosquitoes bred in the stagnant puddles that stood all over town.

After the excitement of the horse was over, Aunt Hilda and the girls went outside to work in the yard. Matti walked upstairs to his family's attic bedroom and found Mother staring into her trunk, unaware of the recent commotion. The hand-carved trunk had been a wedding gift from her grandfather.

Mother was touching the hem of her favorite blue dress. When she saw Matti, she quickly dabbed at the corner of her eye with a hanky. Though Father often got misty-eyed, Mother rarely cried. "You're home already," she said. Grandmother's ruby brooch was in her hand. "I was going through some of my things." She wrapped the brooch in a cloth and slipped it back into the trunk.

Mother's other prized possession lay before her: the bellpull from her father's home. A porcelain bell painted with gilt and delicate blue flowers was tied to a green velvet rope. This bell had hung in a corner of her home when she was a young girl. One pull on the velvet cord would call a servant.

When Matti was small, he often asked Mother why she didn't have servants anymore. She avoided his question, but as Matti got older he eventually learned why. Mother had grown up in the coastal city of Rauma. Her father was a successful lace merchant. But after the death of his wife, he turned to gambling and drinking. Mother's life of silk dresses and silver tea services faded.

"Please don't tell your father that you've seen me like this," Mother said as she gave Matti a hug. "I never expected all this after we'd had such great hopes."

"I know," Matti said.

Wilho's death was difficult for Mother. She missed him keenly, and had to comfort Hilda while also dealing with Timo. On the Saturday after the funeral, Timo stopped at a saloon and never came home for supper. Mother was uneasy, but Father insisted that "a little socializing" would do him good.

Later that night Matti woke to the sound of Mother crying in the kitchen. "How could you drink?" she kept saying to Timo, slumped in a chair. "After what your grandfather did to Hildy and me?"

From that night on Timo spent most of his free time visiting the bars. If Mother tried to talk with Timo about it, Father said, "Let the boy be."

Mother joined the local temperance society, the *Pohjan Leimu* or Northern Light. She also turned to her faith, and the teachings of a man named Lars Laestadius. Though Father teased her about Laestadians being so strict that they were "opposed to smiling," Mother shared their belief that drinking and gambling were evil, and that dressing in bright colors and looking into mirrors showed a vanity that displeased God. That was hard on Kari and Anna, who loved to tie pretty ribbons in their hair.

One evening Mother took Matti and Timo and the girls to see a traveling Finnish preacher who was speaking at the hall in Tower, a mile west of Soudan. The preacher had a deep, thundering voice, and he wore a plain suit.

Mother nodded politely through the whole service, and when the time came to take up a collection, she pulled out her purse and handed Anna and Kari each a coin. Timo, who was sitting next to Matti, reached into his pocket as if he were going to give some money, but he only jingled his coins instead. "Just checking to see if I have enough to wet my whistle." He winked at Matti. "All this preaching has given me a powerful thirst." Then before the preacher had even begun his final prayer, he said, "Give Mother my best," and slipped out the side aisle.

Everyone in the family dealt with Wilho's death in their own way. While Mother prayed and Timo drank, Anna and Kari were full of questions. "Why do people have to die?" the twins asked. "Will we die soon?"

Mother answered every question the same way: "It is God's will."

Father tried to cheer them up with his teasing and storytelling. He told them how the world was a golden egg at the beginning of time, how an eagle brought the gift of fire to the world, and how a hero named Lempi wore out his skis chasing down the magical elk of Hiisi. They enjoyed the stories, but Matti could see that the girls had a hurt that needed mending.

As soon as the girls were alone with Matti, they asked, "Why did Wilho have to die?"

Matti wanted to tell them that God had made a terrible mistake in taking Uncle Wilho, but he could only say, "It's a puzzle I can't understand."

Matti thought of the many times he and his uncle had gone fishing on Lake Kallavesi back home. When the fish weren't biting, Wilho would lean against a tree and laugh at Father, who paced up and down the path and rebaited his hook every few minutes. "Relax, Leo," he'd say. "They call it fishing, not catching. The fun is in the waiting."

Lately Matti had trouble with waiting, too. Each day he felt their dream of owning a homestead drifting farther away. The more time Matti spent surrounded by the engine smoke and steam whistles and piles of cold, red rock, the more he felt that he would never escape the mine.

Shortly after May Day, or *Vappu* in Finland, the men had just come home after the midnight shift. Father and Timo had finished their coffee and were heading upstairs to bed when Mother took Matti aside.

Lowering her voice, she asked, "How would you like to help me with a little project in the morning?"

"What sort of project?" he asked.

She winked and motioned for Matti to take a seat. "It will be our secret."

Chapter 5

The next morning, Matti felt as if he had barely fallen asleep when Mother tapped his shoulder. "Are you ready for our adventure?" she whispered. Her eyes were bright. "See you downstairs." She tiptoed away.

Matti tossed his quilt aside and dressed as quietly as he could. The girls had already left for school, and Timo and Father were snoring on their straw ticks spread across the attic floor.

After a cold breakfast, Mother and Matti stepped out the back door. Up the hill the main engine house sent plumes of smoke skyward. A steam shovel near the trestle dumped ore onto the stockpile, raising a cloud of fine, red dust. Matti shuddered. Every time he heard the clatter of rock on rock, it reminded him of Wilho's accident.

"I'm glad we're getting an early start," Mother said.

Matti nodded, half asleep. He was amazed at her. Normally Mother was so cautious that Father teased her about needing to have a dollar in her pocket when she was only shopping for a dime's worth of groceries. "So where are we going?" Matti asked.

"Winston City," Mother said.

Aunt Hilda often talked about Winston City. The town was built in 1866, a wild year when gold was discovered near Lake Vermilion. But the gold rush turned from boom to bust the following year, and the prospectors left as fast as they had come.

Their walk took them down Tower's board sidewalks, past two dozen sleepy saloons, and out into the countryside. The day was hot and so sunny that Matti squinted in the harsh light. He tried to hold his breath whenever a horse or wagon passed, but there was no avoiding the dust. By the time they reached the abandoned town site, Matti's hair felt gritty, and his lips were cracked and dry.

At Winston City the only hints of the original town were a dozen collapsed tar-paper shacks, some rusting machinery, and a few piles of broken bottles and rotting timbers. South of the town site stood a broken-down saloon called Sally's. A tattered canvas awning stretched across the front. Mother clicked her tongue in disgust at a disheveled lumberjack snoring on the porch. A sleeping dog raised one eyebrow.

The building on the opposite side of the road had a long sign hanging from the eaves that read WINSTON'S TRADING POST AND EMPORIUM. The oldest part of the store was built of logs, but the next two sections were sided with rough-sawn boards. Each addition was taller than the one before it, making the building look like a half-opened telescope. The far part had a LIVERY STABLE sign. A low porch ran the entire length of the building.

Matti was amazed at all the supplies inside. Copper kettles, cast-iron pans, logging chains, ropes, and leg-hold traps hung from log beams. The shelves in the front of the store displayed work clothes, boots, and tools, while the racks in the rear were stocked with food. Mingled with the scents of candy and spices were the odors of freshly tanned leather, last fall's potatoes, and a pickle barrel.

Mother walked toward the main counter. A short, wiry man stood behind a glass case that housed ammunition, hunting knives, chewing tobacco, and cigars. The wall behind the counter was papered from top to bottom with embossed stock certificates that read MINNESOTA MINING COMPANY.

Matti stepped up to the counter. He'd promised Mother that he would do all the talking, but he was having second thoughts.

"Top of the morning to ye," the man said, twisting the end of his handlebar mustache. "Billy Winston's the name. What can I do for you?" Billy's skin was darkly tanned, his uncombed hair had a reddish tint, and his eyes were deep blue. When Matti didn't answer right away, Billy said, "Speak up, lad. Has the cat got your tongue?"

"Cat?" Matti repeated, wondering if he'd heard right.

"Forget it, son," he chuckled. "How can I help you?"

Wanting to get his English words right, Matti spoke slowly. "Good morning to you," he said. "I am Matti Ojala."

"It's fine to meet you, Matti Ojala," Billy said. Nodding toward Mother, he asked, "And who might this pretty young lady be? Your sister?"

"No," Matti said, wondering if he'd misunderstood. "This is my mother."

Matti didn't know he was talking so loud until Billy stepped back and said, "Hold it down, son. My hearing is fine.

I'm just amazed that this fine flower of womanhood could be old enough to be anyone's mother."

"It is the truth," Matti said.

Though Mother nodded, Matti could tell that she wasn't sure what Billy was talking about.

A pyramid-shaped chunk of quartz and granite stood on top of the counter. Matti stared into the milky crystal and saw what looked like flecks of gold.

"If you're thinking there's gold in that rock, lad, you're right." Billy grinned. "The trick is getting it out." Billy's words had a musical lilt to them, and his r's rattled as they rolled off his tongue. Matti studied the golden specks.

"If you could come up with a way to separate that gold, you'd be a rich man," Billy continued. "The stock behind me is proof that lots of fellows have tried." He waved his hand toward the wall that was covered with hundreds of fancy-bordered Minnesota Mining Company stock certificates. "Why, every piece of equipment back along that trail was brought here for the sole purpose of extracting gold." Billy ran a thick finger over the crystal. "Try as they might, they couldn't build a stamp mill tough enough to break up the quartz without breaking the machine, too. So," Billy asked, "what can I do for you folks?"

"My mother would like to make a trade."

"What did you have in mind?"

Mother unfolded her handkerchief and showed Billy the sparkling ruby brooch. He shook his head. "It's a pretty bauble for sure, but I'm in the fur and livery business. Give me a marten or a fisher pelt and I can tell you the value in two shakes of a dead lamb's tail, but I don't know a lick about—"

"What do you have there, William?" A lady stepped through a curtained doorway and leaned over Billy's shoulder.

"It's nothing, Clara," Billy said.

"It looks like something to me," she said. Her voice was low and breathy. She looked twenty years younger than Billy. Her black hair was pinned up with a pearl comb, and her dress was a satiny green. She rested one hand on Billy's shoulder and leaned closer to the brooch. Her perfume was so soft it almost wasn't there.

Matti tried not to stare as she blinked her big green eyes, and extended one finger to touch the gold prongs of the ruby setting and the circle of diamonds that surrounded it.

"I'm sorry, folks," Billy said. "You might try the jeweler in Ely, but I couldn't ever—"

"William, may I have a word?" she interrupted.

She led Billy down the counter and whispered something. He began to nod. Returning, he said, "What sorta goods were you thinking of swapping for?"

"We would like to trade for a horse and a wagon, please."

"That's a bit steep," Billy replied, stepping back as if Matti had talked too loud again. "I—"

"William?" His wife's voice was cool this time.

"But," Billy added, "I'm sure we can work something out. I don't have a workhorse right now, but I could trade a pair of mules and a farm wagon."

Matti translated the word *wagon* for Mother, and she nodded. But when Matti saw Mrs. Winston hold the brooch up to her dress, he said, "Be patient, Mother," in Finnish.

Taking a chance, he said, "And we would like that gun, please."

"Gun?" Billy frowned.

Matti pointed toward the rack.

"That's an 1873 Springfield rifle. I couldn't begin to throw that in. It's worth three doll—"

His wife stepped forward again. "That sounds fair,

doesn't it, William?" She touched the ruby with her fingertip. "And I'm sure this young man could use a box of cartridges."

Billy was about to object, but his wife patted his forearm and said, "Giving up one little gun won't hurt, will it?"

"It's a rifle, dear." Billy shrugged his shoulders and extended his hand. "You drive a hard bargain, sir," he said, "and you've got a good eye for firearms." After he shook Matti's hand, Mother leaned forward and whispered, "Good job!" His face flushed with pride as Billy reached under the counter for a box of cartridges. Then he stepped toward the gun rack. "This is my all-time favorite hunting rifle." He opened the action and handed it to Matti. "They call her a Trapdoor Springfield. These 45:70-caliber bullets will take down a deer or a moose or caribou, but if you load her with bird shot, she makes a great duck and partridge gun."

As Billy showed Matti how to load the rifle, Mrs. Winston gathered up the brooch and disappeared through the curtained doorway.

CHAPTER 6

Billy talked the whole time he showed Matti how to hitch the team to the wagon. "Miss Maude here is a lady," he said, "but Katie leans toward the feisty side. That double bell cut on her tail warns folks to watch her close because she is both a kicker and a biter."

Matti helped Mother into the wagon. As he started down the road, she patted his shoulder. "Our wagon!" They grinned at each other.

Matti watched the mules carefully. Though Katie had a strange habit of turning her head and looking at him every few minutes, the team kept a steady pace. As they drove past the gold town ruins, Matti asked, "How do you suppose a fancy lady like Mrs. Winston ever ended up living at a wilderness trading post?"

"Didn't you notice Billy's eyes?"

Matti frowned. "What do you mean?"

"Every woman dreams of having a man who is dedicated to her heart and soul," Mother said. "One look in that man's eyes told me that he would do absolutely anything in the world for his Clara. And you know, he's a real charmer."

Matti still frowned. Mother had clearly seen something in Billy that had passed him right by.

When Matti parked the wagon in front of Aunt Hilda's house, the whole family came running out. "Where on earth have you two been?" Father said. "And what are you doing with that wagon?"

When Matti reached into the back of the wagon and handed him the rifle, Father looked confused.

"They call it a Trapdoor Springfield," Matti said proudly. "It will come in handy when we move to our homestead."

"What?" Father's eyebrows went up.

"You should have seen how clever Matti was," Mother said. "I would have settled for the wagon, but he got us the rifle, too."

"There's no way we have enough money saved to start a homestead."

"We won't need much money," Mother said, "now that Matti's helped us get a wagon and a rifle."

Matti showed Maude and Katie to Father. Before Matti could warn him about Katie's moods, she laid back her ears and kicked at his leg. Father dodged aside. "I see we've got a spirited little lady here," he said. "What a strange trim job on her tail."

"Mr. Winston said the double bell cut warns people that

she kicks and bites," Matti said. "But he guaranteed she and Maude are a well-matched team."

When Father patted Katie's neck, she *eeoow*ed and bit at him.

Anna and Kari squealed, but Father laughed. "Easy, gal."

"It would be fine to break some fresh ground," Father said, "but there are a million things that we'd need. We couldn't—"

"Don't be such a worrier, Leo," Mother said. Everyone laughed because that was what Father usually said to her. "Hilda's promised to give us her kitchen range, her utensils, and all sorts of—"

Father shook his head. "No. We—"

Hilda interrupted this time. "The only thing I ask in return is that you see me to the train." Father opened his mouth to speak, but she said, "It's been decided, Leo."

Father studied the women with a half smile. "So how long have you and Miss Minna been planning this?"

Mother and Hilda both chuckled. When Mother got stubborn, Father called her Miss Minna after Minna Canth, a writer from Kuopio who was famous for supporting women's suffrage.

"It may just work," Father said. "We do have a little saved." His brown eyes darkened. "I'll never forget the first time I had to write down my landlord's name in place of my own. Timo was just a baby back then, but I swore that even if I had to plow another man's land for fifty years, the day would come when my son would be free to reclaim his rightful name." Now he was smiling. "If Timo stayed on at the mine, and Mother kept the girls here, Matti and I could put up a sauna and live in it while we worked on our cabin."

The whole family laughed. Once Father got sauna building on his mind, there would be no stopping him.

Two days later Father went to the courthouse and filed a homestead claim. He returned home even more excited. "Our land is only nine miles south of Tower," he said. "Best of all, it's on the shore of a lake called Sampo. Can you believe it?"

"There's a lake in Minnesota named after the magic mill of the *Kalevala*?" Matti asked. From the time Matti was little, Father had told him tales of how the hero Väinö had used his powers of song and magic to defeat his enemies and capture the Sampo.

"And it's right down the road," Father said.

"Since the Sampo was famous for yielding both gold and grain," Matti said, "maybe we're finally heading for golden shores after all."

CHAPTER 7

The whole family rode to the train depot to say goodbye to Aunt Hilda. Everyone was on the verge of tears until Anna got the hiccoughs, making them laugh. Matti was glad to see that Aunt Hilda laughed the hardest of all. He hated to think of her going, but returning to Finland might help heal her pain.

That evening Mother was silent during supper. While Father teased the girls and made them giggle, Mother stared out the kitchen window toward the depot. As Timo sipped his coffee, Matti helped Mother and the girls clear the table. "Don't worry, Mother," Matti said. "When we sell the first crop from our farm, we'll send Hilda a ticket so she can come and visit."

"That's sweet, dear," Mother said. But Matti sensed that she thought she would never see her twin sister again.

At dawn the next day Father and Matti loaded their wagon and set out for Sampo Lake. "Clear a good field for our rye and potatoes," Mother said as she kissed them each goodbye.

For most of the way the road ran parallel to the railroad grade. "With a straight route like this we should reach Sampo Junction in an hour or two," Father said. He whistled to himself as Matti drank in the sights and scents of spring. The ditch banks were lined with marsh marigolds. Clusters of white blossoms covered the chokecherry bushes, and catkins hung from the birch and alder. A rich pollen smell filled the air.

"These ladies have an even gait," Father said. "They'll be a perfect pair for plowing, if I can only get used to this harnessing." Like Matti, Father was used to driving mules harnessed in a line rather than side by side.

When they reached a badly washboarded part of the road, Father pulled on the reins and yelled, *"Ptrui! Ptrui!"* but the mules continued forward.

"Say 'Whoa' if you want them to stop," Matti said.

"Whoa!" Father shouted. But his accent was so strange that the mules still ignored him. "Stupid American mules," he hollered.

Matti yelled, "Whoa!" and the mules immediately stopped. Father shook his finger at the back of their heads. "Once you gals get to our homestead," he said, "your first job will be to learn proper Finnish."

Though Maude lowered her head at Father's scolding, Katie turned and stared at him, looking bored.

"Well, even if those mules are illiterate," Father said, "you got us a fine wagon." He patted the oak seat and began whistling again.

A half mile farther on, the road veered away from the railroad and narrowed. For the next half hour the wagon bounced over rocks and lurched through mudholes. Once the left wheel got mired in a hole, and they had to cut a long pole to pry up the axle and block the wheel. Tiny black gnats buzzed around Matti's head, biting his neck and face and chewing the backs of his hands.

When they reached a logged-over area, the bugs were better, but the trail was even rougher. The wagon barely fit between the stumps and the brush piles, and Katie looked over her shoulder as if checking to see if they knew where they were going. "You follow your nose, like your good sister Maude, Miss Sassy," Father called.

Just when Matti decided that Katie had been right to worry, Sampo Junction appeared. Matti had expected a real train depot, but the junction consisted of one side track and a single building that wasn't much bigger than a switch shack. Father introduced himself to the stationmaster, Eino Saari.

"You're lucky to catch me in," Eino said. "We're only a whistle-stop in the summer when the logging camps are shut down." Eino was a short man with a gentle smile and yellow hair that stuck out from under his engineer's cap. A fellow homesteader, he was happy to welcome them to his "neighborhood." But when Father asked for directions to Sampo Lake, Eino frowned. "Did you file on the north or the south side of the lake?"

Father pulled his map out and showed Eino the mark that the man in the courthouse had made.

Eino shook his head. "The lake is right over there." He pointed over the tracks to the west. "But—"

"Is something wrong with the north side?" Father asked.

"The land is fine, but a big stretch of swamp lies between your land and the main road."

"They didn't mention that at the courthouse," Father said.

"They never do," Eino said. "You won't have trouble after the freeze-up. But it would be rough getting in there now."

"Is there a place we could store our wagon?" Father asked.

"A man named Black Jack Mattson lives on the south shore. He might be willing to watch your things for you," Eino said. "The only problem is he's a bit strange."

"Strange?" Father said.

"He's not dangerous," Eino said. "He's just an old bachelor who likes to keep to himself. We call him Spirit Jack."

When they got within view of Black Jack's house, Father said, "What do you think?"

Matti stared at the crude log cabin. The homesteads near Tower had been surrounded by cleared fields, but Black Jack's house was crowded right into the trees. Other than a rocky path between his cabin and the lake, his property was unbroken pine forest.

Father put the break on the wagon. "It can't hurt to ask."

Black Jack's log cabin was roofed with moss-covered sheets of birch bark. Smoke drifted from a rusty stovepipe. When they reached the front door, a gray dog charged around the corner with his teeth bared. Matti crouched and extended an open hand. Luckily the dog stopped and sniffed him.

Matti was scratching the dog's ears when the door opened. Black Jack's hair was long and scraggly. His cheeks were sunken, and a wild gray beard hung down to the middle of his chest. Despite the heat, he wore wool pants with suspenders and a long-sleeved wool undershirt.

Black Jack snarled, "What's this?" His brow was furrowed, but as he watched Matti petting his dog, his mouth turned up in a smile. "Looks like Louhi's found a friend," he said. "That mutt usually makes meat out of strangers."

"Did you say Louhi?" Father brightened. Louhi was the famous witch in the *Kalevala*.

"What else would you call a dog that lived on Sampo Lake?" Black Jack said. As Black Jack shifted his feet, Matti noticed that his left leg was a wooden peg from the knee down. Matti tried not to stare, but Black Jack said, "Haven't you ever seen a man with a stump? It might not be pretty, but it makes for a fine pile driver." He pounded his wooden leg down so hard that a tin plate rattled inside the cabin.

Then he added, "You look like honest Savo folks. From the north I'd wager."

Father nodded and shook hands. "That we are," he said.

Black Jack invited them inside. Along with a pile of dirty cups and plates, his kitchen table was cluttered with woodworking tools. The air smelled of freshly planed pine, and curled shavings were piled up around the table legs. A lard can beside the table served as a spittoon, while a second can at the foot of his bed stank like a chamber pot. The only other furnishings were a cooking range, a three-legged table, and two half-log benches.

"Coffee?" Black Jack offered.

"No thanks," Matti said as Black Jack wiped out a cup with his shirtsleeve and filled it from a stained iron pot. Matti tried not to grin as Father struggled to swallow the thick black brew. Even less appetizing was an open kettle of stew that looked as if it had been standing on the stove for many days. Black Jack saw Matti looking at the food-encrusted sides. "You hungry? I keep a stewpot cooking all the time. When it gets low, I just toss in more venison and potatoes."

When Matti shook his head, Black Jack poured himself a cup of coffee and said, "What brings you fellows to Sampo Lake?"

"We've filed a homestead claim," Father said.

"I suppose those fools in the courthouse forgot to tell you about the swamp on the north shore, eh?"

Father nodded his head sheepishly. "I should have looked closer," Father said, "but when I saw *Sampo* on the map, I couldn't resist."

"That's why I came here myself." Black Jack grinned. "I figured a Finlander had no choice but to settle in a place named after the *Kalevala*. It would be a lot quicker for you fellows to row across the lake. If you'd like to borrow my boat to haul your tools, you're welcome to it. It's no more than a half mile across, and it would save you the trouble of wading through that bog."

Black Jack showed them to the edge of the lake. Three large boulders were set in a half-circle beside his overturned boat. Each was supported by three smaller stones. Matti said, "You must be from the east?"

"That so?"

"We studied pictures of stone cairns like this in school."

"This is just my little rock pile," Black Jack said.

As they helped Black Jack turn his boat over and push it into the lake, Matti stared at the weird stones. They looked too heavy for five men to lift. Black Jack might pretend that this was just a rock pile, but Matti's teacher had told him about ancient monuments like these, built by Finns said to have magical powers, and to worship animals and trees.

Black Jack poked a pair of oars into Matti's stomach and said, "Make yourself useful." After Matti and Father had loaded the boat, Matti climbed into the stern and fit the oars into the oarlocks.

As Father pushed off the boat, Black Jack said, "You fellows take all the trips you need. I'll row her back the last time."

It took Matti only fifteen minutes to row across the bay.

He nosed the boat into the one pocket of sand in the rocky shoreline. Father jumped out and jerked the bow forward, nearly tipping Matti out of his seat. "Have you ever seen a finer piece of land?" Father called.

Matti turned to look. Nearly every stick of timber had been cut down. Matti was used to the green slopes of Puijo and the stately pines that surrounded Lake Kallavesi, but this shore was a tangle of brush and hundreds of gray stumps. The few big pines that were left stood on a rocky ledge to the east.

"Why didn't the county office tell you this land had been logged off?" Matti asked Father. "They let you file a worthless claim!" But Father was striding up the hillside so fast that he hadn't heard a thing. "You'll just have to return to the court-house and explain the mistake," Matti called.

Ignoring the brush and the clouds of mosquitoes, Father knelt halfway up the hill and touched the matted grass. "Look, Matti," he said, "a deer bedded here last night. There must be game everywhere." His eyes scanned a forest to the northwest. "There's birch for firewood and pine for a log cabin."

"But what about these stumps?" Matti frowned at the rocky, root-laced ground.

"We'll plow between them," Father said, turning his eyes to the west. "And look at that low cedar swale."

Matti smacked two mosquitoes on his forearm.

"Cedar means logs for our sauna, and birch means *vihtas* aplenty," Father said. Matti finally smiled at the word *vihtas*. Father was famous for the fine sauna whisks that he tied out of birch branches.

On their way back to the boat, Father praised everything from the "gentle slope of the ground" (in Matti's opinion, steep and rocky) to the "perfect pitch of the goldfinches" (Matti heard ordinary birds). He stood at the water's edge and placed his hands on his hips, and said, "We even have our very own beach." Matti shook his head. Father's "beach" was a five-foot-wide patch of sand surrounded by lichen-covered boulders.

It took four trips to row their tools and supplies across the lake. Black Jack came along on the last trip. "I'll troll a hand line," he said, "and catch us some dinner." Though Black Jack smelled worse than his crusty old stewpot, he did catch two gold-speckled walleyes. Every time Matti splashed an oar, he cackled, "Thanks for the shower." Matti felt like telling him that a little water would do him good.

When they got to shore, Black Jack knelt at the water's edge and ran a short piece of twine through the gills of the fish. Then he tied the line to a root. "Now you and sailor boy will have fresh fish waiting when you get back."

Matti jerked on a logging chain that he was dragging up the bank. The hook hit his shinbone. "You all right?" Father asked.

"I'm fine." Matti clenched his teeth together and tried not to limp as he felt blood run down his leg.

As Matti rowed back to Black Jack's cabin, the pain made him pull crookedly. "If Mutti Boy had captained the ship that brought you to America," Black Jack said to Father, "you'd still be trying to make landfall." Matti ignored him and rowed as hard as he could. He hated Jack's evil laugh. "Mutti Boy"? What right did he have to tease him about being a captain? Only Wilho could do that. Wilho was kind and good and everything that this man was not.

Black Jack caught a bass for his own dinner on the way back to his cabin. After Father thanked him for his help, he and Matti parked their wagon under a big pine and unhitched the mules. Katie planted her feet and refused to move. When Father tried to pull her forward, she jerked the bridle out of his hand

and trotted back to the wagon. "Why don't I start down the trail with Maude first?" Matti said. "Katie might decide to follow."

Matti's plan worked, and Father said, "That's using your head. As the old saying goes, One hour of thinking equals two hours of work."

As they passed by the depot at Sampo Junction, Eino Saari called, "Good luck swimming through that swamp."

The road was covered with the cleft tracks of deer, and huge pine stumps stood on both sides. It was easy traveling at first, but suddenly the road narrowed to a shoulder-wide trail.

Father studied the thick stand of spruce that loomed ahead. The ground was cool and mossy, and the air had a fresh pine smell. Chickadees twittered in the shade. Matti would have enjoyed the relief from the heat, but the mosquitoes and gnats made it impossible.

As Matti swatted the bugs away from the brim of his cap, he heard a loud snort. Katie jerked back and brayed hoarsely. A huge cow moose and her gangly-legged calf stood no more than thirty yards away. The moose flicked her black ears and stared. The calf had enormous ears and a huge, blunt snout. "There's a face only a mother could love," Father said as the cow led her baby away.

Soon they were slogging through ankle-deep mud. Just as Father said, "This isn't too bad," they reached a still pool. Father probed the water with a stick and frowned. "We can't risk one of the mules breaking a leg." He peered toward the higher land to the north.

"Maybe we should leave the mules at Black Jack's?" Matti asked.

"We need them to skid our cabin logs," Father said. He stared at the swamp. "It looks like our only choice is to go around."

"Through that?" Matti grimaced at the twisted mass of tamarack and alder. His shin was throbbing from the cut.

"*Sisu.*" Father winked. "After coming all the way from Finland, we can't let a little detour slow us down."

An hour later Matti's face was swollen from bug bites and cut from thrashing through branches. His shirt was soaked with sweat, and his pants were spattered with mud. He was ready to give up hope when he saw a glimmer of blue.

A few minutes later Father and Matti knelt at the shore and splashed water over their faces. Matti cupped his hands and drank deeply. "Leave some water for the fish," Father said. To cool the bites, Matti dipped his whole head under. Katie waded into the lake and plunged her nose in, while Maude drank more delicately, wetting only her front feet before she tasted the water.

While Father was looking over the property again, Matti soaked his handkerchief in the lake and rinsed off his bloody shin. Though the cut wasn't deep, a red-and-purple lump had swollen up.

"We'd better make camp before dark," Father called. He chose a flat area between two white pines that was carpeted with fallen needles. To make a lean-to they cut a ten-foot-long pole and nailed it between the trees. Then they tied a piece of canvas around the pole, stretched it at an angle toward the ground, and weighed down the end with rocks. Finally they piled their tools and supplies under a second tarp.

"Do you want to clean the fish or build the fire?" Father asked.

"The fire." Matti hadn't eaten since breakfast. He gathered some fist-sized stones from the shore and arranged them in a ring. Then he collected birch bark and a pile of dry twigs and branches. A single match got the blaze going. Father set a flat rock inside the fire ring for his copper coffeepot. Though Mother had to leave all her cookware back in Kuopio, Father had insisted she bring their coffeepot. "Why don't you do the honors?" he said, tossing Matti a sack of coffee beans and clamping his coffee grinder to a log.

"No wonder that pack was so heavy."

"A man can't live without his coffee," Father said.

"But you just had a cup with Mr. Black Jack," Matti teased.

"All the more reason for you to get cranking. I can't wait to clear the taste of that awful mud out of my mouth."

When the fire had burned down to coals, Father got out a cast-iron pan and dumped in a scoop of lard. Fresh walleye fillets were soon sizzling. Next Father sawed off a hunk of rye bread from the loaf that Mother had sent, laid a golden-brown piece of fish on top, and handed it to Matti.

The smell of birch smoke and the hot iron pan made Matti homesick. On summer days his family used to have a fish fry on the shore of Lake Kallavesi. They cast their lines from shore and swam and played. Toward evening Father built a fire, and Wilho told stories. Matti could see his uncle walking up from the shore. "Give me a plate quick, Helmi, before *Kapteeni* eats up all the fish."

When supper was finished, Father sat back against a pine tree with a contented sigh. He pointed up the hill. "Our house will go there," he said, "and"—he waved his hand back to the left—"the hay and horse barns there. But we'll put the first and most important building right here beside the lake."

"Our sauna," Matti said.

Father smiled.

In Finland their *savusauna*, or smoke sauna, had been built by Matti's great-grandfather out of hand-hewn logs and stone. For four generations Matti's family had used that same sauna as a bathhouse. Over the years it had also served as a gathering place on Saturday nights, a birthing room, a place to heal the sick, and in sadder times, a room to prepare the dead for burial.

The sky was lit with purple-pink streaks of light, and the treetops burned red gold. "The daylight hangs on just like back in Kuopio," Matti said. Matti had loved to climb the old wooden tower on Puijo. With the sun still at his back, he used to watch the moon rise over the green islands of Kallavesi. The whole sky glowed as rowboats made their slow way home, and the tall steamships from Savonlinna turned to silvery ghosts on the horizon.

"It's like the land of the midnight sun," Father agreed. "And there's a sight sent straight from heaven." He pointed toward the tallest of the pines. "That tree reminds me of the golden fir of the *Kalevala*. Remember the one with the flowering crown that Väinö felled to bring light to the world?"

"How could I forget?" Matti said, grinning at how Father called the epic hero Väinämöinen "Väinö." As if he were his personal friend.

"We'd better sack out," Father said, "if we intend to skid logs tomorrow." After checking to see that the mules were safely hobbled, they washed their faces and brushed their teeth with rough birch twigs. Then they rolled out their blankets on the pine straw. The lake was silver black and dimpled with rings from fish that were rising to take bugs.

Matti was so tired that he didn't even bother to unlace his boots before he lay down. As he closed his eyes, a mosquito droned past his ear and landed on his temple. Matti smacked himself hard.

"Be careful you don't knock yourself out." Father chuckled. "Just think of it as your bedtime song." Matti gritted his teeth when the buzzing started again. "The critters should go away after dark," Father continued, "but we'll have to live with them until we get our sauna built. It's too bad that Timo can't be here to help us tomorrow."

Father's last words sounded slow and sleepy, but they burned Matti like a slap. Timo, Timo, was all Father ever thought about. A moment later Father was snoring.

Every time Matti relaxed, another mosquito attacked. Even though the air was hot and muggy, Matti was ready to pull the wool blanket over his face. Then the buzzing suddenly stopped. Father was right. With the coming of the full dark, the mosquitoes had left.

Chapter 8

Sometime during the night, Matti felt a tugging on his boots. He turned on his side, but the feeling didn't stop. Matti was confused by the smell of pig fat and rancid garbage that burned in his nostrils. Where could such an awful stink be coming from?

Matti opened his eyes. Father was snoring deep and ragged, but the woods beyond their bedrolls were silent. What was that awful smell? Was someone trying to steal his boots?

Turing to his left, Matti blinked in the moonlight. A dark shape came into focus, and he froze. A bear was licking the side of his boot. Matti wanted to jerk back his foot, but he held his breath and stared as the rough tongue drooled over his ankles. Soon his socks were warm and sticky.

Should he whisper to Father? Should he reach for the rifle he'd leaned against the tree? As Matti's mind raced, he remembered that he and Father had just greased their boots with waterproofing oil. Maybe the bear only wanted a taste of the fresh oil.

The bear sat back on his haunches and licked his left paw. Now that he was done with his boot grease snack, would Matti be his main course? The bear dropped back down and leaned closer to Matti's face. The stench gagged him. At the first glint of teeth he would grab for the rifle.

The bear shook his head and sniffed. Warm spittle dripped onto the back of Matti's wrist, but he forced himself to remain still. Finally the bear ambled off toward the woods. Matti's heart pounded long after the shuffling had faded into the underbrush.

The moment Matti turned to wake Father, Maude and Katie started braying. Matti took a deep breath for the first time in what seemed like an hour. Though he was angry at the mules for calling only after the bear disappeared, he couldn't help admiring their wisdom. Hobbled mules—even old tough ones—might be tempting.

Just then Father sat up and blinked. "What is it?"

His eyes widened when Matti told him about the bear. Father lit a lantern and made sure the Springfield was loaded. As they walked to check on the mules, Matti imagined the bear crouched just beyond the yellow light, staring at him.

Matti slept fitfully after that. Father always said that a bear never hurt a man unless he got between a mother and her cub. But what if this bear hadn't heard Father's theory?

"Rise and shine," Father called.

Shivering, Matti opened his eyes. Father had already

started a fire and was crouched beside the rock ring, stirring a steaming pot of porridge. Matti looked at the ground beyond the lean-to. The pine straw was dusted white. "Did it snow?" he asked.

"It's just a little frost." Father brushed the log beside him. A cool breeze blew across Matti's blanket. "Are you tired from wrestling bears all night?"

It hadn't been a dream, then. Matti looked down at his boots. Though they'd been spattered with mud when he went to bed, the bear had licked them clean. "We're lucky he didn't get into our food cache," Father said. "This evening we'll string our knapsacks up in a tree so we don't have to worry about him pilfering our food."

Right after breakfast Father and Matti began to cut and skid logs. Since their sauna would only be eight by sixteen feet, Father chose smaller cedar from a low area on the west edge of the property. "We'll save the bigger trees for shingles," he said.

Matti's sore leg made it difficult to keep up. They felled the trees with a crosscut saw, and while Father skidded the first logs back to the homesite, Matti limbed and topped the remaining trees with his axe. Father grinned all day long. If Matti slowed down, Father prodded him up with old sayings. His favorite was "Hard work is the mother of happiness."

The hot weather and the bugs made the work doubly hard. By lunchtime the air had turned humid. Despite the heat, Father needed his coffee several times a day. At lunch he warmed it up over the fire by "kicking the pot," or adding a spoonful of fresh coffee to his breakfast brew. Matti preferred water, but no matter how much he drank, he was always thirsty. The scent of pitch burned in his nostrils and gave him a dull headache. Tiny black flies swarmed everywhere, hungry to bite every inch of exposed skin.

The one pure joy for Matti was the sun. After crouching all winter in the dusty darkness of the mine, the light and the earth scents and birdsong were a constant gift.

On the morning after they'd skidded and peeled the last of their sauna logs, Matti woke to a tugging at his feet. Thinking the bear had come back, he turned to reach for the gun. Then he saw Black Jack's dog.

"What's this?" a coarse voice called. "Are we catching up on our beauty sleep, Mutti Boy?"

Matti looked up at Black Jack's scraggly beard and yellow teeth. He wore the same wool pants and half-buttoned wool underwear shirt.

"Ah! Company." Father crouched by the fire. "Coffee for you, sir?"

Black Jack took a cup of coffee. "I thought I'd lend you fellows a hand," he said, stumping over to inspect the foundation stakes that Matti and Father had driven into the ground. A flat rock was bedded at each corner, and leveling strings were stretched between the stakes. "Looks like you're set to go. Now we need to roust this loafer out of the sack. Hasn't Mutti heard that a lazy boy is the devil's pillow?"

Matti groaned. Father's quotes were irritating enough in the morning, but now he had to put up with Black Jack. Matti gobbled some dry bread while their neighbor walked back to his boat.

Black Jack returned with two axes and a peavey, a sharp-spiked tool mounted on an axe handle that makes it easy to move logs. He unbuckled the leather sheath from his broad axe and said, "Need a shave?" Black Jack held the polished steel so that the sun glinted into Matti's face; then he dropped the axe. Matti's eyes widened, but just as the blade was ready to bite into Black Jack's leg, he turned the head and let it clang against his wooden stump. "Now"—he handed him the peavey—"fetch us some logs."

Matti hurried after Father, who had already walked up the hill to harness Maude and Katie. "We'll need the longest and straightest logs to start with," Father said as he hooked a log chain to the mule hitch. "Can you skid them down for us?"

Matti nodded. He looped the chain around the first log and started down the hill. But the mules were used to longer pulls and didn't want to stop at the foundation. "Whoa," Matti yelled. "Whoa."

"I thought those mules understood Englanninkeili?" Father said.

"For a minute Mutti looked like he was going for a morning swim." Black Jack laughed as he helped Father set the log on the cornerstones. Then Father and Jack each made a pencil mark on their end and picked up their axes. Matti was amazed at how fast Black Jack cut his notch. With his peg leg planted firmly on the ground, he set his boot on the log and swung with all his might. Wood chips were soon flying.

Matti knew Father prided himself on keeping his axe sharp, but Black Jack's was sharper. Black Jack also didn't have to worry about cutting himself. Once he swung his axe so close to his peg leg that he cut a shaving from the tip. "I'd better be careful I don't sharpen that stub," he said, "or I won't be able to walk without getting stuck in the dirt."

"Ready?" Black Jack called as the last chips flew to rest at Father's feet. Father nodded and said, "Get the cant hook, Matti." He waved toward the long-handled tool with the hinged hook.

Matti buried the point of the cant hook in the middle of the log, and half a turn later, the first log fell into place.

Father and Black Jack both knelt to check if their

ends lined up with the rock. Then Black Jack called, "Let's have another."

Once the four sill logs were in place, the work fell into a rhythm. The mules soon learned to stop on their own, and Matti helped the men hold each log in place while they scribed the corners for their dovetailed cuts.

Matti was surprised that Maude, the quiet mule, took a liking to Black Jack. Whenever she stopped with a log, she nudged his back until he turned and scratched her ears. "Hey there, gal."

The whole time Black Jack swung his axe, he whistled a strange tune. Matti tried to place the melody, but it sounded like nothing he had ever heard. When Matti got ahead with his skidding, he asked, "What's the name of that song?"

Black Jack said, "Idle hands are the devil's workshop," and handed him a second axe. It had a single-bitted blade and a curved handle that made it possible to flatten the outside of the logs without skinning his knuckles.

"A hewing ax?" Matti asked.

"So Mutti Boy knows some tricks already?" Black Jack raised his eyebrows. "But work on the side opposite us. My legs don't need any more hewing."

Matti was impressed at how fast the walls rose. Father had guessed it would take a week to finish the log work, but with Black Jack's help, the time would be cut in half.

By lunch the wall got so high that the men had to cut their notches standing on top of the corners. Black Jack showed Matti a neat trick. Pulling a headless nail out of his pocket, he tapped it into the bottom of his wooden leg. When Black Jack pressed his weight down on the log, the nail anchored him so firmly that he could swing as hard as he had on the ground.

The sun was getting low by the time Father and Black Jack called it a day. Black Jack declined Father's offer of dinner and started to walk down to his boat, but he stopped halfway. After frowning at the sky, he stumped back up the hill and said, "I think we'd better move that shelter of yours, Mutti Boy."

"Why would we do that?" Matti hated being called Mutti Boy.

"Listen to your elders," he said. Then without another word he took Father's mall and knocked loose the pole of the lean-to.

Father looked up from his fire. "What in the devil?"

Black Jack grinned. "Mutti Boy and I have a little job to do." He rolled up the canvas as if it were Matti's idea.

Father frowned at Matti, who could only shrug his shoulders.

With the big hammer still in his hand, Black Jack walked a dozen paces up the hill. "We'll nail it right here," Black Jack said, motioning for Matti to hold the crossbar between two trees. "Now you can move the bedrolls and the supplies up here." Then with a gruff good-night he was gone.

"I have no idea what that was all about," Matti said.

"Maybe he's just strange like Eino Saari claims," Father said.

They walked to the lake to wash up. Matti took off his shirt and shook out the wood chips and sawdust. He knelt at the shore and splashed water over his arms and chest. His hands were coated with cedar sap, so he used sand to cut through the grime. As he washed, Black Jack's strange tune kept playing over and over in his head.

"Don't get yourself too clean," Father called. "The mosquitoes love a well-washed fellow."

After Matti crawled into his blankets, his back itched as

if he'd been rolling in a hayloft. He shook out his shirt again, but the itching wouldn't go away. He thought he would never get to sleep. Then a pair of loons started calling to each other across the bay. Their song surged up the scale in pure, clear notes, rising in volume, until it reached a wild, laughing frenzy that echoed off the rocky hills above Sampo Lake. Suddenly the song fell away, only to rise again and again. In the quiet between the loon calls, an owl hooted up the ridge and mosquitoes began their nightly hum. In the midst of this wilderness chorus, Matti's tiredness overtook him, and he drifted off to sleep. The next thing Matti knew, Black Jack was walking toward him with a bright-bladed axe. "It's time for a shave, Mutti Boy," he mumbled, offering a seat in a barber chair. Before Matti could say no, Jack grabbed his hand. Matti woke to a loud rumble of thunder. Whitecaps were crashing against the shore, and the canvas roof was rattling like a flag.

Father sat up and shouted, "You okay?"

"So far," Matti yelled as a wall of rain blew into shore. Just then a lightning flash lit up the lake, followed by a thunder-clap and the shuddering crash of a tree falling near the sauna.

Crouching near the low end of the tarp to stay dry, Father and Matti peered into the dark. Matti couldn't tell if the walls were still standing. The wind and rain kept pounding down.

When Matti woke the next morning, Father was studying the big red pine that had fallen in the night. The root ball was twice as tall as a man and tangled with rocks and dirt.

The crown had fallen right where their lean-to used to be.

Beneath the treetop Matti could see the depression of his old bedroll in the pine straw. "Would you look at that?" Father shook his head. Matti nodded, wide-eyed. One of the wrist-thick branches had buried itself right where his chest would have been.

Just then Matti heard a small, squeaking noise. He knelt to see a baby crow lying on his side, his feet pinned down by the crisscrossed branches. Matti pulled away the twigs of a crushed nest and picked up the bird. His head was all beak, and his spindly feathers were plastered to his back. Matti was surprised when the bird wobbled to his feet and cocked his head. His eyes were pale blue like a baby's. Then he stretched out his wings and cawed weakly.

"That's a tough little critter," Father said, "but he sure is ugly. I don't see the mother anywhere. I wonder if—"

"So our young slugabed is up for a change," a voice boomed behind them. Matti turned to see Black Jack stumping up the hill. "Looks like you've had a little blowdown."

Matti looked into Black Jack's eyes. "How did you know that tree was going to fall?" he asked. "You saved my life."

Black Jack ignored the question. "I see you've been bird hunting. Are we having crow for breakfast?"

"There was a nest in the tree."

"You'd better set him off by himself in case his mother comes back." Then he nodded toward the sauna. "So are we gonna gawk at baby birds all day or do some log work?"

The little bird balanced himself in Matti's palm and cawed in a high-pitched scratchy voice as he carried him to the edge of the clearing. He set him beside a tree stump where his mother could find him.

After a quick cup of coffee, Father and Black Jack picked up their axes. The air was soon filled with cedar chips and Black Jack's strange whistling. Between skidding logs and hewing the walls, Matti never got a chance to rest.

When they took a break, Black Jack visited with Maude

while Matti walked over to check on the crow. He looked more listless. Since there was still no sign of the mother, he picked him up. The crow cawed weakly. "What could we feed him?" Matti asked.

"Try some oatmeal," Father said. But when Matti offered the bird a tiny piece, he turned his head.

"Let's try it like his mother would," Father said. He put a bit of water-soaked oatmeal on the tip of his little finger and pried the bird's beak open with his other hand. With a quick poke he shoved the food down its throat. Matti was afraid that Father would choke him, but the little crow's eyes suddenly opened wide, and he cawed for more. Matti couldn't believe how huge and red his throat was. When Matti held out the next piece, he snatched it so fast that Matti jerked back.

"If that bird had teeth he'd take your finger off, Mutti Boy."

"He's got *sisu* for sure," Father said.

By the third day, the crow was strong enough to hop after Matti, and he had to be careful not to step on him.

During their lunch break Black Jack pulled out a bright penny and set it on the toe of his boot. The crow hopped over and grabbed it in his beak. Then he carried the penny to the base of a pine, scratched a hole, and buried it.

"You've either got yourself a thief or a banker, Matti," Father said.

"Same difference," Black Jack said.

Once the wall was chest high, the log work got trickier. Not only was it harder to hew the sides, but it was also harder to lift the logs and scribe the notches. Using two poles for a ramp, the men looped a rope around the middle of each log and rolled it up the wall. The first time Matti tried pulling from inside the building, the log came up so quickly that he tripped and fell. Black Jack tipped his cap. "That's some fine dancing." The little crow cawed from a nearby rock, as if he too were laughing.

By suppertime Black Jack and Father decided that the walls were high enough. "A few rafters and roof boards," Black Jack said, "and you'll be ready for your first sauna."

Father nodded. "We'll get to the roof when we can," he said, "but Matti and I are working on the road tomorrow. When my eldest son, Timo, comes on Sunday, the three of us will start corduroying the low spots."

"That's one job I'll leave to you folks," Black Jack said.

Father invited Black Jack to share some fried side pork and beans for supper. Black Jack used his *puukko* to eat instead of a spoon. As he cut his bread into pieces and dipped them into his beans, Matti noticed white scars on the back of his hand.

When Black Jack saw him staring, he said, "It looks like an animal got me, doesn't it?"

Matti nodded.

"The tar makers used to play a game when I lived up in Oulu. They were a strange bunch who spent their winters back in the forests, boiling pine tar and packing it into wooden barrels. When spring came they built long, narrow boats and rode the rivers all the way down to the harbor. They raced one another the whole way, shooting rapids that no one else dared and yelling like crazy men as they passed under Oulu's sixty bridges. We called them *puukkojunkkarit,* or knife wielders, because they got liquored up and played a crazy game. Being young and foolish, I joined in. They started by stabbing one another in the hand. Each thrust went deeper, and to make it more painful, they pushed the blade real slow. You weren't a man unless you could take a knife right through your hand." Black Jack held up his palm. A line of scars matched the ones on the back of his hand.

"How could you stand it?" Matti said.

"It hurt plenty," he said, "but like those old sword fighters in Germany, we looked on our scars as tokens of pride. It's a wonder that we didn't bleed to death."

When Black Jack stopped and took a sip of coffee, Matti asked, "So how did you know that tree was going to fall?"

He paused as if he were thinking hard. Then turning with his eyes wide, he said, "A bear whispered in my ear."

Black Jack and Father both laughed.

By the time Black Jack said good night, the moon was already rising in the south. "Looks like it's gonna be a pretty day tomorrow," he said, checking the sky as he climbed into his rowboat. "But I don't make no guarantees when it comes to weather forecasting."

Since Matti hadn't hobbled the mules yet, Maude walked down to the shore to see Black Jack off. She waded into belly-deep water and *eeoow*ed until he patted her one last time. "Good night, Mistress Maude," he said. Then just before he pulled on his oars he tipped his cap to Matti and called, "Good night, *Kapteeni*."

CHAPTER 9

Just before sunrise Matti woke with claws digging into the top of his head. The bear! His eyes popped open. The baby crow was pulling at his hair with his beak.

"Ow!" Matti yelled. As he sat up, the crow hopped to his shoulder.

"Looks like your friend wants breakfast." Father spoke from the far side of the fire pit.

Matti wanted to sleep another hour, but he got up. The sky was gray, and a fine rain was dappling the surface of the lake. While Father walked up to check on the mules, Matti balled up some bread and offered it to the crow. He opened wide and cawed. His throat was red and ugly and glowed like a cave.

Father returned, dropping an armload of wood beside

the fire. "Mr. Black Jack was smart not to guarantee his forecast," he said.

Matti grinned. The rain offered proof that Black Jack couldn't predict things any better than he could. Yet when Matti looked down the hill and saw the huge pine, another part of him wanted to believe in Black Jack's powers.

"You ready to clear the trail?" Father asked, flicking the last few drops of his coffee into the fire.

Matti nodded. Though he didn't like the idea of working in the rain, he knew they needed to open a trail before Timo arrived on Sunday. According to Father's plan, they would first build a sauna, which would serve as a temporary house. Next they would plant their crops, improve the road, and build a root cellar. Only then would they start on the main cabin.

"We'll cut a rough trail to that logging road," Father said. "Then Timo can help us widen it into a proper wagon road."

Father made it sound as simple as drawing a pencil line, but as Matti recalled the swamp, he knew it would not be so easy.

The first part of the road went through mixed birch and popple where the brush mainly needed to be cut back. A fine mist fell, making the mosquitoes and gnats vicious. "*Sisu*, Matti," Father said when he slapped at his face, "they've never bled a man to death yet."

By midafternoon their work slowed to a crawl. As they hacked through the tightly spaced spruce and tamarack trees, pitch stuck to Matti's hands and tickled his nostrils with a sweet acid smell.

The main road was within sight when they reached the lowest part of the swamp. The ground was pockmarked with puddles, but Father was still excited. "Now we'll see what we're made of," Father said. "The woods, she gives us the full test."

The last hundred-foot stretch was more work than all the trail they had cleared so far. Father decided that this section would have to be corduroyed by laying logs side by side to build up the roadbed. The water was so cold that it numbed Matti's legs and feet. Once his boot kicked up a loose chunk of ice.

On the second afternoon they finished the rough clearing. When they got back to camp, the crow flapped toward Matti, cawing for food. After he ate he hopped up on a log and cocked his head. His eyes were bright and filled with mischief.

"Do you miss your momma?" Matti asked as the crow preened his feathers to a shine with his bill.

Matti was thinking of Mother in Soudan, and hoping she was safe, when Father said, "What do you say we take the afternoon off and rig up a fish trap? I'll bet we can catch something tastier than pork and beans."

"Anything that doesn't involve chopping sounds good to me."

Father got out a roll of chicken wire, his side cutters, and some bailing wire. He formed one piece of the mesh into a cylinder and wired it together. Then he took two more pieces and made cones that tapered to an opening the size of his wrist. After wiring a cone to both ends, he made a hinged door in the side.

They set the trap under a fallen log in a creek that flowed out of the west end of the lake. The bank was thick with meadow grass. "This will make fine hay," Father noted, chewing a green stem.

After they were done, Father gave Matti permission to take the rifle and hunt for a squirrel or a rabbit on the far side of the river. Matti followed a trail that led along the west shore. Near the end of the bay a big popple had fallen across a second trail that veered east. When Matti noticed the roof of Black

Jack's cabin through the trees, he decided to stay on the main trail. Though squirrels were usually chattering everywhere, now that Matti was carrying a gun they had all disappeared.

Just when Matti was ready to turn around, he saw a partridge. Before he could shoot, the bird ducked its head and ran. Matti followed close behind, but every time he raised his gun the bird dodged behind a rock or tree.

With his head bent low and his gun pointed forward, Matti suddenly burst into a clearing. He found himself staring at the rear of a log building. "Hey there, laddie," a voice called.

Matti turned, accidentally aiming his gun at Billy Winston. "Take it easy." Billy pushed the barrel to one side.

"I'm sorry." Matti quickly lifted up the gun.

"Are we tracking a bear or looking for dragons to slay, maybe?" Billy said. He had a slop pail in his hand.

It took Matti a long while to translate *dragon* in his head. He hadn't spoken English since he'd left Soudan, and Billy's strange rolling *r*'s made him doubly hard to understand. Just when Matti decided that Billy was joking, Billy glanced at the rifle and said, "Hunting season doesn't open for two months, you know."

Would he have Matti arrested for poaching? "I was only—" Matti began, talking louder than he meant to.

Billy smiled and set his pail down. "Don't worry, lad. Nobody cares how you homesteaders fill your soup pots. So how are Maude and Katie doing?"

"Katie's moody like you warned," Matti said.

Billy nodded. "Have your folks filed a claim near here?"

"No." Matti shook his head. "Our land is a long way off at a place called Sampo Lake."

"We're neighbors, then," Billy said. "Without knowing it,

you took a shortcut. There's an old Indian trail that leads from Sampo Lake to the Pike River. Your place is no more than three miles away from mine. To get home by road you'd have to go all the way back to Tower, but it's only a short jaunt through the woods."

"So the path between here and Sampo Lake is like the bottom of a"—Matti searched for the correct English word—"a triangle?"

"That's right." Billy nodded. "I can tell you're a smart fellow. Have you ever thought about working as a clerk? I could use someone who knows Finnish. My French and Ojibwe are passable, but that Finn talk ties my tongue in knots. Lots of the farmers and lumberjacks around here go all the way to Tower so they can trade with someone who speaks their language."

"I could ask my Father," Matti said.

"Good," Billy said, slapping him on the shoulder. "If it's all right with him, you can start next Saturday. I pay four bits a day."

"Next Saturday?" Matti was shocked that he would want him to begin so soon. A half a dollar a day was only a fourth of what he'd made in the mine, but every penny would be helpful.

"I'll see you then, la—" Billy started to say "lad" but stopped and said, "Matti, wasn't it?"

"Yes." Matti smiled.

Knowing that Father would be worried if he were gone much longer, Matti unloaded his gun and trotted toward home. The more Matti thought about clerking in the store, the more he hoped that Father would let him try. It would be fun to meet new people. After working beside Father for so long, Matti could guess which story Father was going to tell before he even opened his mouth. Matti needed to get away before he began finishing Father's sentences the way Anna and Kari did for each other.

The shadows were lengthening by the time Matti reached the log bridge at Sampo Creek. He checked the trap and found a good-sized northern. Though he hadn't had any luck with his hunting, he'd at least be bringing supper home.

CHAPTER 10

When Matti told Father about Mr. Winston's offer, he hesitated. "We've got a heap of work to do," he said, "with the road, and the plowing and planting soon to come."

"You said we need money."

Father nodded. "But it wouldn't be right to take your wages."

"My money could be a seed fund to help with the planting."

Father scratched his beard and thought. "I suppose you could try it."

At five o'clock the next morning, Matti left for the depot to meet Timo. Matti waited for the train, anxious to tell Timo about his new job.

At six o'clock the train went by without stopping. Matti paced back and forth in front of Mr. Saari's shack, wondering if Timo had misunderstood their plans. At seven o'clock he gave up. Just as Matti was turning onto the logging road, he saw Timo strolling down the tracks. Matti was glad to see him until he realized that Timo wasn't even hurrying.

"Hello, little brother," he said. "How's life in the woods?"

"Why weren't you on the train?"

"I was short of funds," Timo said, yawning, "so I walked."

"Nine miles?" Timo looked as if he had spent the night in a saloon. He smelled of stale beer and cigar smoke, and his eyes were bloodshot. Knowing how Mother despised drinking, Matti wondered if she and Timo were getting along.

"It's easy to get an early start if you don't go to bed." Timo was proud of himself.

"You're late" was all Matti said.

Matti thought Timo would appreciate the work they had done on the sauna, but when the walls came into view, he said, "I can't believe the old dreamer stopped reciting poems long enough to pick up an axe."

Matti couldn't believe his ears. Father had always gone out of his way to help Timo. His dream was to start a farm that he could pass on to his firstborn son. "If it weren't for Father you'd be marching in the czar's army right now."

"Well, well," Timo said. He was staring at Matti as if he was about to say more when Father shouted, "Timo," and ran forward to shake his hand. Though Matti could tell that Father wanted to comment on Timo's appearance, he asked, "How are Mother and the girls?"

"Mother sends you her love," Timo said, "and little Anna and Kari are growing so fast that you'd hardly recognize th—"

Timo stopped when he saw the lake for the first time. Blinking his bloodshot eyes, he said, "This is like coming home. We could be at Savilahti or Kallavesi this very minute."

As Timo walked to the lake, he reported on the family and his work in the mine. Then Father slapped him on the shoulder and said, "Are you ready for a little road building?"

They started in the wettest spot. Limbing pairs of big tamarack for stringers, they bedded them lengthwise in the mud and spiked smaller, eight-foot-long logs side by side across the top.

Father clapped his hands. "How fine it is to be working beside my son—my sons. It reminds me of the times we cut firewood on the road to Rytky."

Timo, standing behind Father's back, rolled his eyes.

Later when Father commented on how his hero Väinö could shatter rocks and fell a forest with the power of his magical songs, Timo yawned and said, "Fairy tales won't help us chop trees, Father."

Matti waited for Father to speak to Timo about his disrespect, but he let it pass. Father would never allow Matti to talk like that, yet he never corrected Timo. Still, by the middle of the morning Matti could tell that Father was getting impatient with Timo. If Timo wasn't whining about his headache, he was complaining about the bugs and the mud.

Finally Father set down his axe and turned to him. "Were you expecting servants and a rose garden?" he asked.

By the time they paused for lunch, Matti could tell that Timo was feeling the full effect of going a night without sleep. He looked pale, and when Father and Matti cut big slabs off the rye loaf that Mother had sent, Timo only nibbled at his piece. Matti threw the crow a few crumbs, and Timo frowned. "Why would you ever want a pet crow?"

Matti told the story of how he'd saved the crow after the

storm, but Timo said, "You should have put him out of his misery. They call a flock of crows a murder for good reason."

"He may be a pest," Father said, "but there's nothing murderous about that little fellow. Your brother's taken fine care of him."

Cawing, the crow hopped up on the log beside Timo and pecked at his bread. But Timo tossed his piece to the ground and mashed it under his boot. "There's some dessert for you, birdie," he said. Matti could see the color rising in Father's neck, but he didn't say anything.

All afternoon, every time Father said something, Timo acted bored. When Timo and Matti were limbing a tall spruce, Father began quoting a favorite passage from the *Kalevala* about the giant tree with a hundred branches that kept the world in shadow from the beginning of time.

Shaking his head, Timo set down his axe and interrupted Father. "It's time for me to head back to Soudan."

The next morning Father made no mention of Timo's visit, but Matti could tell that he felt bad. However, once they started working, Father was soon humming to himself. A short while later, when Matti got mad at a knot that resisted a half dozen hard swings, Father was back to his old self. "Remember, Matti"—he pointed toward the tree—"there is no limb that can resist a patient axe."

Through clenched teeth Matti said, "Easy to say."

Father asked, "What do we get when we add patience, strength, and stubbornness together?"

"*Sisu,* Father." Matti finally grinned. "*Sisu.*"

By midweek, after Father and Matti had corduroyed the worst spots in the road and started on the sauna floor and roof, the weather suddenly turned stifling hot. "It looks like Minnesota has two temperatures—cold and hot," Father said.

Working with a long-handled whipsaw, Matti got covered with itchy sawdust as they ripped the boards one by one from spruce logs. Father left an opening in the floor for the stone hearth of the fireplace. "I can't wait to get our main cabin built so this can become our *savusauna.*"

"Why bother to build a bathhouse"—Matti wiped the sweat from his forehead—"when this weather is as hot as a sauna?"

As they worked on the roof, the crow kept watch on the ground. If a nail clattered down the side of the building, he hopped over and picked it up. The first time Father was impressed. "Look, he's fetching a nail for us," he said.

But when the crow pecked a hole in the ground and buried the nail, Father yelled, "Useless bird."

"Patience, Father," Matti teased.

The crow cawed proudly and scratched more dirt on top of his cache. Father had to laugh.

The next day the crow walked over to the ladder and flapped up to the first rung. Though he teetered and nearly fell on each rung, he finally made it to the top. When he reached the roof, he cawed and spread his wings. Matti noticed that his eyes had changed from blue to brown. His voice was getting deeper and louder, too.

To Matti's surprise the crow walked up the roofline, stuck his beak into Father's nail pouch, and pulled out a nail. Then he waddled to the edge of the roof, dropped the nail, and flapped back down the ladder. When he found his treasure, he buried it in another hole.

Father shook his head. "Your crow might be worth his salt if you could only teach him to use a hammer, Matti."

CHAPTER 11

On Matti's first Saturday at the store, he left early to allow extra traveling time. After breakfast was done Father wished him luck and asked, "Have you got your compass and matches?"

"I'm not going to get lost," he said.

"I said, Have you got your compass and matches?"

Matti shook his head. Father reached into a jar and gave him a handful of his "emergency matches," waterproofed with candle wax. "Always carry these with you when you go into the woods."

The walk went faster than Matti expected. Since the front door of the store was still closed, Matti sat down on the steps and waited.

A short while later Matti heard footsteps. He stood

up and said, "Good morning, Mr. Winston," as the door swung open.

"What in tarnation . . ." Billy jumped. "Have you been sleeping out here all night, lad?"

"No, Mr. Winston. I just got here sooner than I planned."

"Call me Billy." He waved Matti inside. "My real name isn't Winston anyway." For a moment Matti thought he wasn't understanding Billy's English. "I was christened William Angus McKenzie the third," he explained, "but the folks who come to the store figure I'm a Winston because that's the name out front. It's simpler to answer to Winston than to correct everybody."

"William," a singsong voice called from inside. "Is the tea ready?"

"I'll be there in a minute, dear," Billy called. Turning to Matti, he said, "We only got married last April. Clara was a Hughes girl. She grew up in a big house on Summit Avenue in St. Paul where they never got moving until the afternoon." Before Billy stepped toward the living quarters in the rear, Matti studied his eyes, trying to see a glimmer of the all-out devotion that his mother had mentioned. Though Billy's eyes were a lively blue, they looked like regular eyes to him. Matti couldn't imagine his father ever serving Mother tea in bed. Even when the twins were born, Mother got up the next day and helped with the grain harvest.

Billy returned and showed Matti around. "Your main jobs will be stocking the bins and shelves and sweeping the floor," he said. "If a customer comes in while I'm busy, help them as best you can. Of course, if he's a Finn, you can step right in."

"What you got there?" a gruff voice sounded from behind Matti. "A little Finlander to run your candy counter?" Matti turned to see a huge lumberjack in a red wool shirt, green suspenders, and "high-water" pants that were cut off above the tops of his boots. As he took a seat on a nail keg beside the stove, the floor creaked.

"Never you mind, Karl," Billy said. "Matti has agreed to help me with my clerking."

"Looks like he'd do better in a millinery shop." Karl laughed. Matti tried not to blush and did his best to listen to the rest of Billy's directions. Billy waited on the first few customers himself. He showed Matti the cash box and the ledger book where he recorded his charge accounts. Matti noticed that most of the folks enjoyed visiting and were in no hurry to leave. But one tall fellow came in and handed Billy a list and never said a word. Once the order was filled, the man held out a handful of coins. Billy took a quarter and three pennies. Then the man tipped his cap and left.

"Sven's one of my best customers," Billy said. "Comes in every other Saturday and always pays cash."

"Doesn't he ever talk?" Matti asked.

"No," Billy said. "Unlike some patrons of this establishment"—Billy made sure that a short, red-bearded man who had joined Karl Gustafson on a bench beside the stove heard him—"he never complains."

The short man hooted, "A highlander like you would be lost without a little bellyaching."

"The scary thing about Sven," Billy said, "is that his wife is the quiet one."

A minute later a short, scowling man walked in. "Here's your first customer," Billy whispered. "His name is Kaarlo Tuomi."

Mr. Tuomi was carrying a kerosene can with a small potato stuck in the spout for a stopper. He looked angry, but when Matti said *Hyvää huomenta,* he smiled. As Matti filled his order,

Mr. Tuomi asked where he was living, who his parents were, and what province in Finland he'd come from.

Billy complimented Matti after Mr. Tuomi left, saying, "That's three times more than he usually buys."

Mrs. Winston had watched Matti the whole time, too. She surprised him by asking, "What does *hyvää huomenta* mean?"

"Good morning," Matti said.

Mrs. Winston repeated it slowly and asked, "Is that right?"

"Close." Matti nodded.

"Clara's been to finishing school," Billy said. "That means she knows how to order soup in six languages."

Mrs. Winston ignored Billy's comment. "You may not realize it, Matti, but you and I have a lot in common."

"We do?"

"I'm just as much a foreigner in this place as you are. Why, I felt more at home when I visited Paris than I do in"—she paused and her eyes narrowed as she looked out the front window—"in these woods." She shivered as if *woods* were the coldest word in the whole wide world.

"Now, Clara," Billy said, "I told you it would take a while for the local folks to warm up to a city gal. They just need time." Between customers Mrs. Winston asked Matti to teach her how to say *please, thank you,* and *May I help you?* in Finnish. In return she helped Matti with his English when he got stuck. *D* and *b* sounds were difficult for him, and he had trouble with *a, an,* and *the,* because none of these existed in Finnish.

When Billy went out to the barn later, Matti was feeling confident. An Ojibwe brave walked in. Though he wore a wool shirt and lumberjack pants, his hair was tied back in a ponytail. Matti asked if he could help him, but he just stared. Finally the man said, "Where is day after tomorrow?"

It sounded like a strange riddle. Was his English that bad? "Where's day after tomorrow?" the big man repeated, twice as loud.

Matti was blushing when the side door opened and Billy came back. He shook the brave's hand. "I should have warned you," Billy said to Matti. "Some of the older Ojibwe call me Day After Tomorrow. That was the nickname they gave my father. When he started this trading post, he traveled all the way to Duluth for supplies. If the Ojibwe asked him when he was coming back, he'd always say, 'The day after tomorrow,' and the name stuck."

By the end of the day, Matti's head was swimming with names and faces and ledger columns. When Matti finished sweeping the floor and got ready to go home, Billy said, "Are you going to take your wages in cash or trade?"

Matti blinked at yet another mysterious use of an English word. "What would I trade?"

Billy laughed. "Trade means you can use your hours as credit to buy goods from the store."

"I will ask Father what he thinks," Matti said.

When Matti got home, Father was hobbling the mules for the night. As Matti walked up to help him, Katie brayed as if she was glad to see him. "How was your day?" Father asked, pulling the first knot tight.

Since Matti had been speaking English for most of the day, it took him a moment to switch back to Finnish. "Fine," Matti said. "It's a real busy place. Homesteaders come from miles around to trade at Billy's store."

"Any Finns?"

"A couple. But Billy says there'll be lots more when they find out he has a Finn clerk."

"He should give you a raise then," Father said.

"I've only worked one day." Matti had hoped that Father would be more positive. "He asked if I wanted to take my wages in cash or trade."

"Is that some shopkeeper's trick?"

"No." Matti smiled. Now it was his turn to explain an English expression.

CHAPTER 12

As soon as the last roof board was nailed in place on the sauna, Father and Matti cut out a small window opening in the wall facing the lake. Then Father tied some cedar boughs at the end of a stick to make a crude broom. He handed it to Matti and said, "Give our little castle a sweeping, and we'll be ready to keep house."

Just before dark Father and Matti rolled out their blankets on the floor. "Sweet dreams," Father said.

"Good night," Matti said, enjoying the luxury of having no rocks or roots grinding into his hips. Matti was almost asleep when a pesky mosquito drilled him in the neck. Then he heard another and another buzzing nearby. Father cursed and slapped twice.

With no windowpane in place and no door, the sauna was a haven for mosquitoes. It was also much hotter than their lean-to. "What do you say we move back to our old house?" Matti asked.

Father tossed his blanket off. "I was just about to suggest the same thing."

The next morning Father and Matti turned their attention to the fields. Eino Saari and Black Jack had warned Father that frosts came to Sampo Lake through the end of May, so he was in no hurry to get the seed planted too soon.

Since Father couldn't afford a factory plow, he and Matti built one. They began by sawing an ash log into a timber and shaping the end into a gentle curve. Then they bolted on a steel plate, two ash handles, and an iron ring for the hitch.

When Father started the mules down the first furrow, Matti thought it would be easy going. The ground was a mix of loam and sand, and the plow dug in easily. Father smiled as the sod rolled over. The familiar smell of the newly turned soil brought memories of springs past to Matti. From the time he was little, he had helped his father and mother during planting time.

Father was saying "This will be great dirt for potatoes" when the point of the plow hit something. The handles jerked up and nearly pitched him to the ground.

"It felt like I hit an anvil," Father said.

Matti fetched a pick and shovel, and he and Father uncovered a boulder as big as a water bucket. "Let's hope there aren't too many nuggets this big," Father said as they rolled it to the edge of the clearing. Then clicking the mules to life, he added, "But you know that the *Kalevala* calls us Finns masters of a land of stumps and stones. This feels like home already."

Only a few paces later the plow got stuck next to a pine stump. Father dropped to one knee and swore. "I thought these roots would be rotted enough to break loose." Matti got an axe, and while he chopped, Father kept the mules pulling. When the plow jerked forward, the root snapped up, knocking off Matti's cap and plastering his face with dirt. Father laughed as Matti spit out the grit. The crow flapped down to investigate. He looked as if he were going to pick up Matti's cap, but he plucked out a worm instead.

It took Father and Matti an hour to chop and dig their way to the end of the first two-hundred-foot-long furrow. Then just as Father turned the mules around and headed back toward the lake, the plow stopped again. Suddenly Father wasn't smiling. "How I'd like a few sticks of dynamite to persuade these rocks," he said.

Matti drove his pry bar into the ground, and sparks flew as he hit solid granite. A wisp of rock dust rose into the air. The deeper they dug, the angrier Father got. By using two bars and a shovel, they finally pried the boulder out of the hole. But when Father tried to roll it off to one side, it dropped back in.

"Blast these rocks," Father cursed. Katie turned her head and flicked her ears. Matti had never seen Father so mad. Father kicked at the boulder and missed. His other foot turned, and he slipped into the hole, twisting his left leg under his right. Father was wedged so tight against the rock that he couldn't move.

Katie let out an *eeoow* as if she were laughing.

Father's eyes turned black and glowering, and he looked ready to explode. Finally he took a deep breath. "Help me out of this hole, before those mules fall asleep."

Once Father was back on his feet, Matti said, "Why don't we cut a long pole to pry with?"

"It would snap right off," Father said.

"My science teacher in Kuopio taught us that a lever can move anything."

"Fetch a pole if you like." Father shrugged his shoulders. "For now I'll plow around this pesky boulder."

Matti trotted to the edge of the woods and felled a fifteen-foot aspen with his axe. He trimmed the branches and chopped off the top, leaving a stout ten-foot pole.

When Matti returned, Father stopped the mules and watched. Matti fit the limber end of the pole under the boulder and pried down. The boulder started to roll up out of the hole. As Matti leaned his full weight down, Father raised his eyebrows in approval. Stepping forward, he said, "Let me help," but just then the green aspen snapped off. Matti fell cheek first into the newly plowed ground, and his right elbow smacked a buried stone.

Pretending he wasn't hurt, Matti jumped up and brushed off the dirt. Father joined Katie in her laughter this time.

CHAPTER 13

When Saturday came again, Matti felt guilty about leaving Father to do the field work alone, yet he was looking forward to his job at the store. As Matti said goodbye, the crow flapped onto his shoulder. Matti shooed him away, but he flew right back.

"Looks like he wants to be a shopkeeper, too," Father said.

Matti hiked down the trail, enjoying the cool morning breeze. At times the crow glided ahead. Other times he rode on his shoulder. The peace of the woods made Matti lonesome for Kuopio. This was the time of the year when he and his friends Paavo and Juha caught dozens of *hauki* in the lake. Though Paavo always managed to fall in the water at least once on every trip, they brought home sackfuls of fish to share with their neighbors. If only Paavo and Juha could come and visit him at Sampo Lake.

When Matti reached the store, the crow perched on the porch railing and studied the merchandise in the window. The front door was already unlocked. "Morning, Matti," Billy called, stepping outside. "Have you recruited a new customer?"

"He's my pet." The crow cawed and flew to Matti's shoulder.

"Once those hatchlings fix on you, you're stuck being their momma."

"He's feeding himself already," Matti said.

"He looks plenty healthy," Billy said as he watched the crow preen his wing feathers. "You ready to get to work?"

Matti said, "Yes sir," and stepped into the store.

Since word had spread that Billy had a new "Finn clerk," lots of Finnish folks came to meet him. The hardest people to understand were those who spoke a mixture of Finnish and English, which Billy called Finnglish. When a man came in and said, "Kivit for me tat *kahvi*," Matti was stumped. Blushing, he said, "*Anteeksi*," or "Excuse me" in Finnish. Only when the man switched to Finnish did Matti figure out that he meant "Give me that coffee."

Most of the customers were friendly except for the ornery lumberjack, Karl Gustafson, who had made fun of Matti his first day. When Karl came in after lunch and bought some chewing tobacco, he paid Matti with a handful of dirty pennies, saying, "I want to test your young Finlander, Billy, and see if he can count." Karl thought that was real funny until Matti noticed he was one penny short. Then he grumbled about "boys too smart for their britches" and dug for another coin.

After Karl left, Billy said, "Don't you pay that fellow no

mind. He's been as crabby as a cat with his tail in a wringer ever since a bum leg made him quit lumberjacking last year."

Through the morning, as Matti waited on customers and listened to Billy speak with the French Canadians, Norwegians, and Swedes who came into his store, he realized that these were folks just like his own family. Matti decided that was why Mrs. Winston made the customers so nervous. They'd left their home countries to escape rich landowners who'd lorded over them their whole lives, and Mrs. Winston's fancy ways reminded them of the world they'd fled.

Matti was still confused by Billy's strange way of talking. Instead of saying goodbye to the customers, he'd often call "Keep your powder dry" or "Watch your back, *hivernant.*"

Just before lunch Billy asked Matti to come to the livery stable to help him. As Billy stepped into the barn, he waved his hand to his right. "I got me a fine pair of Missouri mules in yesterday."

Hurrying to keep up with Billy, Matti cut close behind one of the new mules. The mule lashed out with his hind foot and kicked him in the same shin that was still bruised from being hit with the logging chain. "Owww," Matti groaned as he fell.

"What on earth?" Billy turned to find Matti lying on the hay-littered floor. "Don't you know enough to stay clear of a strange animal?"

"But the tail isn't clipped funny like Katie's," Matti said.

"Did you think we put a warning sign on every barnyard beast in America?"

Matti limped through the rest of the day, trying not to show his pain. Things went well until the middle of the afternoon, when Matti heard a shriek from the porch. He looked out and saw his crow diving at Mrs. Winston. He hurried out.

"Mind your manners," Matti hollered, and the bird

glided over and landed on his shoulder. Two customers were grinning.

Mrs. Winston said, "Is that bird your pet?"

"I rescued him after a storm," Matti said. "He wouldn't hurt you. He just wanted to see that pretty ring you're wearing."

"This?" She held up her left hand, and the crow cawed.

Matti took a step toward her so that the crow could see the sparkly diamond. He cocked his head and leaned over and pecked at the stone. She pulled back her hand, and everyone laughed.

"That bird has fine taste in jewelry, Clara," Billy said.

"Well, he can't have it," she said. Everyone laughed again.

Billy walked up to Matti after his wife had gone inside and put his arm around his shoulders. "I'd like to thank you, Matti."

"Thank me?" Matti said.

Billy nodded. "That's the first time she's gone near a wild creature since she moved here. I don't care if it's a mouse or a magpie. Being that she grew up in the city, she's afraid of anything furred or feathered." As the customers walked back into the store, Billy asked, "Did I ever tell you how I met Clara?"

Billy went on to tell the story of how Miss Clara Hughes had come north to vacation with the Congdons, one of the wealthiest families in the Midwest. She and the Congdon girls had gone on a steamboat ride to the Cook end of Lake Vermilion. Billy was returning from a trading trip at Wakem-up Village when he met Clara on the boat. "The weather was still and blue that day," he said. "A pair of ospreys were circling over Norwegian Bay, and Clara asked me what kind of birds they were. We struck up a conversation and hit it right off. By the time we reached Big Bay, the moon was huge and sparkling on the water." Billy paused. "I was smitten. A week later we eloped. At first Clara's father threatened to disown her, but things gradually settled down."

Just before quitting time the door swung open and Matti heard, "Hey there, Mutti Boy."

It was Black Jack, with his dog Louhi at his side. "Since when have you been working at Miss Clara's store?" Black Jack stumped past him and walked up to Clara. "How's the prettiest lady between here and Helsinki?" His English was rough but understandable.

"Why, Mr. Mattson," Clara replied. "How nice to see you." To Matti's amazement she held out her hand and Black Jack shook it. "So what can we do for you?" she asked.

"My stewpot is low on potatoes."

"I believe we can fix that," she said.

After Black Jack had paid for a sack of potatoes, Mrs. Winston turned to Matti. "Since we'll be closing soon, why don't you help Mr. Mattson carry his potatoes home? You're neighbors, aren't you?"

Matti thought about using his sore shin as an excuse to avoid spending time with Black Jack, but how could he refuse to help a one-legged man?

When they stepped outside, Matti said, "I didn't know you spoke English."

"I don't speak English," Black Jack said as Matti bent to pet Louhi.

"But . . ." Matti frowned.

"When I first came to this country, I learned the only two phrases I've ever needed: 'Please pass the potatoes' and 'My, aren't you a pretty lady.' I haven't found a place where one or the other didn't work."

As Matti shouldered the potato sack, his crow flapped down from a tree and perched on top of it.

On their way home Black Jack spent half the time cackling at his own jokes, and half the time whistling the same strange tune that had accompanied his chopping. Matti asked him about the music again, but Black Jack said, "What music? You must be hearing things." Then he cackled so loud that he scared the crow.

When they reached Jack's cabin, Matti set the potatoes on the doorstep. Anxious to get home and rest his aching shin, Matti said goodbye and turned to go.

"Don't you have time for one cup of coffee?"

Matti searched his mind for an excuse. "Father worries if I don't get home before dark."

Black Jack nodded.

But before he turned to leave, Matti asked, "How did you know that tree was going to hit our lean-to during that storm?"

"It's like this, Mutti Boy. I hold up my finger and . . ." He grinned as if he were about to say something silly. Then he stopped. "To tell you the truth, I don't know how I do it. The scary thing is there's no way for me to predict when it's going to come. Sometimes I just see things. When the feeling is strong, it's like I've been blind up until that moment."

He paused as if he was waiting for Matti to laugh at him. When he didn't, Jack kept going. "I grew up as a beggar boy back in Finland. My father died in a logging accident when I was only eight years old. The night before it happened, I had a terrible dream where I saw a load of logs tip over on him. I begged Father not to go to work, but he patted my head and said he'd see me at supper.

"I'll never forget the look on my mother's face when the man came to tell her about the accident. Her eyes flashed toward me for just a second; then she broke down sobbing.

"Times were hard from that day on. By doing sewing and needlework Mother did her best to take care of me and my three sisters, but she barely earned enough for us to survive. Then when I was ten years old, my mother and one of my big sisters died in a flu epidemic. The family was split up between relatives. I was sent to live with my aunt and uncle.

"I got along fine with my aunt, but my uncle was a mean brute. One day I had a feeling that something bad was going to happen. I warned him to be careful, but he only made fun of me. The next morning a rope broke in the hayloft, and a metal hook dropped and broke his arm. When I tried to help, he accused me of cutting the rope and trying to kill him. Before I could say anything more, he picked up a hoe and swung at me. I ducked. The handle broke over my back. When he raised that hickory to crack me in the head, I took off running."

Black Jack stopped suddenly. He was staring toward the lake as if he was trying to shake a dark picture out of his head.

"And?" Matti asked.

"And I soon grew up and learned that it was wise not to ask so many questions of my elders," he said.

On his way home Matti kept thinking of how fortunate he'd been to have Wilho. He couldn't imagine an uncle being so mean that he would drive his own nephew away.

CHAPTER 14

On Sunday morning Father and Matti were hitching the mules to the plow while they waited for Timo to arrive. Matti's leg was almost totally healed, and he was glad that Father hadn't noticed his injury. Matti was irritated to find himself whistling just like Black Jack. When he stopped himself, he heard a small sound. At first he thought it was raindrops, yet the sky was clear. Then he noticed small bits of leaves on the ground. He picked up a piece and saw that the edges had been chewed.

Father held out his palm. Black flecks, not much bigger than grains of pepper, were falling from the trees. Matti looked into a popple and saw a thin caterpillar dangling from a silk streamer. Then he saw another and another. He pointed and said, "There must be thousands."

"I'll be . . . ," Father said, blowing the black specks out of his hand. "This must be caterpillar manure. It would take millions."

While Father finished harnessing the mules, Matti picked up one of the caterpillars. It had a black back marked with an even row of white dots. A pale blue stripe ran down its sides. As it crawled across Matti's hand, its tiny mouth parts opened and closed.

"What's so interesting?" It was Timo, arriving an hour late.

"Just some hungry worms," Father said, shaking Timo's hand. "You want to plow or pick rocks?"

Timo chose to drive the team. Though Timo looked as rough as he had the week before, he didn't whine much until they hit a bad patch of ground. After they uncovered a half dozen rocks in a row, Timo threw down the reins and said, "There's more boulders than dirt in this field."

"Timo sounds as crabby as that character from the store that you told me about, Matti," Father said. "What was his name? Karl something?"

"Karl Gustafson."

"Maybe we should change Timo's name to Crabby Karl."

Timo cursed and said, "Let me try that lining bar."

In the next hour Timo took a turn with the lining bar and then the shovel before he switched back to driving the team again. Matti decided that if he had a choice, he would rather do the work himself than put up with Timo's grumbling.

When Timo and Father walked down to the lake to get a drink, Matti trotted over to the ash swamp and cut another pole. He hadn't given up on his lever idea yet. Knowing that ash was nearly as strong as oak, he trimmed and topped the tree and dragged it back to the field.

"Are we going to pole-vault over the field or plow it?"

Timo asked. Father chuckled and told Timo about Matti's previous try.

Ignoring their laughter, Matti fitted the tip of his ash pole under the boulder that Father had given up on the other day, and he placed another, shorter piece of ash crossways at the edge of the hole to act as a fulcrum. To Matti's relief the boulder rolled up, and with a little help from Father, out of the hole.

"Would you look at that," Father said, patting Matti on the back. "Wilho always told me you were smart as a whip. I should have listened to him."

"The round ones are always easy to roll," Timo scoffed.

"It's smart to use your brain instead of brawn." Father beamed at Matti. "The *Kalevala* teaches us that the one who triumphs is 'he who has the greater knowledge.'"

"Spare us the poems, Father," Timo said, picking up the reins and starting the mules.

When they stopped for lunch, Matti gathered a handful of caterpillars and brought them to the crow for a snack. Father said, "Your crow can finally earn his keep."

Though the crow always ate the bugs and worms that Matti fed him, when he saw the caterpillars, he hopped away.

Father shook his head. "He'll be useless forever."

"That's the truth," Timo said.

"At least he's not as useless as these caterpillars," Matti said.

"Bugs are another matter," Father said. "I guarantee you that some critter is lunching on these right now."

Matti promised himself that he would prove Father wrong. What animal would ever eat the repulsive caterpillars?

All day and all night the caterpillars munched away. Leaf

bits fell from the trees like jagged green snowflakes. Caterpillars fell into Matti's oatmeal. They crawled down his shirt, and their silk strands caught in his face and hair. In a week they had doubled in length and chewed the popple and birch half-bare.

As much as Matti disliked the caterpillars, Mrs. Winston hated them even more. When he arrived at the store the following Saturday, Matti was surprised to find her out on the porch. "This is war, Matti Ojala," she said. Her hair was tied back with a kerchief and she wore a plain cotton dress for a change. "I'm getting rid of these filthy worms," she said, pausing to squash a cluster with her broom, "if I have to mash every one myself."

"Dearest," Billy pleaded as she swept more caterpillars off the porch. "There's no stopping those worms. Killing a few of them is like trying to melt a glacier with a blowtorch."

She stomped her foot down in front of his boot. "There's one less for us to worry about."

Though Matti normally had a strong stomach, the sound of the caterpillar being smashed under her shoe made him queasy. Billy wrinkled up his nose, too, and turned away. "We'd better check that flour bin, Matti," he said.

Matti's English was getting better, but he was still confused by some of the strange words that Billy used. When Billy was adjusting a shelf later that morning, he stood back and complained that it was "catawampus." When Matti looked at him funny, he said, "It's just another way of saying something's crooked."

That same day Billy said some people were "straight shooters" and others "heels." Mrs. Winston explained that it had nothing to do with either marksmanship or boots. She also translated two of Billy's expressions: "the whole kit and caboodle" and "take it with a grain of salt."

Mrs. Winston continued her war on the worms throughout the day. At quitting time she called Matti to the back counter and asked, "Could you do me a favor?"

Matti hoped it didn't have anything to do with caterpillars.

"Would you drop this off at Black Jack's cabin on your way home?" she said, handing him a sack. "He loves licorice."

Matti agreed, but he could barely keep his mouth from falling open. Mrs. Winston was sending candy to Black Jack!

When Matti knocked on Black Jack's door, he wasn't surprised by the gift. "Clara's my sweetie," he said as Matti set the package on his shaving-littered table.

The cabin was an even bigger mess than Matti remembered. Wood chips and sawdust were piled ankle deep under the table. His spittoon looked as if it hadn't been emptied in a month. The same coffeepot and stew kettle stood unwashed on the kitchen range.

As Black Jack picked up a rasp and a carving knife from a stool so that Matti could sit down, Matti noticed a thin spruce panel lying on the table. The wood was cut in a graceful arc, and beside it was an open catalog that showed an assortment of carving tools and a diagram of a stringed instrument. "You're building a violin?"

Black Jack nodded. "It's going mighty slow. I couldn't afford to buy any fancy tools, so I built a forge out of an old cream separator and made them myself." He picked up a little hooked blade and a thickness gauge. "See," he said, holding them next to the picture in the catalog, "they're a perfect match. I'm even making all the parts by hand. I've cut the sound post setters from the tips of an old hayfork, and I've got a book of formulas for mixing the stains and varnishes."

"When did you learn to play the violin?"

"I picked it up on my own," Black Jack said. "My father was a great fiddler. If he heard a song once, he could play it. On winter evenings he'd hold me on his lap and let me pull the bow across the strings while he did the fingering. His violin was the one thing that my mother set aside for me. But when I went to live with my uncle, he sold it to pay for my keep."

Louhi started barking. "He must be ready for his supper," Black Jack said. "Would you care for a bowl of stew?"

Looking at the blackened pot out of the corner of his eye, Matti said, "Maybe some other time."

"Suit yourself," Black Jack said, picking up the violin panel. "But don't forget to check your fish trap on the way home."

Though Matti hadn't caught a fish in the creek all week, he was happy to bring two fat northerns home to Father for supper.

CHAPTER 15

The morning finally arrived when Father and Matti left to pick up Mother and the girls. The day before, Father had made a door for the sauna and measured the window opening so that he could buy a sash in town. The road had dried out so well since spring that it took less than three hours to drive to Soudan.

Anna and Kari squealed when they saw them. They set down the dishes that they were packing into a wooden crate and ran forward to greet Father. Since Matti hadn't seen the girls in such a long time, he'd forgotten how much Kari acted like Aunt Hilda and how much Anna took after Mother.

Anna and Kari wrinkled up their noses as they hugged Father and Matti. When Mother got close, she frowned, too.

"What's wrong?" Father asked.

Mother cleared her throat. "Have you gentlemen by any chance taken a bath lately?" she asked.

"Our sauna chimney won't be finished for a while," Father said.

"So you haven't had a bath this whole time?"

"We dip in the lake every evening," Matti said.

"Do you use soap?" Anna and Kari were holding their noses.

"What's soap?" Father gave Matti a dig in the ribs and leaned forward and kissed Mother.

She pushed his unshaven cheek away. "The first order of business will be to take a razor and a washcloth to you wild men. For now, how about a little breakfast?"

"We've got to get going," Father said, but when he saw the disappointment in Matti's face, he said, "You go ahead."

"I saved you a treat," Mother said as she reached for the butter crock. Matti smiled as she took a spoon and dropped a big eye of butter into a steaming bowl of oatmeal. Matti hadn't tasted butter for a month.

As Matti ate, Mother said, "I just got a letter from Hilda. She's doing as well as we could expect. She's taken a room at our old neighbors the Koskelas' and says that she doesn't miss America a bit. One good sign was that her letter sounded angry. She hates the Russians so much that she said she'd sign up as a soldier herself if there were ever half a chance to fight them."

Father frowned suddenly. "Is that lazybones Timo still asleep?" he asked. Stepping toward the stairs, he yelled, "Timo, get yourself out of the sack!"

"Leo," she interrupted him. "Timo isn't here."

"Don't tell me he's still out gallivanting. I'll teach him—"

"He moved out last week."

"What?"

Mother nodded. "He said he was sick of being treated like a child, and he wanted to be out on his own."

Father paced to the window and stared up the hill at the head frame above the main shaft. "He's staying on at the mine?"

"And he's taken a room at Mrs. Korpi's boardinghouse."

"That ungrateful pup." Father still stared out the window.

Matti couldn't believe Timo's selfishness. How would they break all that ground and build their log cabin without his help? The one time the family really needed him, he had walked away.

"He did leave half of his last paycheck," Mother said, "but I haven't seen him since."

"After all the work," Father said. "How could he ever—"

"He's young, Leo. Perhaps we need to give him time."

"But what good is a farm without a son to pass it on to?"

What about me? Matti thought as he loaded the last box onto the wagon. Aren't I a son, too?

Just then Kari came around the corner with a storybook in her left hand, and a huge yellow cat tucked under her arm. He was so long that his tail dragged on the ground.

"What's this?" Father asked.

"It's Yrjo."

"Yrjo the cat?" He pretended to frown. "Where are you taking him?"

"To our homestead," Kari said as Anna nodded.

"He's too big to fit into our wagon," Father teased.

"He can ride on my lap," Kari said.

"Or my lap," Anna said as she petted Yrjo's ears.

Father sighed loudly. "We'll just have to take the moocher with us, then."

"What's a moocher?" Kari asked.

"That's another name for a cat," Father said.

* * *

On the trip back to the homestead, Matti drove the wagon while Mother and Father chatted about their farm. The girls rode in back and kept an eye on Mother's dishes. Father went on about Timo, still not believing that his son—"a serpent's tooth," he called him—could be so ungrateful.

When Mother first glimpsed Sampo Lake, she clapped her hands. "Our very own lake?"

"Almost," Father said. "We share it with one neighbor, Black Jack."

As the girls climbed out of the wagon and started toward the lake, Matti's crow swooped down from the branches of a red pine. Matti expected him to land on his shoulder, but he dove toward the girls instead. Kari screamed as the bird pecked at her hair ribbon. Yrjo jumped out of her arms and dove under the wagon. The crow pulled Kari's bow loose and flew to the tree with his prize.

Father and Matti laughed, but Kari ran crying to Mother.

"He's only a pet," Matti said, but Kari was crying too hard to hear him. When she finally settled down, the crow flew back and landed on Matti's shoulder. Kari and Anna both squealed.

"He won't hurt you," Matti said.

Kari blinked away her tears and stared. When Anna tilted her head, the crow tipped his head, too, and stared at her.

"What a wise bird," Mother said. The crow landed on her shoulder and pecked at her hair comb. "Oh no you don't," she said.

The girls giggled as the crow glided to the ground.

"What's his name?" Mother asked.

"I haven't named him yet."

97

"Such a fine trickster deserves a special name." She smiled. "How about Wilho?"

For a moment everyone was silent. Then Father nodded. "He's certainly clever enough."

At first it made Matti sad to think of naming his crow after Uncle Wilho. But he realized he could never find a more fitting name. It reminded him of a story that Mother used to tell him about a little boy and his grandfather. After the grandfather died, his spirit visited the boy as a swan. If Wilho had chosen to join them at Sampo Lake, he couldn't have picked a better form.

With Mother's arrival life immediately became orderly. She clucked her tongue in disgust when she saw the dirt on the sauna floor and put Anna and Kari to work with brooms and a scrub bucket. "But we just got here," Kari whined.

"Work before play, Miss *Ruusunukke*," Mother said. There were no complaints from then on, for neither of the girls wanted to be called a silly rose doll.

The sauna was so small that Mother decided to store most of Hilda's furniture outside under a tarp until their main cabin was finished. The only things she brought inside were her trunk, her spinning wheel, the kitchen table and chairs, and the straw ticks for sleeping. She announced that the men's camping was over and everyone would be sleeping inside. Mother also made good on her promise to trim Matti's and Father's hair, and she insisted that from now on washing didn't count unless they used soap. She gave Anna and Kari a good scrubbing beside the lake, and she threatened to do the same to her two lumberjacks, as she had taken to calling Father and Matti, if they didn't take care of themselves.

Mother set up her cookstove and her kitchen utensils under the lean-to. For the summer she would do all her cooking outside. "We'll call it our canning kitchen," she said. They would move the stove inside the sauna once the weather turned cold.

Rather than drinking right from shore, Mother had Matti fetch a pail of water from the lake and hang a dipper beside it. Matti also had to get two buckets after every meal for the dishes. When Matti carried up her dishwater the first time, she frowned into the bucket. "What do you see in that water, Matti Ojala?"

He looked down. "Snails?"

She nodded. "And I think I saw a small minnow. You and your father are going to have to build a dock so you can fill the buckets out in deeper, cleaner water. In the meantime, would you hike up the hill and see if you can find a rowan tree for our yard?"

Father turned to Matti and said, "Why don't you and Ti—" He stopped before the word *Timo* came out and said, "Let's see if we can fetch one." There was a tradition in Finland of planting a rowan, or mountain ash, in the courtyard of every new home. Though Father thought it a waste of time, he didn't complain when it took a good part of the morning for them to find a small ash and replant it.

On her second morning at Sampo Lake, Mother turned to Matti over breakfast and said, "Who has the nearest cows?"

"I think Mr. Saari keeps cows. He's the stationmaster."

"We will have to pay the Saaris a call this afternoon," Mother said. "You can show me the way."

When Matti admitted that he hadn't been to the Saaris', Mother scolded him for being unsociable. After stopping to get directions from Mr. Saari, Matti found the Saari cabin was only a mile east of the tracks. Mrs. Saari was working in her garden and didn't look up until her dog started barking. She looked amazed to have visitors. Three boys, the youngest barely tall enough to reach her apron strings, were helping her, but the moment they spotted Mother and Matti, they ducked behind the barn.

Mrs. Saari's white-blond hair was tied back and covered with a kerchief. Her face was round and tanned, and she was so short that she barely came up to Matti's chin. Mrs. Saari said, "I thought it was the peddler coming up the road."

Mrs. Saari was so shy that she averted her eyes when she spoke. "Please come in and have some coffee," she said, still looking down.

Having seen Black Jack's cabin, Matti was nervous, but the Saari house was as clean as a hospital. The wooden floors were scrubbed to a soft shine, and sunlight streamed through blue-curtained windows.

"How bright and airy," Mother said.

Just then one of the boys peeked through the window and ducked back down. "I'm sorry," Mrs. Saari said, "but my boys are a bit shy."

Though the cabin was clean, it was crowded with every sort of utensil imaginable. Stone crocks stood in the corner. Pots and pans hung from hooks over the kitchen range. Rows of jars and glass bottles crowded a shelf. A spicy scent drifted from wire baskets above the stove that were filled with herbs, dried roots, and flower petals. An iron kettle with a medicine smell simmered on the stove.

Mother noticed a black case and several small cups cut from the tips of cow horns. Beside the case lay two ivory-handled razors. "Why, you're a *kupparimummu!*" she exclaimed.

Mrs. Saari nodded. "My grandmother taught me."

Matti recognized the instruments. The *kupparimummu* or cupping woman back home cured the sick through bloodletting and special poultices. No one went to the doctor without first seeing her.

Over a cup of coffee Mrs. Saari agreed to sell Mother a pail of milk three times a week. Matti wasn't paying attention to their conversation until Mother said that in exchange for the milk, Matti would give the Saari boys English lessons after the harvest season.

"How could you do that?" Matti whispered to Mother as Mrs. Saari led them to the barn.

"Do what?"

"Say I could teach English," Matti said.

"You'll do just fine," she said.

As Mrs. Saari handed Matti his first pail of milk, Mother said, "Now we'll see how strong my Matti is."

Matti thought Mother was joking at first, but only a short while later the pain in his arms was no laughing matter. The weight was all on one side, and the handle cut into his fingers. Yet he wasn't about to complain about carrying a milk pail.

From then on every Monday, Wednesday, and Friday Matti set off for the Saaris' at dawn. Though it wasn't fun hauling the heavy pail, the rewards were worth it. Mother used the fresh milk for oatmeal, for her special fish-and-potato soup, and for Father's favorite rye pudding. She also made squeaky cheese (Kari could eat a whole plate of it) and *viilia,* a creamy yogurt.

After a week of stretching his fingers to the breaking point carrying milk pails, Matti decided to use his head. He took a short spruce pole and hewed a flat spot to fit the curve of his shoulder. Then he tied a rope to the end to make a carrying yoke, or as Father teased, "Matti's horse collar."

Father and Matti finished Mother's dock on the hottest day of the year. Matti's shirt was plastered with sweat, and his neck itched from sawdust. After they nailed the last plank in place, Father knelt and splashed water on his face. Then he took off his boots and put his feet in the lake.

Matti stripped to his shorts and took a running start from shore. "Clear the deck," he yelled. Sprinting past Father, Matti leaped as far as he could. With his knees tucked to his chest, he hollered, "*Sisuuuuu,*" hitting with a splash. Father chuckled when Matti surfaced. The prickling chill of the water shocked Matti's tiredness away. He tipped back his head and floated. The sun and the blue water reminded him of how it felt to dive into Lake Kallavesi on a hot summer day.

"We're coming swimming, too, Matti," Anna and Kari called. He waved to them. Then he turned and swam parallel to the shore, taking slow, deliberate strokes and breathing deep and easy. For the first time since Wilho's accident, Matti felt that America wasn't such a bad place after all. Perhaps there was hope that Sampo Lake might soon feel like a real home.

"Is the missus home?" A croaking voice interrupted Matti's thoughts. He looked toward the dock. Black Jack was rowing his boat and doing his best to spoil the peace of a perfect day. Maude *eeoow*ed a greeting to Black Jack from the top of the hill.

"That would be me." Mother's voice was a whisper compared to Black Jack's. The girls dove behind Mother's dress.

Black Jack saluted Mother and said, "Nice to meet you." Then he reached down and pulled up a dripping stringer of fish. "I wanted to welcome you to Sampo Lake and bring you some supper." He climbed out of the boat.

"Why, thank you," Mother said. As she took the fish, Anna and Kari clutched at her waist and tried to stay hidden.

"Do I see some young cubs rustling behind those petticoats?" Black Jack called. "Why don't you little ones come here and say hello to Black Jack?" As he leaned sideways to look at the girls, they squealed and ran to Father.

Father caught the girls in his arms. Then he said, "How about a cup of coffee, Jack? I'll kick the pot for us." When Black Jack agreed, Father walked up to the big iron pot that he always kept simmering on the stove. Then the two of them sat on a log facing the lake and visited.

When Anna and Kari got over their shyness, they ventured a little closer to Black Jack. With a sly grin Black Jack pointed at one of the twins and said, "You must be Anna?"

"How did you know I was Anna?" she asked, looking startled.

"You look exactly like an Anna," he said.

"Most people can't even tell us apart."

"Well, people don't pay proper attention then. You look exactly like an Anna, and that other edition over there"—he pointed his finger at Kari, who was still hiding behind Mother—"looks just like a Mathilda May."

Kari shook her head. "I'm Kari," she said.

"My apologies, Mistress Kari. I won't make that mistake again."

By the time Black Jack left, the girls got up enough courage to walk him down to his boat and say, "Good afternoon, Mr. Black Jack."

As Black Jack rowed off, Matti turned to Father and said, "Did you tell Black Jack Anna's name?"

"No." Father shook his head and glanced toward Mother.

"Don't look at me," she said. "I've never met the man before."

CHAPTER 16

By the first week in June, Father and Matti had plowed only half the ground they'd hoped to, yet it was time to seed their crops. "If only that Timo had helped more," Father said. "It's a thankless son that walks out on his family during planting time."

They hadn't seen Timo for two weeks, and Matti could tell that it pained Father a great deal. Though he used to speak of Timo as his eldest and the carrier of his good name, these days he was more likely to call him "that rascal" or "that ne'er-do-well."

Wilho was a pest on the day that they sowed the rye. From the moment Matti filled the canvas shoulder bag, Wilho followed his every move. Since Matti had worked so hard to buy the seed, he didn't want the crow to eat it all up. As Matti broadcast the rye, Wilho hopped alongside him. Father shooed him away, but Wilho caught the seed in his beak before it even hit the ground. And as Father raked the dirt, Wilho pecked between the tines.

Father stopped and pointed his rake at Wilho and said, "This isn't lunchtime, useless." But he couldn't help laughing when Wilho flapped up and perched on the rake handle so that he could peer into Matti's seed bag. "With his taste for rye," Father said, "I'd wager that crow has some Finnish blood in him."

While Matti and Father seeded the fields, Mother and the girls planted a vegetable garden. Mother also did her best to make the sauna into a real home. She hung a curtain over the window and set lace doilies on the table. Every morning she and the girls piled the straw ticks in the corner and swept the floor. Though Matti had been looking forward to the arrival of his family, the sauna was suffocatingly crowded. Father snored like a ripsaw, and the girls were both restless sleepers. Anna often woke up crying from a bad dream, and Kari seldom lay still. After Matti got his face scratched by Kari's toenails twice in the same night, he decided to sleep with Yrjo in the lean-to.

Along with the curtains Mother sewed flour-sack dresses for Kari and Anna. Though the girls rarely fought, they got into an argument over the sack material. "I want the Gold Medal label on my dress," Kari said, having learned that gold and medal were both good things in English.

"It's my turn," Anna pleaded.

"I wish we could afford some nice gingham," Mother said, "but for now we have to share."

"Why don't you cut it down the middle and put one word on each dress?" Matti said.

"Now that's sensible," Mother said. "We'll draw straws to see who's our gold girl and who's our medal girl."

On Friday afternoon Mother made a shopping list for Matti to take to the store the next morning. Though Matti used his wages as merchandise credit, he always had to spend a little of Mother's money, too. She wanted only a few groceries and some thread, yet Matti could tell that she was worried. Mother pulled out her coin purse and counted her money. "We could do without the molasses," she said.

"Don't be such a worrier," Father said. "The berries will soon be ripe for canning, and we'll have enough potatoes to fill two root cellars when the harvest comes."

When Mother handed Matti the list, he could tell that she was still uneasy. Mother might worry too much, but Matti could understand her fears when Father rushed forward so often without thinking.

When Matti started for the store the next morning, the caterpillars were worse than ever. Matti normally enjoyed his walks, but he decided that he would rather be stuck inside the sauna with his giggling sisters on a rainy day than have to hike through the caterpillar-infested woods. The tops of the birch and popple were wriggling masses of caterpillars. Leaf bits and droppings fell on his cap, and the nearly invisible silk caught on his hands and face. For the last two days, the wind had washed piles of dead worms onto the shore. Matti and the girls had been hauling bucketfuls to the garden for fertilizer, but the stink was still awful. Mother's little rowan tree was chewed bare.

Though Matti arrived at the store on time, a homesteader had already parked his wagon out front. Billy was filling his order. "Would you load those things, Matti?" Billy waved toward the goods he'd piled on the counter.

But when Matti picked up a bolt of cloth and started out the door, Billy hollered, "Hold your horses, lad."

Matti stopped and frowned. "What horses?"

Billy and the farmer nearly split their sides laughing. "That just means stop," Billy said. "You've got the wrong bolt there."

All day a steady stream of customers came through the door. The store was so busy that Karl Gustafson gave up his seat on the nail keg and went home because people kept trampling on his toes.

At closing time Matti cleaned up as usual by sprinkling sawdust on the floor and sweeping it up. When he stepped out the back door to empty his bucket, he was startled to see a bear. Recalling the huge bear that had slobbered over his boots last spring, Matti was about to duck back inside. Then he noticed a cub sitting on the ground, pulling a branch across its lips and licking it off.

Mrs. Winston opened the back door. "What is it, Matti?"

When he pointed to the bears, she froze.

"Just watch," he whispered, hoping that she wouldn't scream.

The bears were feasting on caterpillars. Totally content, they bent down one clump of brush after another and slobbered up great gobs of the fuzzy worms. "Good Lord, Matti," she said, "is it just me, or do those bears look like they're smiling?"

"They're grinning like picnickers," he agreed.

"And so are you."

"Father told me that some critter would enjoy eating the things, but I didn't believe him."

"They must chew up hundreds of pounds of those worms." Mrs. Winston smiled. "I think I've finally found some friends in my battle with the caterpillars."

Chapter 17

Matti normally didn't care for cats, but he felt sorry for Yrjo. Every time Yrjo stepped outside, Wilho dove and pecked his head. The only place Yrjo found safety was inside the sauna.

All that changed one day when Anna and Kari talked Mrs. Saari into giving them a pet rabbit. The floppy-eared creature was as big as a small dog, but the girls were afraid an owl or a fox might get him. So Mother let him stay inside at times. His favorite food was milk. One day when Mother poured some leftover milk into a bowl, the rabbit started drinking alongside Yrjo.

"Look," Kari called, "Loppy and Yrjo are friends." But the minute the rabbit saw the milk was gone, he jumped on top of Yrjo's back and started kicking the daylights out of him. The cat took off running, and the minute he got out the door, Wilho flew down and pecked him on the head.

Yrjo finally discovered one place where no one would pester him, underneath Mother's cookstove. Whether there was wood burning in the firebox or not, he curled up and took a nap.

One day Mother got tired of setting out buckets in the sauna whenever it rained, and she told Father that it was time to finish the roofing. Since it would have taken too long to split cedar shingles, Father decided to make a temporary roof out of birch bark. Uncle Wilho was the first to teach Matti about birch bark. One spring when Matti was small, Wilho had caught him peeling bark. "The tree will die unless you time it properly," he scolded.

Wilho then showed Matti how to study the trees until the bark was ready to release. Father would have taken the hatchet and gotten the bark for Matti, but Wilho was a patient teacher. For several days in a row he watched Matti make a tiny slit down the side of a birch. Each time Wilho shook his head. Finally a thin layer of bark curled back from Matti's cut, and Wilho smiled. That winter Wilho showed Matti how birch bark could be shaped into a bowl or a berry basket, and how it could be woven into shoes and packsacks that were stronger than canvas and lighter than leather.

On the day that Father and Matti harvested the bark, birch sap stuck to their hatchet blades and their hands. Even as the sweet scents of earth and sugar lingered in the air, Matti felt a great sadness sweep over him. For with Uncle Wilho gone, spring and the wonder of the white bark leaping free would never be the same.

Matti's crow found new ways of getting into trouble. One day when Father and Matti were skidding some firewood, the twins discovered a patch of wild strawberries. Anna asked Father if they could move the plants to the garden.

Wilho had spent the morning alternately perching on Matti's shoulder and riding on Maude's back (Katie, of course, would not permit such a thing). Wilho watched the girls as they dug up the blossoming plants and carried them back to the garden. He then flew over and watched the girls replant the strawberries and water them with buckets they carried from the lake.

After lunch the girls showed Mother their new project. "We'll make a fresh strawberry pie as soon as..." Mother stopped and frowned.

Matti looked up the hill. Wilho had pulled up every one of the strawberry plants and piled them beside the garden. Wilho crowed proudly when he saw everyone walking toward him.

"Bad bird," Kari said, but Wilho only cawed louder.

"He's getting too smart for his own good," Father said.

To keep Wilho from repeating his "helpful" trick while the girls replanted, Matti took him for a walk. Matti followed the trail toward Sampo Creek. Wilho glided ahead, exploring the forest. Then he flew back and landed on Matti's shoulder.

Just as Matti was ready to step into the meadow, he heard a whoosh of wings. Wilho let out a screech and dug his claws into Matti's shoulder. Matti looked up to see the cold, yellow eyes of an owl only inches away. Wilho pumped his wings to escape as the owl hissed and stretched his talons toward Wilho. Bony wings struck the side of Matti's head, and talons closed on empty air.

Matti was trembling as he took a deep breath and watched one black tail feather float to the ground.

"Wilho," Matti called, softly at first, afraid that he might attract the owl. Then he trotted down the path, calling louder. He saw the flicker of a bird ahead and dashed forward, but it turned out to be a woodpecker.

Matti walked a long way beyond the creek, calling the

whole way. Had the owl circled around and caught Wilho? Matti scanned the trees, but there was no sign of him. When it was nearly dark, Matti turned toward home. Under the shadowy cedars Matti hiked, his mind fixed on the memory of the cold, yellow fire that had burned in the eyes of the owl.

When Matti was almost within sight of the sauna, he heard a familiar caw. There was Wilho, standing at the edge of the garden with the strawberry plants neatly piled at his feet again.

CHAPTER 18

The next Saturday when Matti arrived at the store, he saw a group of lumberjacks gathered in front of Sally's saloon. They were looking at something in the grass and laughing.

A fellow wearing the red-stained clothes of a miner was lying flat on his stomach with his pockets turned inside out. Karl Gustafson prodded the ribs of the sleeping man with the toe of his boot. "Is it alive?"

"He's been testing knockout drops," another man said, laughing.

"Ya," his grizzled buddy agreed. "Those boys pitched him right here last night after they picked his pockets clean."

Matti was chuckling along with them until he realized that he was staring at his own brother. "Timo!" Matti cried, kneeling down beside him. He rocked Timo's shoulder and said, "It's me, Matti."

Timo groaned and rolled over onto his side. He smelled like stale beer, and his forehead was plastered with bits of grass. A crushed ant hung from his lip.

"Matti?" He squinted up.

"Are you all right?"

"What happened?" Timo asked. His tongue sounded thick.

"I'll be right back," Matti said, running to the store to get a glass of water and a wet cloth.

As Matti sponged off Timo's face, he came to his senses. He groaned, "I've been robbed."

"How did you get way out here?"

"Last night I met a couple of fellows in the saloon in Tower," he said. "They asked me if I wanted to ride out to Sally's and have a few drinks. The next thing I know, I'm lying here in the grass." Tears welled up in Timo's eyes.

Timo—crying? He'd always been the tough man. Matti had seen him cut his leg open with a scythe and never whimper. "You can earn more money," Matti said.

"Money?" Timo looked confused. "The money's nothing. Matti . . . It's Wilho that gets to me. I can't shake the nightmares. I hear that ledge breaking loose again and again. I see his eyes, so desperate to push me clear." Timo stopped and wiped his face with his shirtsleeve. "Liquor's the only thing that shuts it out."

Matti stared at him. "Timo . . . ," he said slowly. He'd never imagined that his brother might feel like this. He'd never thought about what Wilho's death had been like for Timo.

Timo reached to pull out his watch, but it was gone. He stood up and blinked. "What time is it?"

"Going on six-thirty."

"Nooo," he groaned. "I'm supposed to be at the mine. Maybe I can catch a ride with that wagon." The fellows who'd been laughing at him had just started down the road. Timo took a few quick steps then trotted back. "Thanks," he said, handing Matti the water glass. "And I'd appreciate your not saying anything about this."

Matti had one of his busiest days ever at the store. He waited on customers and carried orders out to wagons nonstop. When several Finnish fellows showed up at once, Mrs. Winston decided to wait on one of them. He was a cranky fellow named Risto Ryti.

Matti was impressed to hear her say "Good morning" in Finnish. Though she'd been practicing a few words, she'd never tried them on a customer before. Risto stared at her funny, but he gave her his order. Things went well until she handed him his sack and said, "Bless you."

Risto puffed out his chest and said, "Bless yourself."

He marched out the door, leaving her nearly in tears. "What's wrong?" she asked. "I've heard lots of farmers say that to you."

"Mr. Ryti is a Socialist. He doesn't like to be blessed."

"But—"

"Most people think that Finns are all alike," Matti said. "But we pride ourselves on being independent thinkers. My neighbor back home had two sons. One was a minister and one an atheist, but every Sunday they sat down to family dinners together."

"I suppose I wouldn't want anyone saying that everyone from St. Paul is the same," she said. "My Summit Avenue neighborhood is as far removed from this little store as Paris is."

Matti tried to think of something to cheer her up. "But there is one thing that all Finns have in common," Matti said.

She raised her eyebrows. "And pray tell, what might that be?"

"It's called *sisu*. Let me tell you about it."

CHAPTER 19

Once the rye was sown and the last of the potatoes were planted, Father said, "If we work fast, we can have the fireplace in our sauna done by Midsummer's Eve."

"Don't we deserve one day off?" Matti asked. He wanted to say, "Why should I have to work so hard when Timo is doing nothing?" but Father said, "There'll be time enough to rest in the grave. Besides, a sauna cures a man better than a doctor or a drugstore."

To build the hearth for their *savusauna,* Father selected rocks from the piles at the edges of the field, while Matti carried buckets of sand and water to mix the mortar. Together they fitted the rocks in place for the firebox and smoothed the joints with their fingers.

"Now for the *kiuas*," Father said, referring to the smooth, round stones that were piled on top of the firebox and splashed with water to make steam. When Anna and Kari volunteered to help gather the stones, Father said, "These must be strong enough to pass the test of fire and water." He rejected three stones for every one that he pronounced fit, but Matti had the girls pretend that it was a treasure hunt.

Next Matti and Father built three cedar benches at the end of the room. Father planed the top of each bench and rounded the edges with a rasp. Working with slow, steady strokes, Father said, "In the sauna a man must conduct himself as he would in church."

"You're not going to take a sauna in the house we're sleeping in?" Mother asked.

"Midsummer's Day only comes once a year."

"What about our beds and dishes?"

"For one day we can store them outside. Right, Matti?"

Matti nodded. Back in Finland, Midsummer's Day celebrated the longest day of the year. To bring good fortune, birch wreaths were hung in windows and laced to the horns of cows. At midnight the townspeople gathered by the shore of Kallavesi and lit a huge bonfire. Then they sang and danced until dawn.

Kari yelled, "We're going to have a sauna party," and she ran to tell Anna.

The final job was to cut the *savuluukku,* or smoke hole, in the gable and fit it with a small door. "Now we must invite our neighbors," Father said. On Saturdays back home Father needed only to call "The bath is ready" across their stone fence to fill the sauna with friends. Father never missed his weekly *savusauna.* Though it made Mother angry, Father called the sauna his private chapel. "It's better than a real church because there are no noisy ministers to interrupt my prayers."

Father sent Matti to invite the Saaris and Black Jack. Everyone was pleased by the invitation. Mrs. Saari offered to bring a kettle of soup and some black bread. When Black Jack asked if he could bring some food, Matti told him, "Your company is all we want."

On Midsummer's Eve morning Father said, "The honor is yours," and handed Matti the matches. Back home it had been Matti's job to keep the fire stoked all day Saturday so that the *kiuas* would be hot by evening. Matti opened the smoke hole and lit the birch bark and kindling. Though he crouched low and tried to hold his breath, there was no way to feed the fire without gulping smoke.

When Father inspected the fire later on, he nodded his approval. "By supper it will be hot enough to cook an egg in my hand." Father took soaked birch boughs out of a pail to make *vihtas,* or whisks, to slap the skin and increase circulation. Just as Father began tying the boughs, Matti heard a familiar voice: "Do you use a special knot to tie those *vihtas*?"

"It's Timo," Kari shouted, and she and Anna ran forward to greet him. Mother put her head out the door.

"And what brings us the honor of such a visit?" Father asked.

"I know I've let you down, Father." Timo spoke more softly than usual. "But the mine had me shaking so bad I couldn't stand it. Every time a chunk of ore dropped, I thought of Wilho. That rockfall was meant for me, you know."

"Don't say that," Mother said, giving him a hug.

"It's the truth," Timo said. "But I've hired on as a wagon driver in Tower now. It feels so good to be out in the air again."

Timo brought a letter from Aunt Hilda. She'd joined a theater group back in Kuopio, and she was also working for a suffragette organization. Hilda thought they had a good chance of winning women the right to vote in the next few years. As Mother read the letter, Matti wondered if it was wrong of Hilda to be so busy so soon after Wilho's death. But maybe that was the only way Hilda could fight off her sadness.

After the Saaris and Black Jack arrived, everyone shared a supper down by the lake. Along with her black bread and soup Mrs. Saari also brought fresh buttermilk. Black Jack's conduct was unusually polite, though he scared Anna when he asked, "Why are you so quiet? Have pirates cut out your tongue?"

After supper Matti doused the fire in the sauna. Once the smoke purged, he rinsed the soot from the benches and closed the *luuko* to hold in the heat. While the ladies took their sauna, the men built a bonfire down by the shore. As Father piled the fire high, Black Jack and Mr. Saari told about Midsummer celebrations of their youth. Black Jack pulled out a small bottle of whiskey and offered the men a drink. Everyone took a sip except Timo, who winked at Matti and said, "I swore off the stuff after I had a bad fall the other day."

"That's a gentleman's choice," Black Jack said. "Maybe we should liven things up with a little fire leaping."

Just then Mother returned to veto the idea. "Scalding oneself," she said, "is not my idea of livening things up, sir."

"But wouldn't you like to see a peg-legged lumberjack leap a bonfire, Mrs. Ojala?" Black Jack offered.

Matti could tell that Mother smelled whiskey on the men, but she only said, "The sauna is all yours, gentlemen."

As soon as Black Jack took off his clothes, he hobbled to the water pail and splashed a dipperful on the hot rocks. A rush of steam hit Matti. Then Black Jack climbed to the top bench and said, "Throw on another dipper."

"Are you sure?" Father asked.

"I've got to make up for lost time," Black Jack said. "I haven't had a sauna since I hiked up to Ely last spring."

When Father poured on more water, the steam was so hot that Matti and Timo had to cover their faces with wet cloths, but Black Jack was all smiles. "We sure fit these joints tight," he said, running his finger between the logs. "Say, Mutti Boy," Black Jack continued, "have you heard about the Finnish farmer who was famous for taking hot saunas?" Matti could tell that Father was disturbed, because he liked it quiet in his sauna.

When Matti shook his head, Black Jack said, "One day the devil got jealous and invited that farmer to try the fires of hell. The moment he passed through those smoky gates, he started smiling. Every time the devil threw more coal on the fire, the farmer bowed and thanked him. Finally the devil cursed and ordered him out of hell, saying that he and his kind would be unwelcome in Hades forever after. So—"

"So," Eino Saari interrupted, "that's why every Finnish farmer is guaranteed a place in heaven."

"You've heard the tale?" Black Jack chuckled.

"My father used to tell me that story when I was little and I didn't want to take a bath," Eino said.

Black Jack grinned a devilish grin and said, "Toss me a *vihta*." His shiny clean face looked almost handsome.

CHAPTER 20

On the second Saturday in August, Matti was weighing a sack of horseshoe nails when a familiar voice interrupted him. "How's the life of a storekeep?" It was Timo. "I'd like to introduce a friend of mine." To Matti's surprise a beautiful girl was extending her hand. "Ida," Timo continued, "meet my brother, Matti." Ida's white-blond hair was tied back with a blue kerchief that matched her eyes.

Matti wiped his hand on his apron and shook her hand. "Nice to meet you, Matti," she said. "My uncle speaks highly of you."

"Your uncle?" Matti asked.

"He trades here all the time. His name is Arvid Koski."

"He's a fine man," Matti said.

The three of them chatted for a few minutes about Matti's work at the store and Timo's new wagon-driving job. Then Timo said, "We'd better be heading back to Tower. I need to return my boss's wagon." As Timo turned to leave, he said, "Let's keep this between you and me?"

Matti nodded. Why would Timo want to hide Ida from anyone? If Matti ever had a girlfriend, he would want the whole world to know. But he was proud that Timo was willing to share his secret with him.

As the summer drew on, new leaf growth filled in the trees, and rain washed away the caterpillar droppings. Berry picking kept the whole family busy. They'd barely finished canning the last of the strawberries and raspberries by the time the blueberries ripened.

In their spare time Father and Matti continued to plow new ground. "If we get a head start on next year's planting," Father said, "we should have a few extra bushels of rye and oats to sell."

Matti's time at the store was a vacation compared to the work he had to do at home. One Saturday, at the invitation of Mrs. Winston, Matti brought Mother and the twins along. Though the walk tired Anna and Kari, Mrs. Winston perked them up when she said, "Could I interest either of you in a cinnamon stick?"

Since Anna and Kari were used to Mother's plain gray dresses and her kerchiefs, they stared in wonder at Mrs. Winston's deep blue dress (Matti was glad that she hadn't worn Mother's brooch as she sometimes did). They admired her high-piled hair and pearl comb. Despite the difference in their styles, with Matti to translate Mother and Mrs. Winston talked warmly with each other. Mother inquired about the summer trade at the store, and Mrs. Winston asked about the prospects for fall crops. Both ladies were glad that the caterpillar invasion was over. After Mother had finished her shopping and was ready to go home, Mrs. Winston stuck some licorice in a bag as a treat for Anna and Kari.

Later that afternoon Matti was walking home when a voice startled him. "Hey there, Mutti Boy." It was Black Jack, returning from the river with his fishing pole. "How about a cup of coffee?" Before Matti could think of an excuse, Black Jack had started up the trail. He had no choice but to follow.

Black Jack's house was smellier than ever. As Matti bent to pet Louhi, he looked at the table. "Your violin's almost done."

"No, not nearly," he said. "Though the pieces are matched and glued, I'm only halfway there. The final shaping and finishing is what takes the time. And then it takes some good hard playing to mellow the sound."

Matti said, "I never heard the rest of your story. What happened after you left your uncle's house?"

Black Jack leered as if he were going to make a wisecrack, but stopped. "You remember how my uncle broke that hoe over my back?"

Matti nodded.

"After I lit out, I wandered from village to village, begging for crusts of bread. Winter came. I slept in haystacks and ditches. One night I froze my foot. It turned black and the skin broke open, but I had no money to pay for a doctor. By the time a kind minister offered to help me, it was too late.

"After I recovered from the operation and got fitted with my first stump, that same minister lined up a job for me in a charcoal factory near Oulu. I worked in the plant for five years, doing my best to learn the business. I even got promoted twice. I was renting a room from a nice widow lady. She was the one who gave me the name Black Jack, because my face was always covered with charcoal dust.

"I hadn't had any visions for a long time. Then one night I had a dream that a fire was going to start in the plant. I went straight to the foreman, but he said I was crazy and refused to tell the boss. Later that week a fire burned down the factory. I felt awful for not going directly to the boss. The real shocker came when the foreman accused me of setting the fire. He went for the police, and I ran. I wanted to tell the truth, but I was afraid of being put on trial for a crime I didn't commit. So I took my small savings and left for America."

Matti stared at Black Jack. "I can't believe a man could be that wicked."

"There's plenty of meanness in this world," Black Jack said, "but I figure everything has turned out for the best. There's no way I could have owned property like this in Finland." He waved his hand toward the lake. Then Black Jack changed the subject. "So is Wee Willy Winston learning you anything at the store?"

"I'm picking up a few things," Matti said, smiling at the thought of how upset Billy would be if he knew Black Jack called him Wee Willy.

"And how's my pretty Clara?"

"I'm not sure." Matti paused. "She seems lonely some-times."

"I feared that," he said. "Her first winter is going to be tough. When a lady's used to bright lights and big cities, it can get mighty bleak and cold out here."

"Does it snow a lot at Sampo Lake?"

"No more than in town," Black Jack said. "But the drifting is a lot worse. When a wind gets to kicking out of the north-west, it buries this place good."

On his way home Matti recalled the snowdrifts last winter that had covered up the first-floor windows of Aunt Hilda's house in Soudan. If the weather was more brutal out here, how would Clara Winston ever stand it?

CHAPTER 21

Since Father and Matti wouldn't be able to clear a hay field until the next year, they cut wild hay for the mules in the river meadow. They started at dawn, when the grass was still damp and easy to cut. Father began by pulling a file from his pocket. "A dull tool makes the work go twice as hard," he said as he sharpened two short-handled sickles. Then he made a quick pull through the grass. The stems fell in a neat row. Leaning over to drink in the scent, he said, "There is nothing sweeter than dew and fresh-cut grass."

When they stopped for a midmorning break, Matti's back ached. "It's too bad we don't have long-handled scythes," he said.

As usual Father answered with a proverb: "Even the greatest king must learn to kneel."

Matti groaned. Father's constant good humor was almost as bothersome as Timo's incessant complaining had been. Matti wished that just once Father would admit a job was hard.

After sunrise it turned hot, but there were too many horseflies for Matti to work without his shirt. Bits of grass stuck to his neck and arms. "Itching will only make it worse," Father said, but Matti scratched between his shoulder blades and pulled at his shirt. At noon Mother and the girls arrived with a picnic lunch and a jar of warm coffee.

When Anna saw the long rows of cut hay, her eyes got big. "Are Maude and Katie going to eat that much in one winter?" she asked.

"That and a good lot more," Father replied. "And if it gets real cold this winter, Mother is going to stretch our rations by boiling up some hay soup for you two young fillies."

"Yuck." Anna wrinkled up her nose. But Kari pranced up and down the rows. "Look, Father! Anna and I are ponies."

It took two days to cut the meadow. While that hay dried, Father and Matti hiked to the railroad and cut more hay along the tracks. Timo stopped by on Sunday and helped for most of the day. Matti was impressed that his eyes were still clear and sober.

After the hay had dried, Father made two rakes with long spruce handles and wooden teeth. Then they raked the hay into piles, and Father rigged carriers out of birch saplings and wire. With these "harnesses" slung over their shoulders, the whole family helped with the hauling. Father heaped a mound of hay on top of Kari first. When she walked off with hay hanging all the way to the ground, everyone started laughing. "What's wrong?" she said, turning to face them. They laughed all the harder. Though Matti could hear her voice, her face was totally hidden. "You look like a sheepdog peering through a long mop of hair," Matti said.

"You're a walking haystack." Anna giggled. "All we can see is two little feet."

"Save your laughter, Miss Anna," Father said. "You're next."

When the hauling was done, they piled the hay in waterproof stacks. Starting at the bottom, Father laid short poles on the ground. Then he set a tall pole in the middle and laid the hay in one direction so that it would shed water. Wilho even tried to help by dropping a few strands on top.

The girls were good helpers, but as they got more tired, they walked slower and slower. On her last trip Anna's legs gave out, and she sat right down in the middle of the path. When Kari saw Anna disappear under the hay, she laughed until she fell down, too.

It was hot and still on the evening they finished the last haystack. After they were done, the girls shook out their dresses and did what Kari called an "itch dance." Then they all went swimming.

Though the water near shore was lukewarm, out deeper it was still cool enough to make Matti shiver. While the girls splashed in the shallows, Matti floated at the edge of a drop-off. Even as his shoulders relaxed in the sun, his legs felt the prickling of the dark cold below. The scent of dew mingled with fresh-cut hay, and a loon called across the lake.

Matti looked back at the shore. Wilho crowed from the peak of the sauna roof and flapped his wings. Matti smiled. With its single curtained window their log sauna looked like a toy house set on a needled carpet under the tall red pine. For a moment the girls were quiet enough for Matti to hear the crackling of birch bark and kindling as Mother stoked up the stove in her outdoor kitchen. Woodsmoke rose in slow black puffs and clung to the lower branches of the pine before it drifted up and away. When Mother waved at Matti, he was so relaxed that he could barely lift one lazy hand to wave back.

Through late summer the family raced to store up enough food to last the winter. They canned berries and wild plums and green beans. They dug up their potatoes, carrots, and rutabagas for winter storage. Mother put up dozens of jars of chokecherry and pin cherry jelly. Father and Matti each shot a deer, and Mother canned the venison along with the suckers and northerns that Matti regularly brought from the fish trap.

The job that Matti dreaded most started after they'd butchered the last deer. It began when Mother asked Matti if he would walk her to the store so that she could do some shopping. Though Mother usually waited for Matti to pick things up when he went to work, this time she wanted to shop for herself.

When they got to the store, Billy was carrying a bucket of lard and a package to a wagon for Ester Olafson. He set his load down and greeted Mother. "So nice to see you again, Mrs. Ojala." Then he introduced her to Mrs. Olafson. Matti did his best to translate while Mother and Mrs. Olafson chatted about their homesteads. As the ladies were bidding each other goodbye, Matti glanced into the store and saw that Clara Winston was wearing her green dress.

He took a chance and interrupted. "If you tell me what you want, Mother, I can run in and get it for you."

Mother looked surprised at Matti's impoliteness, and she was about to say something until she turned and saw Mrs. Winston standing in the doorway, wearing her brooch.

Matti knew that some ladies would have ducked back inside or tried to cover up that brooch, but Mrs. Winston never blinked. "Good morning, Mrs. Ojala," she called, standing tall and proud. "How nice of you to stop by and visit." Matti translated.

And Mother, standing just as tall and proud, said "Good morning" right back as Mrs. Winston welcomed her into the store.

Mrs. Winston asked about the girls, and Mother commented on the lovely weather. They spoke so fast that Matti stumbled with his translating, but that gave them something to chuckle over. And they made him blush when they agreed that he was a fine young man.

Mother finally got to her shopping list. "Would you have a bottle of lye?"

"Not soap making," Matti groaned.

"Get ready to stir," Mother said. "You're lucky that you don't have to make the lye by hand out of ashes."

"So that's why you wanted to do your own shopping today," Matti said, and both women chuckled.

On the way back home Mother said, "Mrs. Winston is a very pleasant lady, Matti. You're lucky to be working for such nice people. And that Billy is absolutely charming."

"You said that the first time you met him."

"So I did. It's hard to explain. He looks like a typical woodsman, but there's something in his manner. He has a way of giving a woman his full attention that makes her feel"—she paused to think of the right word—"special."

As soon as they got back to the cabin, Mother filled her largest iron pot with chunks of deer tallow. After it melted down, she poured the warm fat into a crock and carefully added lye and water. Then she handed Matti a wooden spoon. Matti knew the routine all too well. He had to stir without stopping—

Mother wanted no lumps in her soap—until the gooey mess in the jar got stiff enough to support his spoon. Though Anna and Kari both offered to help, Matti couldn't take a chance on them spattering themselves with lye. Matti had burned his hand once, and he was careful to stir very slowly. The job was tedious, still, Matti was grateful that the deer tallow didn't smell as bad as the hog fat they'd rendered back in Finland.

It took nearly two hours for the soap to thicken. Matti's wrist ached as if he had been peeling logs all morning. He helped Mother pour the mixture into shallow dishes to cool, and was ready to go help Father when Mother said, "Since we've got the pot all greasy, we may as well do one more batch."

Matti moaned.

All summer long Mother had written down the family expenses in a notebook. Every Friday she showed Father some numbers before she got her coin purse and counted out money for Matti's Saturday shopping. Father always waved his hand and said, "Go ahead." Mother's face showed that she didn't always agree, but she'd give Matti her shopping list. Things were so costly at the store that even with Matti's discount the money didn't go far. The biggest expense was canning jars. Mother bought a case nearly every week. When Matti hauled the jars home in his packsack, he had to be especially careful. Once he tripped and broke a half dozen, which he replaced with his own money.

The last two projects that Father and Matti completed before winter were the root cellar and the mule barn. Father planned on making the barn big enough to store Aunt Hilda's furniture under better cover than a tarp once the weather turned bad.

They built the cellar on a hillside, exposed to the full afternoon sun. It was easy digging until they hit the rocks.

"Rocks, rocks," Father mumbled, cursing as he reached for the pick, "every blessed way you turn on this farm." Matti hid his grin. For once Father wasn't reciting a poem about the honor of digging in the dirt.

Two broken shovels and a day and a half later, Matti and Father had finally dug a deep enough hole. They set timbers for the walls and built shelves for canning jars and bins for their root crops. To seal the cellar from the weather, they laid boards and birch bark on the roof and shoveled three feet of dirt over the top. Father's good spirits returned by the time they hung the inner and outer doors. "She's locked as tight as the magic Sampo in Louhi's castle," Father said, referring to the gold grinding mill in the *Kalevala* that the hero Väinö sailed north to capture. "Remember the bronze door that the evil witch Louhi secured with nine locks?"

"You've never let me forget," Matti said. "And over the years the Sampo grew roots out under the earth, the ocean, and the mountains, making it a challenge for Väinö to win it back."

"Yet he taught that witch a lesson and dug the Sampo up." Father nailed the last hinge in place and stepped back to admire his work.

"But in the end Louhi attacked Väinö's ship, and he lost the Sampo in the sea," Matti said.

"Don't forget that Väinö's loss was humankind's gain," Father said. "For when the broken fragments of the Sampo washed ashore, they brought wealth and prosperity to our people."

"Let's hope Sampo Lake yields us the same fortune," Matti said.

"If a man works hard enough, he can make his own magic."

The mule barn ended up being more of a loafing shed, or

a three-sided building with a flat roof. It, too, faced south, and they hung a tarp across the sunny side for a door.

Once the crops were harvested, Matti had to begin another job he'd been dreading. He was careful not to bring up the subject, but one morning as he was getting ready to go to the Saaris' and pick up the milk, Mother said, "You'd better bring your English book with you today, Matti. It's time that you start those lessons we promised." Groaning, he grabbed his knapsack and English grammar book. For once he wished Aunt Hilda had never sent him that book.

When Matti arrived, Mrs. Saari seated her boys around the kitchen table. Their names were Ukko, Ahti, and Taipio, and they were six, seven, and nine years old. Matti pulled out his book. "Let's start with . . ." Then he stopped to think.

How could he make learning fun? His time at the Soudan School had been torture. The teacher had called him Matthew instead of Matti, and whenever he spoke Finnish, even if it was only an accidental thank you, she rapped him on the knuckles with a ruler.

After a long pause Matti turned to Mrs. Saari and said, "Would you have a wooden box top?" Matti remembered Mother's story about how her own school didn't have enough money to buy slates, so they practiced their spelling in a sand-filled tray.

"Yes," she said, "but—"

"And a stick," he added. "We need a stick, too."

Little Ukko's eyes got big.

"What's wrong?" Matti said.

"Are you going to beat us, Matti?"

"No." Matti laughed.

After Mrs. Saari found a wooden box top, Matti and the

two younger boys went outside and filled it with clean sand while Taipio whittled a pencil-sized stick with his jackknife. Matti set the tray back on the table and handed Ukko the stick. Then he guided the little boy's hand to spell *U K K O.*

"Do you know how to read that word?" Matti asked.

Ukko shook his head.

"Those letters spell your very own name," Matti said. Ukko smiled so proudly that Ahti and Taipio were both anxious to take a turn with "Matti's writing box."

Matti breathed a sigh of relief. Perhaps playing schoolmaster wouldn't be quite so bad after all.

CHAPTER 22

As flocks of birds passed by on their way south, Matti noticed that Wilho became restless. One by one the songbirds disappeared, leaving only the chickadees and nuthatches behind. One evening a raft of bluebill ducks settled on the lake. Wilho sat on a boulder at the water's edge and studied the ducks for a long time.

Later that same day a flock of crows flapped along the ridge behind the farm. When they called toward the lake, Wilho flew to the top of a dead pine and stared after them. Wilho kept his perch all through supper. Just before dark he flew down to see if Matti had saved a snack for him.

"You don't have to worry about that bird flying south," Father said. "He would miss your mother's cooking too much."

Once Matti's "school" was up and running, Mrs. Saari invited him to bring Anna and Kari along. The first time Anna and Kari gave an answer in exactly the same words, Matti thought nothing of it, but the boys just stared.

"It was like two people talking with the same mouth," Ukko said.

As soon as Mrs. Winston found out that Matti was teaching the Saari boys, she donated some storybooks and old newspapers for reading material. Anna and Kari liked the storybooks best, but the boys begged Matti to read stories out of the *Tower Weekly News*. Little Ukko, who wanted to be a policeman when he grew up, quickly learned to identify crime stories by their exclamation points. Matti started to read an article entitled "Wanted in Tower," but he stopped when he discovered the subject was a murderer named George Barlich, otherwise known as the Austrian Axe Man. He knew Mother wouldn't want him to read the little ones such a story, so he picked an article about new passenger train service instead. But Mrs. Saari told Matti to use whatever the boys found interesting. They spent the rest of the morning spelling words like *murder* and *axe* and *trial* in their sand trays. On the way home Kari and Anna promised not to tell Mother.

When Mother came along with Matti and the girls, the boys were careful to read wholesome stories. But she and Mrs. Saari chatted so much that Mother didn't seem to notice Matti's lessons. One morning the ladies were recalling their hometowns back in Finland. Matti was surprised when Mrs. Saari asked Mother to name the thing she missed most about Kuopio, and she said, "Our local ski hill."

"Whyever?" Mrs. Saari asked.

"The slopes of Puijo are all color and movement. The

people are so totally alive racing down toward the city with their bright caps and their scarves flying back in the wind."

"I miss the life of my village, too—simple things like folks mingling at the market and the fair," Mrs. Saari said.

"At least we have them." Mother nodded toward the busy spellers at the table.

The girls were so excited about mastering English that they often continued their lessons at home. Mother would join in, too, as Matti pointed to the window, the door, and the stove, and the girls said the English name together. To make the game more fun, Matti would point faster and faster. "Floor, ceiling, bucket," the three ladies called out. "Pencil, paper, table, cup . . ."

The fun ended when Father walked in and said, "Matti, talk like a man."

Matti was glad that the work on the farm had slowed, now that he was so busy with tutoring and clerking. One Saturday Black Jack showed up at the store late in the afternoon. "I need to stoke up my stewpot, Mutti Boy," he said. "How's your supply of potatoes?"

"Good afternoon, Mr. Mattson." Clara Winston half-curtsied. "Where have you been keeping yourself?"

"I decided to bring some pretty flowers for a pretty lady," Black Jack said as he handed her a bouquet of fall flowers and bowed as low as his bad leg would allow.

"I thought your priority was your stewpot," she said.

"Mutti Boy," he said, "how do you say 'A man needs to feed his eyes as well as his stomach' in English?"

When Matti translated for him, Mrs. Winston smiled. "I'm flattered, sir."

Matti shook his head. How could such a crude and dirty fellow have a sweet side? Whenever Matti decided that Black

Jack was a complete pig, he surprised him. Jack visited with Mrs. Winston and Billy until quitting time, then he turned to Matti and said, "Are your potato-carrying muscles still in good shape?"

"I thought you'd never ask," Matti said with a chuckle, swinging the gunnysack onto his shoulders. "Lead the way."

As Matti trudged down the path behind Black Jack, he caught an odor of stale tobacco and unwashed clothes. It was a mistake to be walking downwind. All he could do was hang back by Louhi, who smelled a whole lot better. For some reason Black Jack wasn't whistling as he normally did.

Just as Black Jack was about to turn onto the path that led to his house, he stopped and stared to the south. "I feel a powerful storm brewing down that way," he said. Matti couldn't understand what he meant, because the sky was perfectly clear. "I see a terrible wind. A wall of water. People screaming . . ."

Louhi whined softly, and Matti knelt down to pet him as Black Jack's voice trailed off. The rest of the way to his cabin, he was silent, and once Matti carried his potatoes inside, Black Jack thanked him and said good night.

But just as Matti turned to go, Black Jack said, "And Matti—"

"Yes."

"You make sure you keep a close eye on that little Anna."

Before Matti had a chance to ask for an explanation, Black Jack had closed his cabin door.

The next morning the sky was unbroken blue. Matti forgot about Black Jack's forecast until the following Saturday at the store. He was totaling up a grocery order when a fellow sitting by the potbellied stove looked up from the paper and said, "That sure was some storm down in Texas. They say it was the worst in the history of America."

Matti walked over and looked at the paper. A hurricane

had hit a town called Galveston, Texas, and over six thousand people had drowned. The storm blew ashore last Saturday, the very day Black Jack had his strange feeling.

"What's wrong?" Billy asked.

"Would you think I was crazy if I told you Black Jack knew that storm was coming?"

Billy shook his head. "Nothing would surprise me. Everyone in these parts can tell you stories about his predictions. I've seen him stand right here and say that one day men will be driving sun-powered carriages and riding ships off to the stars."

The man with the paper nodded. "I'd believe just about anything where that Spirit Jack is concerned. Last summer he was out at my farm and he looked to the south and said, 'One day that hillside will be a city of lights.' Since there's nothing out there but woods, I would've figured he was as crazy as a coot if I didn't know him better."

CHAPTER 23

After the hay was stacked and the crops were stored in the root cellar, Matti assumed that the field work was done for the year.

On a calm morning when the leaves on the birch and popple had turned bright gold, and Matti was looking forward to a rest, Father checked the wind and said, "This would be perfect weather for burnbeating."

"No," Matti moaned.

"We won't be able to break any new ground this fall," Father said, "but we can at least get a few more trees out of the way."

Father made "out of the way" sound as simple as whisking the ground clean with a broom, but Matti knew there were at least a hundred trees in the patch of woods that Father had chosen.

While Father and Matti felled and skidded the larger birch for firewood, Mother and the girls scattered the branches across the soil. Once the leaves had dried, they set fire to the field. By rolling the smaller trees over the forest duff and beating the ground with flaming branches, they spread the fire through the whole clearing. Anna and Kari guarded the edge of the field and beat the ground with wet gunnysacks when the flames turned the wrong way.

No matter where Matti stood, smoke blew into his face and made his eyes water. His hands and clothes turned black, and his mouth tasted as if he'd been eating charcoal.

No one got a chance to rest until the fire began to die down toward evening. The whole family was coughing as they walked to the lake to wash up. When Anna and Kari pulled their kerchiefs from their heads, everyone laughed. They looked like sooty dolls with white dots for eyes.

Matti knelt by the shore and splashed water on his face. He watched the soot run down his arms in black rivulets. His muscles ached, and his head felt light.

Though the water had a fall chill to it, Kari slipped off her shoes and waded into the shallows. Anna joined her. "Don't get your dresses . . ." Mother stopped. "I guess there's no need to worry about getting these wet," she said, stepping into the water, too. Father took off his boots and joined the ladies in the water. The girls giggled as Father stood in the lake wearing his pants and suspenders. Father flicked a palmful of water at Kari, and she splashed some back.

Suddenly war broke out, and everyone was splashing. Father crouched and swung his arm. Kari and Anna squealed as a wave hit them.

Mother turned and whipped her arms in a waterwheel motion, drenching both Matti and Father.

Father threw up his arms and hollered, "I surrender." Then he dove under the water and tipped both girls over. Kari and Anna gasped as they bobbed back up.

By then they were so used to the water that they decided to take a swim. "This will save me lots of work at the washtub," Mother said, pausing to wring out the hem of her dress.

Everyone was soggy but happy as they stepped out of the water. Except for their faces, which were red from being so close to the fire all day, a stranger could have taken them for a family of picnickers who had jumped into the lake on a lark.

CHAPTER 24

With the coming of the first real cold, Father and Matti carried the wood range into the sauna and ran a stovepipe out the window. Yrjo moved in with the stove, and no matter how hot the fire got, he took his naps right under the oven. When he stepped outside, steam rose off his body from nose to tail.

School was going better all the time at the Saaris'. Since Mrs. Saari was good at teaching math, Matti mainly concentrated on English. By reading the newspapers over and over again, and practicing their spelling in the sand trays, the boys were soon getting good enough at their reading to pronounce the easy words themselves. Though the girls and Taipio were the best readers, Matti always made sure that Ahti and Ukko got a turn when they were reading out loud. Anna and Kari had given up trying to warn Matti about things in the paper that "weren't proper," because the boys had a gift for finding every story about a criminal, a wagon accident, or a wedding dance brawl.

Matti was beginning to appreciate the different personalities of the boys, too. Little Ukko had turned out to be a nonstop talker who showed amazing mental quickness for a six-year-old. His specialty was math. The middle boy, Ahti, was a great practical joker who enjoyed making up riddles and rhymes. Ahti made Matti solve a new riddle every time he saw him. His latest was "Who can marry a hundred women and still be a bachelor?" Even though Matti knew the answer was a minister, he pretended to be stumped. The eldest boy, Taipio, liked it when Matti called him his teaching assistant.

One afternoon when Matti returned from a session at the Saaris', the girls ran off to play. Mother and Father were inside at the table. Mother had a pencil in her hand, and she was shaking her head. "I don't see any other way."

"Other way for what?" Matti asked.

"We've been talking money," Mother spoke quietly. "And things don't look good."

"What about my salary from the store?"

"It helps, but we still come up short," she said.

Father said, "I'm applying for work over at Camp twenty-three."

"But that must be fifteen miles away," Matti said.

"I can ski home every Sunday," Father said. "In the meantime, you'll have to be the man of the house." Father slid his chair back. "We'd better check on Maude and Katie before dark."

Matti was suddenly angry. Was Timo right in calling Father a flighty dreamer? Father had insisted on building his cabin in the middle of this stump-ridden wilderness. And now he was going off and leaving his family alone?

On the way to tend the animals, Matti tried to convince Father not to go, but he only quoted an old proverb: "We live as we can, not as we wish."

Matti's face grew hot. Why couldn't Father talk in straightforward sentences and tell him how he truly felt, as Uncle Wilho always had? Why did he always have to repeat his silly old sayings? But before Matti could say anything, Father added, "A winter of logging won't be so bad. I'd rather fell a few trees for a lumber company than go back to tenant farming."

Maude brayed when she heard them coming, and Father whistled back. "It did feel rotten to be called Perala all those years we worked on the Perala estate," Matti said. Though Matti and Father had always been known as Ojalas to their relatives and close friends, the official town records listed them as Peralas.

Father chuckled and said, "I don't think we'll have to worry about the folks in Sampo Township calling me Leo Camp twenty-three."

On the morning that Father left, the starlight was silver blue. The girls were still sleeping when he shouldered his pack and kissed Mother goodbye. Matti walked down the driveway with him. An owl hooted in the swamp as Father paused to test the corduroy logs of the road with his boot. "We bedded these solid, Matti," he said. "I know I'm leaving the place in good hands."

Matti listened to Father's footsteps as he disappeared down the dark shadowed road. The scent of balsam tingled in his nostrils. He felt cold and alone. After doing Timo's work all summer, now he would have to do Father's jobs as well. Where would he find the strength? In the last year he'd lost his home in Kuopio, his grandparents, his best friends, his uncle, and his aunt. Maybe even Timo. What if Father never returned?

As Matti started back down the driveway, a mule's harsh bray told him that his worries would have to wait. For now there were chores to do.

From the time Matti finished carrying hay and water for the mules until the moment he brought in the last armloads of firewood for the night, he barely had a chance to catch his breath. In addition to his regular jobs, Mother decided that the ashes needed to be cleaned out of the stove. And once the stove had cooled, she looked at him and said, "We may as well take the stovepipe apart and clean that, too." Matti only spilled a little soot when he took the pipe apart, but that was just enough to extend their cleaning project to include the entire cabin. And once the beds were carried outside, Mother decided that this would be the perfect day to restuff them with dried cattail fluff—a lining that Mrs. Saari had recommended as warmer and softer than hay.

It took the second half of the day to gather the cattail tops, shred them, and sew them into the ticks. When bedtime finally arrived, the girls helped spread the beds across the floor. Matti was so tired that he expected to fall instantly asleep, but he lay for a long time. He couldn't figure out what was wrong until Kari finally called from the corner, "Why is it so quiet?"

Then Matti knew what the problem was. "You miss Father's snoring," he said, amazed that the newfound quiet could leave them all so uneasy.

Only two days later Matti and the girls were behind the sauna laying hazelnuts on a rock ledge to dry. It was a clear, cool day, and the lake had just frozen over. Mother was inside preparing lunch, and Wilho was perched on the roof. After watching the girls for a while, Wilho flew down and dropped a nut into the sack they had just emptied. Kari and Anna thought it was funny, but when Matti remembered Wilho's "help" during the strawberry planting, he said, "Bad crow."

Wilho cawed and sat back to watch. A few minutes later he flew down again. Matti was about to yell at him, but instead of grabbing for a hazelnut, Wilho chased off a squirrel that was sneaking toward the rock.

As the squirrel chattered away, Anna said, "Good crow," and she started for the sauna. A few minutes later Wilho glided toward the lake.

He flew back, cawing loudly, and swooped down to pull at Kari's hair ribbon. Before Matti could yell, Wilho wheeled toward the lake, cawing and trailing the ribbon behind.

Matti expected Kari to cry. Instead she stared after Wilho. "Anna's in trouble," she said, running toward the lake. Just then Black Jack's warning about Anna flashed into Matti's mind.

Matti dashed after Kari. When he reached the shore, the ice was an unbroken mirror of blue. Matti followed Wilho's flight until he saw what he most feared—a fractured place offshore. As Matti scrambled down the stony bank, he was stunned. Why would cautious Anna ever do something so dangerous?

The jagged hole was only twenty feet from the bank, but there was no sign of his sister. "Anna," he yelled, looking up and down the shore. "Anna," he yelled again, stepping onto the ice. How could this happen so soon after Father had left the family in his trust!

The ice sagged as Matti inched toward the hole. Mother joined Kari on the shore and shouted, "No, Matti," but he knew there was no time to waste. When Matti got to the edge of the hole, he leaned forward and peered into the water. He couldn't see anything, so he turned and yelled, "Get a branch."

The ice broke. Mother and Kari screamed as Matti went

under. The water was so cold that it burned his face and shocked the breath right out of him. His head ached from the sudden chill, but he forced his eyes open.

The bottom of the lake was photograph clear. Brown weeds stood like dead corn plants in a windless field. Matti looked toward the green depths, but there was no sign of Anna. He surfaced and took a gulp of air.

Ignoring the shouts, he dove back under and turned toward the shallows. His eyes hurt from the cold. He pulled hard with his arms, wishing he'd kicked off his boots so that he could swim better. Sunlight brightened the pebbled bottom near shore. Matti's heart hammered in his chest. His eyes scanned left and right.

When Matti finally saw Anna, his air was almost gone, but he dug his boots into the bottom and pushed forward. Anna's eyes were closed tight. Her lips were blue and half parted. Matti touched Anna's hand and pulled her toward him, knowing he didn't have enough air to make it back to the hole.

The world turned red as Matti planted his feet and pushed upward. The ice didn't budge. Squatting lower, he braced himself and pushed up with his shoulders and back. The ice crackled as he broke through. Matti took a big gulp of air and reached down to pull Anna up. At the same time Mother ran forward, breaking more ice and helping him to shore. Matti fell to his knees, gasping. Mother turned Anna over onto her belly and slapped her back. Nothing happened. She lifted her arms and slapped twice more.

Matti shivered as a gust of wind blew across the bare ice. Just when it seemed as if there were no hope, Anna coughed. Water and mucous spurted out of her mouth and nose. "Go put some wood in the stove, Kari," Mother said. Wilho cawed as Kari ran.

Mother pulled a tick in front of the stove and bundled Anna in a quilt. Anna's lips were still blue, and the only way that Mother could stop her trembling was to hold her in both arms. Kari stayed beside her sister and squeezed her hand the whole time.

Matti couldn't believe how quickly Anna's color returned. In a few minutes she sat up and said, "Why is it so hot in here?"

All at once Mother's strength melted away, and tears began pouring down her face. As Mother wiped her eyes with the corner of her apron, both girls hugged her and said, "Don't cry, Mother, please don't cry."

By suppertime the following evening, Mother noticed that Anna looked flushed. "Lord sakes." She touched her forehead. "You're burning up, child."

Mother put Anna to bed and made her a cup of rose-hip tea. Through the evening Matti and Mother and Kari took turns holding a cool cloth on Anna's face, but her fever got higher.

By the next morning Anna was even worse. Her cheeks were flushed and her eyes were dull and listless. Kari and Matti tried to cheer her up, but she was too tired to do anything but moan.

Mother turned to Matti. "You'd better get Mrs. Saari."

Matti ran down the trail, driven by a fear that no one dared mention. A fever like this had killed his baby sister Senja two winters ago. They'd just returned from the Sunday races on the lake. Little Senja had cheered the galloping horses with their steaming nostrils and their tails flying straight back. A fever set in the next day, and a week later Mother and Aunt Hilda were washing Senja's body in the sauna, preparing for the funeral.

Matti found Mrs. Saari in the barn. She lowered her eyes and whispered good morning. Her shyness vanished at his news. She called to Taipio, "Finish the milking. I'm needed at the Ojalas'." Then she turned and said, "Tell me what happened." As Matti explained the accident and how long Anna had been sick, she packed her supplies in a cloth bag.

Mrs. Saari took control as soon as she and Matti arrived at the Ojalas'. She touched Anna's forehead. Then she looked into her eyes and felt her pulse. Turning to Mother she said, "The best place to heal is a steam room."

"What can we do?" Mother asked.

"Some hot water would help," Mrs. Saari said, slipping off her coat and sweater, "and Matti can stoke the fire."

Mrs. Saari prepared a poultice that smelled of tar and mustard. Then she took out tiny horn cups that were polished to a jewel-like sheen and her razor. Kari gasped when she saw the razor, but Matti signaled that she shouldn't worry Anna.

"More wood," Mrs. Saari ordered Matti.

Once the water was warm, Mother helped Mrs. Saari wash Anna's arms and neck and chest. The temperature in the room rose as the fresh wood crackled. Anna's upper body was soon flushed as bright as her feverish forehead.

"We're ready," Mrs. Saari whispered. She reached for her razor and a cup. Kari buried her face in Matti's shoulder as the bright blade cut a slit in Anna's forearm. "Now to pull out the bad humors," she said, applying the cup to the fresh wound and catching the blood in a small glass jar.

Twice more she made cuts and caught the thick droplets. "There," she said, holding a compress in place, "she should be fine now."

To finish up, Mrs. Saari tied the mustard-and-tar poultice over Anna's chest. Anna had lain silent the whole time, but now she coughed and wrinkled up her nose. "What's that smell?" she said.

As everyone chuckled, Matti could see tears welling up in Mother's eyes.

Chapter 25

The following Saturday Mrs. Winston asked Matti to stop by Black Jack's and deliver a plug of chewing tobacco on his way home. Before Black Jack said hello, he asked, "How's young Anna doing?"

Black Jack nodded as Matti told him about the accident. Matti was about to ask how he'd known about Anna when he noticed that Black Jack was loading his packsack.

"You're leaving?" Matti asked.

"It's time to head for the lumber camp." Black Jack paused to spit into his lard can. "The ice roads will be ready for hauling any day now. That means they'll need their dentist on the job."

"Dentist?" Matti frowned.

"That's the name they give to the fellow who sharpens the saw teeth."

"Sometimes English makes sense," Matti said.

Black Jack picked up his still unfinished violin from the table and wrapped it in a cloth. "I'll have the whole winter to polish up this little lady," he said. "The wood will season with some good hard playing, and her music will get sweeter by the day."

Matti said goodbye to Black Jack, realizing for the first time that he would actually miss the old fellow.

"Thank Miss Clara for the tobacco," Black Jack said, "and you remind her that even if the winter gets tough in this country, the spring is pretty enough to make the wait worthwhile."

After his heroic help with Anna's rescue, Wilho led a pampered life. Anna was especially grateful to him. Though Yrjo became jealous, Anna talked to Wilho all the time, and she saved special treats for him after every meal. Wilho puffed out his feathers and lifted his beak in the air at every compliment.

As proud as Wilho was, Matti noticed that he was getting more restless every day. Late one afternoon a noisy flock of crows roosted in a grove east of the sauna. They called to Wilho, and he cawed back from his perch on the sauna roof. When Matti stepped outside to get an armful of firewood the next morning, the flock flapped out of the treetops and headed south. Wilho flew along with the crows until they reached the far shore of the lake. Then he wheeled to return to the homestead as he always did.

Swooping low, Wilho cawed three times. When Matti waved, he cawed again. But instead of landing on the roof as Matti expected, Wilho turned back toward the flock. Matti watched Wilho ride the sky, working his way higher and higher. Only when the flock was the tiniest of black specks did Matti let his eyes drop. He was happy for Wilho, yet he would miss him, too.

"It looks like our crow has found some friends." Mother had been watching from the steps.

Matti nodded.

"Your aunt Hilda once told me that everything in this world happens for a purpose," Mother said, her eyes still fixed on the sky. "Maybe Wilho's purpose was to stay long enough to help Anna."

Matti looked at the horizon. Above the farthest ridge of rock-rooted pine, the sky was blue and empty. "Like it was Uncle Wilho's purpose to help us move to this country," Matti thought out loud.

"That's right," Mother said, squeezing Matti's hand.

Matti thought back to how angry he'd been at Uncle Wilho's death. It still hurt to think of him being gone, yet he knew that he would always be a better person because of what his uncle had given him. He recalled a day back in Finland when he was a little boy and feeling sorry for himself. Uncle Wilho had tapped his shoulder and said, "Life's too short for that, Matti. If you weep in this house, you weep alone."

A part of Matti would always miss his pet, just as he would always mourn the loss of Uncle Wilho. Yet crying served no purpose.

Just then Mother surprised Matti by chuckling. "Would you look at that?" she said, pointing toward the doorstep. Yrjo was staring into the southern sky, with the closest thing to a smile that a cat can muster.

"There's one member of the family who isn't going to shed any tears today," Matti said.

Chapter 26

In mid-November the weather turned cold, and life on the homestead fell into a winter routine of chopping wood, hauling water, and hiking to the Saaris' and the store. As the snows deepened, Matti became especially lonesome for Finland. When he used Uncle Wilho's skis to pack a trail to the store, he kept wishing that Paavo and Juha could be there to test the hills with him. During the winters back home, he and his friends often went on cross-country ski treks. A Saturday was a disappointment if they couldn't get in a twenty-mile loop before suppertime.

Now that it was winter Timo had switched from driving a wagon to a sleigh, and he was busy six and sometimes seven days a week. Once he stopped by the store and told Matti, "The teamster business is going so well that I might not be able to visit the farm until Christmas. In the meantime here's a little something for Mother's grocery fund." To Matti's surprise he handed him three silver dollars.

Though Matti had dreaded his trips to the Saaris' at first, he found that his tutoring offered relief from the boredom of their dim little cabin. It was pitch dark when Matti rose in the morning to feed and water the mules, and it was dark before they sat down to supper. Lately Anna's and Kari's tempers had matched the ever shrinking daylight. It took no more than a cross look from one or the other to get them quarreling.

Luckily Anna and Kari were getting along better with the Saari boys than they were with each other. Little Ukko was especially fond of Kari. Even when the girls switched coats and dresses to trick the boys, Ukko could always tell them apart.

Since the time of the accident, Anna had become attached to Mrs. Saari. After she finished her lessons she lingered in Mrs. Saari's kitchen and asked questions about the mysterious-smelling herbs and flowers.

At home the girls divided their time between making candles, carding the big bag of wool that Hilda had left with Mother, and tying rugs. Carding the raw wool into "logs" for Mother's spinning wheel was a never ending job. As the fibers whirled through her fingers, Mother kept an eye on her log supply. "Speed up that carding," she'd say, "my basket is getting low." Matti got tired of the constant hum of the spinning wheel and the click of the knitting needles. He was also bored by Mother telling him and the girls how much she missed the loom she had left back in Kuopio.

Mother expected Matti to help the girls with the carding when he was inside, so he made sure he had lots of outside work to do. In addition to hauling milk from the Saaris', he had to split kindling, carry firewood, empty the slop pail, and feed and water the mules.

Matti was also quick to volunteer for trips to the root cellar whenever Mother needed vegetables or smoked meat. During the bright cold days he enjoyed stepping through the doors of the root cellar and smelling the musty odor of unfrozen ground. It was like traveling back to a cool autumn day scented with a hint of rain.

Sawing and splitting firewood became a nearly full-time job in itself. Since the range was made for cooking rather than heating, it used up twice the wood. The small firebox meant that Matti had to cut the wood in short lengths, doubling his time with the bucksaw. Matti or Mother had to get up at least twice every night to load the stove, too. The floor was so cold that Matti's bare feet ached for a long time after he'd climbed back under his blankets.

Uncle Wilho had often said, "The pleasure of firewood comes from the fact that it warms you thrice: once in the cutting, once in the carrying, and once in the burning." Wilho forgot to add hauling out the ashes, an endless task because of their leaky old wood range.

Even a simple job such as filling the water pails became a taxing labor when winter arrived. Matti had to chop through the ice every morning. Even when he laid boards over the top, it had a thick skim by lunchtime. His wet mittens froze to the handle of the pail, and his hands burned from the biting wind. With the effort it took to haul and heat the water, washing clothes was an all-day job for the family.

For fun indoors Matti sang silly songs with the girls (their favorite was about a half-blind tailor who sewed people's pant legs shut), and he showed them a button game, where they spun a button up and down a thread stretched between their fingers. As Matti passed the button on, he made everyone answer a question in English. When it was Mother's turn, he tricked her with a string of *b*'s and *d*'s: "Did the duck drop the bad baby in the brook?"

Mother stumbled with the difficult letters, laughing just as hard as Anna and Kari.

Matti's other winter "jobs" were hunting and fishing. Though Matti pretended it was hard work, he enjoyed getting outside. When he had good luck fishing, Mother boiled up a pot of *kalakeitto,* a fish and potato soup. By carrying the Springfield with him to the store, Matti often brought home a rabbit or a partridge.

On the first weekend that Father returned from the logging camp, Mother cooked roast partridge, and the girls gave Father big welcome home hugs. Father teased the girls, and he thanked Matti for saving his sister from her "ice diving."

Late in the afternoon, however, Father's mood quieted. While he was filling his packsack to return to the camp, Mother asked, "What's wrong, Leo?"

"Nothing," he replied, "but I'm going to be a wood butcher."

When Mother frowned, he explained, "That's a kind of carpenter. We build and repair the sleighs, wagons, and water barrels."

"That sounds like a good job," she said.

"It's a fine job," Father said. "The problem is, I'll have to work weekends. Sunday is the only day we can repair equipment, and we're so far behind that there won't be any days off."

"So you'll not be coming home next weekend?"

"I can quit." Father stood up. "We could get by if—"

"No," Mother said. "We have no choice."

Father nodded. "The boss has promised to give me

time off on Thanksgiving weekend. So I'll be home in just a couple of weeks."

Matti and the twins walked Father all the way to the depot. He knelt and hugged both girls at once. "Be good, you two, and"—he turned to Anna—"no more testing the ice."

Anna nodded as Kari squeezed her hand and said, "We'll make sure she's careful, Father."

Father reshouldered his pack and shook Matti's hand. "I know I can count on you."

The next day Mother sent Matti to the root cellar to get some potatoes. "That father of yours ate up every single one."

Even before Matti got to the cellar, he felt as if something was wrong. Katie was *eeoow*ing strangely up in the barn, and the hay in front of the door was disturbed. He ran to find that the door had been forced open. Deep claw marks scarred the wood. Matti started down the steps and then stopped. Bears should be hibernating by now. But what if one were still inside? He made sure the doors were open wide in case he had to run.

The stink of rotten fish rose from the cellar. When he got inside, the dirt floor was littered with broken canning jars. The bear had licked up every bit of food and raked the potatoes and carrots onto the floor. The haunch of smoked venison that they'd hung from the ceiling was gone, too. Matti thought he'd seen the worst until he looked in the corner and gagged at the big pile of bear droppings.

The joke that Father made last fall about this cellar being the storeroom of the witch Louhi was no longer funny. An evil witch could not have done more damage with a spell. Just then Matti heard something behind him. Had the bear returned?

"Matti? Are you all right?" It was Mother.

It took all day to clean up the mess. The few potatoes and carrots that weren't chewed up stunk so bad from fish juice and bear drool that Matti had to take them down to the lake and wash them. Then Mother spread them in front of the stove to dry.

Kari wrinkled her nose and said, "I don't know if I'll ever be able to eat a potato again after seeing that awful bear . . ." As she searched for a word, Anna said, "Bear slime."

"You'll eat what we have," Mother snapped, but when she saw Kari's eyes well up with tears, she gave her a hug.

While the vegetables dried, Matti took a shovel and scraped the floor of the root cellar clean. Then he nailed some spikes through the door from the inside, leaving the sharp points sticking out.

Try clawing your way past that, he said to himself.

Matti spent every free moment trying to restock their depleted larder. He knew he had to work fast, because fish and game became scarce in midwinter. He hunted each morning and evening, and fished during the day.

Matti didn't want to frighten the girls with their food problem, yet he needed their help. On Sunday night he said, "Beginning tomorrow, we are going to cancel school and have a week-long fishing contest."

Anna looked confused. "Is this an American holiday?"

"Like *Pikkujoulu* or *Vappu* back home?" Kari added.

"This is called Sampo Lake Week," Matti said.

"And we get to fish all week long?" Anna asked.

"Yes."

The girls looked at each other. Then they raised their arms and cheered.

The next morning Matti rigged up two extra jigging sticks and tied on heavy lines and large snelled hooks. When they stepped out onto the ice, Anna shrank back. "Are you scared?" Matti asked.

She nodded. Matti dropped to one knee and put his arm around her shoulders. "I wouldn't take you out on the lake if the ice weren't safe," he said. "Let me show you."

Matti took a few steps, scraped back the snow with his boot, and chopped down with his axe. "Come and see," he said, chopping until he broke through.

Anna looked down into the hole. Matti hooked the edge of his axe on the ice and showed her the depth. "Look how thick it is," he said, "and how solid." Matti jumped up and down.

Matti chopped two holes at the edge of a weed bed and hooked a thin piece of side pork on a line for himself. "Why do you have such a small hook, Matti?" Kari asked, feeling sorry for him.

"I want to catch a fish for bait." A moment later Matti pulled in a perch and cut two strips of meat to bait their hooks.

Kari wrinkled up her nose, but she and Anna giggled when Matti called out, "Let the official Sampo Lake Week begin.

"Now jig your sticks up and down," Matti said.

Matti was just tying on a heavy line and hook of his own when Kari squealed and pulled in a big northern. Then before he could pick up his fishing rig, Anna caught one, too.

"Whose is bigger?" Anna asked.

"Mother will be the judge of the contest," Matti said, slipping the fish into a gunnysack.

The girls kept Matti so busy baiting their hooks that he didn't get his own line into the water at all. Luckily the sun was warm and he could leave his mitts off.

During lunch the girls asked who was leading the contest. Mother said, "It is too close to tell right now."

"But Kari caught two more fish than I did," Anna said.

"That's right," Matti said, "but Mother counts the weight, too, when she figures the total points."

It started snowing that afternoon, so they went inside to help Mother with the cleaning. That evening Matti tried hunting, but the snow was blowing so hard that he couldn't see.

When Matti took the girls out on the lake the next morning, a cold front moved in. The wind shifted to the north, and the girls were soon shivering. Matti chopped a dozen holes, but they had no luck. "Sampo Lake Week is no fun anymore," Anna said.

Kari nodded and said, "I'd rather have school."

Anna finally hooked a walleye, but she wet her mittens as she pulled it in and started crying. Matti gave her his mittens. Then, cradling the gunnysack under his arm and sticking his hands in his pockets, he led the girls back home.

Overnight the snow drifted deep over the meadow and the lake. Matti tried fishing on his own, but he caught only two little perch. To make matters worse, the cold front stayed all week. When Matti told the girls that the contest had ended in a tie, neither of them seemed to care.

If only Timo or Father were home. With a partner Matti could range as far as he needed to in search of fish and game. For now he would have to stick close to the cabin and try to solve the problem on his own.

CHAPTER 27

"Oatmeal again!" Kari said.

"Better a spoonful of porridge than an empty pot, Miss *Ruusunukke*," Mother said.

For days Mother's purse had been empty, and the family had been living off Matti's wages from the store. All Matti could afford to buy on his own was flour, lard, and oatmeal. Since the bear's raid, they had mainly been living on fried bread and oatmeal.

When Matti was chopping wood all by himself, he sometimes got angry at Timo and Father for being gone. Why couldn't Timo at least stop by with a few more silver dollars? Why should it all fall on his shoulders? What made it most difficult was knowing that no matter how hard he worked, it wouldn't matter in the end, because Father would be following custom and passing his farm on to Timo.

But whenever Matti started to feel sorry for himself, he thought about Black Jack. Though Black Jack had been shunned by his family, forced to live as a beggar, and lost his leg, his job, and his homeland, he had refused to give up. If Black Jack had struggled through all that, Matti should at least be able to handle his chores without complaint.

Mrs. Winston helped cheer the girls up by sending them treats. Once she even handed Matti a whole tin of crackers, saying, "That Billy has overordered again. You take these home to the twins."

Mother accepted the gifts in the same way that she accepted their misfortune. "All things are ordained," she told the girls.

Matti preferred to believe that he controlled his own life. Why bother to live if every moment is plotted out ahead of time? Matti tried to cheer the twins up by continuing to play games and tell stories. He was also quick to remind them that Father would soon be returning from the lumber camp with extra money.

When Matti got ready to leave for work the next Saturday, the air was unusually warm. A light breeze blew out of the southwest, and the sky was summer blue. By the time Matti got to the store, his skis were sticking to the warm snow.

Billy and his customers were in a good mood due to the fine weather. However, by midafternoon a low bank of clouds had crept in, and a few wet snowflakes were ticking against the front windows. When Matti carried a sack of flour to a wagon an hour later, the wind had switched to the north.

Karl Gustafson stuck his head in the door and said, "It's snowing so hard back in Tower that the whole town has shut down."

"Is it coming this way?" Billy asked.

"No doubt," Karl said.

Billy turned to Matti. "You'd better spend the night here."

Matti thought about how Mother would worry and shook his head.

"If that storm is coming from the north—"

"I can ski home in just a few minutes."

"Well, if you're set on going, you'd better scoot," he said.

Matti poled down the trail. The track was fast and icy. On the first hill Matti's skis made a loud whirring sound, and he glided twice as far with each kick as he had in the morning. With every turn in the trail the sky darkened and the snow got heavier.

As Matti skied out of a sheltered stand of balsam and turned north, a gust of wind stood him straight up. Matti wheeled his arms to keep his balance, and his cap blew off. When he turned to grab for his cap, his ski tips crossed, and he fell backward into the snow. He laughed out loud.

In the short time that it took Matti to scramble to his feet, the wind had gotten stronger. He couldn't believe how quickly the temperature had dropped. Now that his mitts were wet, he could already feel his fingers going numb.

Lowering his head, he dug in his poles and kicked forward. The wind made it difficult to catch his breath. He stayed low and squinted as the storm-driven snow peppered his face like hot buckshot. It was so hard to see that his ski tip caught in the brush. He spun in a half-circle and almost fell again.

This time Matti didn't laugh. He stopped, panting. The whiteout was nearly total. The wind was whipping straight into his face, and the tops of the pines behind him whistled like a wood flute stuck on a high note. He heard a sharp crack as a branch broke loose and crashed to the ground. Though he could see the ski track at his feet, he was blinded the moment he lifted his eyes.

One thing was clear. He wasn't going to make it home. Matti tried to think things through. He could ski back to the store, or he could take shelter in the balsams and break off a pile of boughs to shield himself from the wind. Then he remembered that he'd forgotten his matches. Without a fire he'd have no chance of surviving the night.

The more Matti thought about what could happen, the closer he got to panicking. He was ready to try a wild sprint toward the homestead when he thought of a third choice. What about Black Jack's cabin? He was close to the southwest shore of the lake. But could he find the trail that led to the cabin?

Matti recalled the fallen popple that Louhi always jumped over when he ran to greet him. If he could find that tree, the cabin would be close. He skied forward, stopping every few feet to shield his eyes and peer to the east. His morning ski tracks had already drifted over, but he did his best to stay on the trail. Just when he was about to give up hope, Matti saw the hazy outline of the downed popple. He took off his skis and stuck them upright in the snow. Then he stepped over the trunk. Using his poles as a blind man would, he tapped at the brush on both sides of the path and stumbled forward. If he stayed on the path, he should have less than two hundred yards to go.

Only a few minutes later, Matti was scared. Had he veered too far south and walked past the cabin? Why hadn't he thought to count his paces? He'd just decided to backtrack to the popple and start over when he saw a hazy shape to his right. He took a step forward; then he ran. He had never been so happy to see Black Jack's filthy shack.

Though it was cold inside the cabin, as soon as he closed the door and blocked the wind, the air felt warm. He stood for a moment and caught his breath. He listened to the icy flakes hitting the door. The wind rattled the birch bark on the roof, and it whistled through the stovepipe.

Black Jack's table was still littered with sawdust and tools and old catalogs. His pot, crusted with the same old globs of stew, stood frozen on the wood range.

Matti was glad to see that the wood box was filled. That would save him a trip outside. He picked up some wood shavings from the floor and got a blaze roaring. As the room warmed, he began to smell something terrible. He looked under the corner of the table, and his happiness at being warm turned to disgust. Black Jack's lard can spittoon was just shy of overflowing and covered with a layer of green fuzz. Matti took it to the door and pitched it out. Not caring to touch Black Jack's soiled blankets, Matti left his coat on and slept on top of the bed.

When Matti woke the next morning, he felt as if something were terribly wrong. He sat up and listened. What could it be? Then he realized that his strange feeling was caused by the complete silence.

The snow had drifted so deep in front of Black Jack's steps that Matti had to bump his hip against the door to open it. As the leather-hinged door creaked open, he squinted into the brightness. Except for the black bark of the pines and the blue-patched sky, the world was without color.

Matti put on his coat and mitts and stepped outside. Just as he started slogging through the knee-deep snow, he heard Katie bray across the lake. The sound carried clearly through the bright air. He grinned. His impatient lady wanted her breakfast.

Matti found his skis, but the snow was so deep that he had to break trail on foot the whole way home. The drifts in the yard were enormous. The snow was level with the top of the haystacks and the wagon box. But the biggest drift of all extended from the eave of the sauna toward the lake. As tall as the roof, it was shaped like a frozen wave arching gracefully toward the ground.

Mother and the girls were standing in front of the sauna door, staring across the lake toward Black Jack's house. Mother was pointing at the smoke plume curling from Jack's chimney.

When Kari turned in Matti's direction, she blinked and yelled, "Look, it's Matti!"

Matti jogged forward as fast as he could while the girls jumped up and down and shouted, "Matti's home. Matti's home."

Matti shoveled a path to the woodpile and carried in two armloads of firewood before he snowshoed to the barn to feed and water the mules. It was tricky carrying the water pails from the lake on snowshoes, but even cantankerous Katie was glad to see him.

Only after he'd fed the animals and gotten more water for Mother did he sit down to a bowl of oatmeal. Though Matti had been eating oatmeal twice a day lately, he had never tasted anything so sweet.

CHAPTER 28

After a week of shoveling snow and hauling wood and water, Matti was anxious to return to the store. With the snow drifted so deep in the yard, Anna and Kari were spending most of their time inside, and they were getting on Matti's nerves. "Play with us," they'd say, but they got bored with every game. The girls were even more restless because Matti had to cancel his tutoring until he had time to break a trail to the Saaris'.

Matti enjoyed the quiet of the morning as he snowshoed to the store. The deep snow reminded him of winters past back home when he and Paavo and Juha had snowshoed to the edge of a swamp and hunted rabbits. It felt good to be alone, even if it took him half the morning to pack the trail. Matti feared that Billy might be upset when he arrived so late, but Billy pumped his hand and said, "I've been worried sick. When that storm blew in after you left, I thought about chasing after you. I should have made you stay overnight."

"I was too stubborn to listen," Matti said. "Besides, it wasn't that bad when I started." Billy motioned for him to take a seat beside the stove so that he could continue his story. Matti was impressed when Karl Gustafson offered him the nail keg and sat next to a farmer on the bench. The old-timers listened intently right to the end, and when Matti told about how happy he was to find Black Jack's cabin, everyone chuckled.

Karl said, "I'll bet you didn't mind Jack's shoddy house-keeping for once, did you, son?"

"I was so cold that I would have taken a stall in a cow barn," Matti said. Then he smiled.

"What's so funny?" Billy asked.

"I just remembered that I forgot to dig Black Jack's spit-toon out of that snowbank."

"Don't worry," Billy said. "I'll loan you a fresh lard can before he comes back in the spring."

As the fellows all chuckled, Matti felt for the first time that he was truly a part of this community of men. They laughed at him as he laughed at himself, for his foolishness in risking his life in the storm, yet they respected him for the quick thinking that had allowed him to survive.

"I wish I could afford to visit away the morning." It was Mrs. Winston, marching toward the front of the store. Matti stood up to apologize. He'd been worried about her lately because she'd been so silent. She surprised him with a hug. The soft, springtime scent of her perfume washed over him. "I'm so glad that you're safe. Last Saturday when I found out that man"—she pointed at Billy—"had sent you home in the middle of a storm, I gave him a piece of my mind."

"That she did."

Everyone chuckled again.

Later that afternoon Mrs. Winston asked Matti how it felt to be caught in the blizzard. When he told her about the cold wind and the fear, she shivered and hugged herself tight. "I can imagine how desperate and cold you must have been," she said. Then she stared out the window. "Can you believe the dark days we've been having? I've never seen such gloomy weather. Billy keeps promising that things will brighten up. 'Wait till Christmas,' he says." Her voice got softer as it trailed off. "Wait, wait, wait . . ." Matti was about to tell her that the winters were even darker back in Finland when she changed her tone and said, "So how's your tutoring going at the Saaris'?"

"Fine," Matti said.

"Would you like a little more reading material?" she asked, reaching behind the counter to retrieve some back issues of the Ely and Tower newspapers.

When Matti saw that one of the headlines described a sawmill accident, he said, "These will be much appreciated."

As Thanksgiving drew near, the whole family prepared for Father's homecoming. Mother planned to serve his favorite dishes: sucker canned in mustard sauce and roast partridge. She'd saved two jars of suckers that the bear hadn't spoiled, and it was Matti's job to furnish the partridge.

One afternoon he hunted all the way up the pine ridge but came home empty-handed. The next morning he tried the swamp. The sky was a dull metal gray as he snowshoed past the cedars. When Matti reached a patch of alder, he stopped to catch his breath. For some reason a song was stuck in his head. The notes played up and down, as if a flute were trilling in the distance. Where did it come from? Then he remembered Black Jack's whistling from last summer. Why couldn't he ever get that old man's tune out of his head?

The day was perfectly still. The sun was touching the treetops with streaks of pink light. Matti set the butt of his gun on his boot. The snow exploded between his legs, and he almost fell over. With a whirring thunder a partridge darted left and then right before it flew to the top of a distant popple.

Matti stood for a long time, trying to quiet his beating heart. A pair of chickadees flitted in the brush, and a raven called over the lake. When he finally calmed down, he lifted his boot and two more partridges flew up out of the snow, scaring him all over again.

Once Matti reached the popple stand, he realized why he hadn't been seeing any birds. At night they slept under the deep snow, and during the day they feasted on buds high up in the popple. In a short while he shot a half dozen birds and returned home.

"Now the meal will be perfect," Mother said when Matti emptied his pack.

They set the table before they went to bed and got up early the next day to wait for Father. Mother had hoped he'd arrive by lunch. But the noon meal came and went and still no Father. They waited all day Saturday, but he still didn't come. Matti and Mother pretended that everything was fine. When they sat down to a lonely dinner on Sunday afternoon, Mother said, "The snow must be too deep for Father to travel," and Matti quickly agreed.

"But doesn't Father have snowshoes?" Anna asked.

Mother had no answer for Anna until a week later, when Matti stopped by Mr. Saari's shack to check on their mail. "The mail is slow sometimes in these parts"—he chuckled as he handed Matti an envelope—"but this one is no fault of the post office."

Matti was excited to see Father's writing, but he had to laugh when he saw the scrawled address. The words were an illegible combination of Finnish and English.

"According to the postmarks," Mr. Saari said, "it went from the lumber camp to Sand Lake and Sturgeon Lake before it got here."

The letter was short and simple. Father couldn't make it home for now because the camp was still behind on its contracts. "But come Christmas," he wrote, "tell Anna and Kari that I'll make it home even if I have to hitch a ride in *Joulupukki*'s sleigh."

CHAPTER 29

Father's letter cheered everyone up, especially the girls, who had wondered if *Joulupukki,* or Father Christmas, would be able to travel all the way to Minnesota from his home in Lapland. The letter also gave Mother an excuse for the small portions of food she'd been serving lately: "We want to have lots of food when Father comes home."

In mid-December Matti noticed a huge smoke cloud to the north. The girls were worried that Father's lumber camp was on fire, even though Matti told them Father was working to the southeast. When Matti got to the store, everyone was talking about the fire that had burned up the Tower Lumber Company and six million feet of lumber. The whole town would have been lost without the help of the firemen.

On the Sunday before Christmas Matti took Anna and Kari out to cut a Christmas tree. The spruce was twice as tall as the girls, and they set it in a snowbank beside the door. Mother and the girls wove decorations out of straw, and Matti shaped a star out of cedar shavings to place on top. Then they strung some cranberries for the birds.

"Can we put candles on, too?" Kari asked.

"We can't spare—" Mother began, but seeing her face, added, "On Christmas Eve you may each light one." That reminded Matti of the cemetery back in Kuopio. On Christmas it glowed with hundreds of candles to honor the souls of departed relatives. He hoped that Timo would remember to light a candle in Tower for Uncle Wilho.

When Matti and the girls went to the Saaris' the following Friday, the boys were sitting at the table ready to begin their schoolwork. But as Matti took off his coat, everyone shouted, "Surprise!"

Mrs. Saari brought out a big plateful of *Nissu Nassu* Christmas cookies. The boys had shaped the spicy gingerbread into the letters of the alphabet to show how well they had learned their lessons. Everyone picked out a cookie to eat. Taipio took the letter *T* and Ahti the letter *A*, but Ukko chose an *M*. Thinking he had confused his letters, Matti was disappointed until Ukko said, "I took an *M* because Matti is my favorite teacher."

"And your only teacher." Matti smiled.

Then Ukko ran over to Anna and Kari and hugged them, too, saying, "And you are my favorite schoolmarms."

Matti wanted to make Father's Christmas special, but it would be difficult to buy a present with the few pennies that he'd set aside. On the Saturday before Christmas Matti was ready to buy a shaving mug, but Mrs. Winston saved the day. "There's one thing that makes every homesteader's eyes light up," she said, "and it's right over here." She led Matti to the far end of the storage room and pointed. "What do you think?"

Matti grinned. *"Täydellinen,"* he said. "That means perfect." Though Matti didn't have enough money to pay for the gift, Billy said, "As your Christmas bonus, I'll sell it to you for the price of a shaving mug." Matti was still smiling after he'd carried his present home and hidden it on a shelf in the mule barn.

Father got home early on the afternoon of Christmas Eve, and Timo arrived shortly after. Mother made a dinner of roast partridge and potatoes, and Father and Timo both brought presents. Father gave hand-carved tops to the girls and an oak breadboard to Mother. Matti got new ski bindings made from harness leather. Timo brought a sack of oranges for the family, and he gave Mother an envelope—"A little something to make up for the salary that I drank up when I was working in the mine," he said. Matti gave the girls stick candy and hair ribbons. And since Mother had been complaining about how bland her cooking was, Matti gave her a package of spices.

Everyone thought the gift giving was done until Matti slipped on his coat and went up to the barn. When he got back, he said, "Now for Father's present."

Father shook his head. "Just being with my family is present enough, Matti." With a grin Matti carried in the wooden crate and set it on the table.

Father stared. "Dynamite!"

Suddenly Father was waving his arms and talking all at once. "Think of the stumps we'll blow. And the rocks . . ." Father looked for a tool to pry up the lid.

"Not inside this house, Leo Ojala," Mother said. "You'll not be blowing us up on Christmas."

"It's not dangerous without a blasting cap," Father insisted.

"Matti," Mother said, "take those explosives out of this house."

After breakfast the next morning Father turned to Matti and said, "We'd better check on Maude and Katie." When Matti started to tell him that he'd already fed and watered the mules, Father said, "You and Timo get your coats. I need some help."

Before they were halfway to the barn, Father said, "I've been thinking. The ground can't be frozen too hard with all this snow."

When Matti saw the twinkle in Father's eye, he knew exactly what he had planned. "Should I get the lining bar?" Matti asked.

"And a shovel?" Timo said.

Timo scraped away the snow from the south side of a stump, and Matti poked the lining bar between the roots. When Matti's second thrust broke through the frost, Father chuckled. He packed a stick of dynamite in place, attached the blasting cap, and measured out the fuse, saying, "I'll give us plenty of time to get clear."

They worked their way down the field, selecting eight of the biggest stumps. Each time Father cut the fuse a little shorter. "If I time these right," he said, "it will be quite a show."

As soon as they were finished, Father went to the door of the sauna. "Get your coats, ladies," he shouted.

When everyone had gathered outside, he said, "Are you ready for some Christmas fireworks?"

"You're not going to blast today?" Mother said.

"We're set to go," Father said. He walked to the farthest stump and took out his matches. The morning shadows stretched long across the field, and the chickadees twittered in the birches.

"Be careful, Leo," Mother called.

He waved to her; then he knelt to light the first fuse. As smoke puffed out of the snow, he ran to the second stump and then the third. Father lit each fuse quickly until the last one, when his match dropped into the snow. Mother wrung her hands and yelled, "Hurry, Leo, hurry!" as he fumbled with another match.

Father raced over. "Watch the sky in case anything flies this—"

The farthest stump blew. Anna and Kari squealed as a tangle of roots and rock flew out of the ground. Then four more stumps exploded almost at once, booming so loud that the girls screamed again. The last three blew within seconds of one another, raining down a cloud of pebbles, and causing the girls to ignore Father's warning and duck their heads.

When the girls looked up, their eyes were wide. Smoke rose from the hillside, revealing a series of blackened circles in the snow. Every stump but the closest one was tipped at a crazy angle. When Father saw the level stump, he said, "That one needs a little help, Matti."

"Do it again, Father," the girls yelled. "Do it again."

"That's quite enough," Mother said. "You put that dynamite away so we can have a civilized holiday."

Anna and Kari asked together, "Can we blow up stumps every Christmas?"

Chapter 30

Though Father and Timo had to return to work the next morning, Father left the best present of all behind—a whole month's wages. Mother celebrated for a week after Christmas, frying either bacon or side pork for breakfast every morning. The twins cheered the "no oatmeal mornings," and Kari enjoyed the meat so much that she told Matti to put a third door on the root cellar, so that the bear couldn't ever get at their food supply again.

On the first day of the new year, the Ojalas got a surprise visitor. Mother had just set out the soup bowls for lunch when Matti heard the mules braying up at the barn. He looked outside and saw Black Jack stumping up the road with a big pack on his shoulders. He had a little ski attached to his peg leg, and he was using a walking stick to keep his balance.

Black Jack banged on the door with his stick, and as soon as it swung open, he kicked off his ski and stomped inside. "It looks like I got here just in time for lunch," he said, wiping his dripping nose with the back of his hand and slipping off his pack.

"You're welcome of course," Mother said, "but we only have a little bread and soup." She was even more startled than Matti was.

"That soup is a blamed sight more appealing than the whiskey and cigars I dined on last night." He was already taking off his wool coat, which was so dirty that the plaid pattern had nearly disappeared. "But before I start on the soup, I need to heat up your Christmas presents," he said. "Sorry they're a week late, but I was tied up in camp until yesterday."

Matti's first fear was that he'd brought them a jar of stew, but he reached into his pack and pulled out a pot for melting tin.

"Hooray!" the girls shouted. It was an old New Year's custom back in Finland to drop molten tin into water and tell fortunes from the cast shapes. "If Matti can find us a pail of water," he said, "I'll get my smelter ready."

Black Jack lifted up a stove lid and fit his smelting pot into the opening. As the tin heated, Black Jack had some soup. He talked so much that he spilled more on his beard than he got in his mouth. But between slurps he told them about his lumber camp, which was much closer than Father's, and explained that he had come home to pick up an adjusting tool for his violin.

Anna's and Kari's eyes got big when the time came for Black Jack to trickle the molten tin into the water bucket. After a sharp hiss Black Jack fished out the first piece of still-warm metal. Holding it to the light, Black Jack studied the shadow it cast on the wall. "Look," he said, turning to Kari, "it's a spring tulip, just risen from the ground. That shape tells me you will be a graceful dancer one day." Next he cast a form for Anna, which took the shape of a long, needle-like object. According to Black Jack, that meant she would become a talented seamstress.

Once he finished with the girls, he said, "Now for Matti and the missus." Matti was disappointed when his casting fragmented into many tiny pieces, until Jack said, "That signals you will be a rich man with many pieces of money." Mother's bit of molten metal formed into a solid glob, which Black Jack called "a perfect image of a grain sack and a symbol of a rich harvest soon to come." Then when he noticed a second smaller piece hanging from the corner of the casting, he said, "And here is a strong sign that there will be a grandchild coming along very soon. Does Mutti Boy have a little girlfriend that he's been keeping from his mother?" Anna and Kari laughed and laughed.

When Black Jack got ready to leave, Kari whispered to Matti, "Anna and I feel bad that we don't have a present for Mr. Black Jack."

"Why don't you sing him one of our songs?" Matti said.

Black Jack grinned as the girls sang about the half-blind tailor who got into trouble for using the wrong colored thread, stitching pant legs shut, and sewing buttons on backward. The last verse told how the tailor became famous when the king's jester hired him to sew a costume that was envied by all the jesters in the land. Jack clapped his hands and said, "Bravo!"

As Black Jack shouldered his pack, Matti warned him that he'd used his cabin for shelter during the storm and accidentally left his spittoon in a snowbank. Black Jack said, "That's good of you to help with my housecleaning."

*　*　*

By January Matti was tired of being stuck inside with the chatter of the girls and the incessant click of their knitting needles. To pass the time he tried weaving a knapsack from birch bark, but it turned out so lopsided that Kari said, "Your sack looks tired, Matti."

A deep cold descended from the north. On his way to the barn the air burned Matti's nostrils and stung his eyes. During the endless black nights, the stars glimmered like white points of ice while the lake buckled and moaned. Sometimes the ice made a sad, far-off rumbling, and other times it cracked like cannon fire. One night Anna said, "It sounds like ghosts crying under the ice." Though Matti smiled, it scared him to think of how close Anna had come to being an ice-trapped spirit herself.

An even louder cracking came from the drying sauna logs. They split in the night as if they had been struck by a gigantic axe blade. The first time it happened, both girls sat up in their sleep and cried out.

The walk to the Saaris' was bitter cold, but Matti's teaching sessions were a welcome break from the monotony. Mrs. Saari had bought five slates for Christmas, so everyone could practice their spelling. Soon even Ukko could print his letters.

To Matti it felt as if winter were never going to end. When Father went off to the logging camp in the fall, Matti had looked forward to a break from his poems and old sayings. Yet now he longed for Father's tales. The girls begged Matti to tell stories, but even when he tried "The Great Ox of Suomi," the girls barely squealed when he told about the seven boatloads of blood.

The stars burning above Sampo Lake on black nights made Matti long for Kuopio. Back home smoke plumes rose from the school, the granite church, the market, and the dark red houses in his neighborhood, painting the evening sky with wisps of gray. Here the single smoke trail of their chimney, pressed down by the cold, trailed flat across the treetops until it vanished in the dark.

But the saddest news of the winter came from Billy Winston. One morning Matti arrived at the store to find the door unlocked. He stepped into the familiar scents of leather, coffee beans, and spices, but no one was around. Matti stoked up the stove and waited on two customers before he heard someone stirring in the back.

"She's gone" was all Billy said as he walked up to the counter. Billy stunk of whiskey and looked as if he'd slept in his clothes. For the first time Matti understood what his Mother meant when she'd spoken of Billy's eyes showing his love for Clara. This morning Billy's eyes were dead and empty. "She told me she couldn't stand the cold and the loneliness another minute," Billy continued, blinking at the glass display case. "Next thing I knew she was on the train to St. Paul."

"I'm sorry," Matti said, searching for something more to say.

"I should've seen it coming," Billy said. "But there was no stopping her once she made up her mind."

Nothing could heal Billy's broken heart. One part of Matti wasn't surprised. He knew that Clara Winston didn't fit into Billy's world. Yet Matti had hoped that she would learn to love the wilderness and want to stay.

Folks soon found out what had happened, and their glum faces made it all the worse. What Billy needed was normal talk to ease him into his life without Clara. But everyone was so unnaturally quiet that he was reminded of his sadness all day long.

Once Karl Gustafson did speak his mind and said, "That woman was way too uppity, if you ask me. Good riddance to her."

"Well, I ain't asking," Billy shouted, grabbing him by the shirt, "and you got no business telling—"

"Okay, okay," Karl muttered, shocked by a side of Billy that he'd never seen. "I didn't mean nothing by it."

When February came, Matti decided to break the monotony of cabin life. On the Tuesday before Lent back in Kuopio, the townspeople held a sliding festival called *Laskiainen*. A contest challenged all the young men and women to see who could slide the farthest down Puijo. The girls went to bed early the night before because, according to custom, the one who made the longest slide in the morning won a spray of flax for her linen weaving.

Once the girls' race was done, the hill was open to everyone. To make the course more challenging, no one was allowed to use a sled or skis (unless two boys stood up on one pair together). Anything else was allowed: sheets of birch bark, blocks of ice, barrel staves, and fir boughs. Lunch was served after the morning sliding, and later on there was a sleigh ride and a dance.

The part of the holiday that everyone enjoyed most was the whip sled, so Matti decided to build one for Anna and Kari. The next morning, as soon as the girls had finished their breakfast, he said, "Who wants to help me chop a hole in the ice?"

"Are we going fishing?" Anna asked. "My hands get too cold."

"No," Matti said.

"Or fetching water to wash clothes?" Kari said.

"No," Matti said. "Put on your coats, and you'll see."

When they stepped outside, Mrs. Saari and her boys

were arriving, just as Matti had planned. Taipio was carrying a long spruce pole.

"What's going on?" Anna and Kari asked together.

"You'll see," Matti said. When he picked up a log and carried it to the lake, the girls cheered. "A whip sled," they cried. "Matti's building a whip sled."

Taipio and Matti chopped a hole in the ice and set the upright log in place. While they waited for the log to freeze, everyone helped shovel a circle clear of snow. Next Matti bored a hole through the middle of the spruce pole, and Ahti whittled a wooden pin to fit the pole onto the end of the frozen log. Finally they tied a short rope to the smaller end of the pole.

"Me first," Anna called. Sitting on a sheet of birch bark, she tucked her knees under her chin and held on tight to the rope. "Faster," she yelled as Matti pushed against the fat end of the pole. The birch bark made a loud scraping sound as Anna sped across the ice. "Faster, faster," she squealed as her scarf lifted off her shoulders and her hair blew out from under her cap. She finally let go of the rope and skidded into a snowbank. As Anna rolled over laughing in the snow, Kari shouted, "My turn."

After Kari was done, the boys each took a turn. Then the boys and girls tried it in pairs. When two of them let go of the rope, they spun in a complete circle before they slid into the snowbank. Even Mother and Mrs. Saari took a short ride. Both of them giggled like young girls. It felt good to hear Mother laugh again.

The twins urged Matti to give the sled a try. "You'll never move me," Matti said, planting his weight on the bark and taking up the rope.

Taipio put his shoulder to the pole, and Mother and

Mrs. Saari stepped forward to help. "Push," Taipio urged. "Push harder."

At first Matti barely moved. "I told you I was too heavy."

But as Taipio and the women put their full weight behind the pole, the birch bark went faster and faster. Soon Matti was flying across the ice.

"*Ptrui*," Matti yelled.

"Speak English," Ukko called from the side.

"Whoa!" Matti hollered. "Whoa!"

When Matti let go of the rope, his weight made him hit the snowbank so hard that he nearly disappeared.

Matti lay perfectly still. He waited until the twins and Ukko came to see if he was all right. Then he jumped up and chased them all the way back to the sauna.

CHAPTER 31

In early March the weather suddenly turned warm. The wind shifted to the south, and for two days the snowbanks melted. It was so warm one afternoon that Matti split kindling without wearing his coat. Anna asked, "Will it be summer again soon?"

"No," Matti said. "We have a good bit of winter yet to come."

"But it's so sunny."

"Just wait," he said.

By the weekend the wind had shifted to the north, and the temperature had fallen to below zero. After the hard freeze the snow crust allowed Matti to ski without following the trails.

Though the conditions were perfect for skiing, they were

deadly to the deer. One evening after Matti fed and watered the mules, he saw a deer run onto the lake near the creek. Steam was blowing out his nose and rising off his back. As he bounded forward, his front legs suddenly broke through the crust.

Yipping and snarling, a pack of wolves dashed out of the cedars in close pursuit. The deer scrambled to his feet and pulled away. But just when it looked as if he would escape, his hooves broke through the crust again.

Matti ran in and got the rifle. "What's wrong?" Mother asked.

"Wolves" was all he said as he slipped a handful of shells into his pocket and stepped outside. Before Matti could raise his rifle, a wolf grabbed onto the rear leg of the deer. Matti aimed at the shoulder of the wolf, but just as he was about to squeeze the trigger, the lead wolf lunged for the deer's throat.

It was too late now. Instead of firing at the wolf, Matti raised his rifle and shot into the air. The wolves turned toward him and stared. One snout was red with blood. They looked ready to charge. Matti levered another shell into the chamber, but before he snapped the action shut, the pack was loping for the far shore.

The deer was barely alive when Matti reached it. The snow was pink with blood. The deer's breath was raspy, and his eyes were half-glazed. Matti ended his suffering.

Though his family could make use of the meat, Matti hated to see any animal die like this. On firmer ground the deer could have easily escaped. It reminded Matti of a spring evening when he was a little boy, when he and Uncle Wilho had seen an owl kill a rabbit. The snow had melted early that year, leaving the rabbit half-white and an easy target. Matti had cried when he heard the rabbit's terrible shriek. Though Wilho had tried to explain how nature sometimes played cruel tricks on her creatures, it had taken Matti a long while to get over his sadness.

When business was poor at the store the following Saturday, Matti had an idea. "Is this your slowest season?" he asked Billy.

"Generally," Billy said. He'd been talking in one-word sentences since Clara left.

"So if you were ever going to take a vacation, this would be the perfect time?"

"What are you driving at?"

"I was just thinking," Matti said. "I'd be willing to look after the store if you ever wanted to take a trip down to St. Paul."

"So you're gonna stick your nose in like every Tom, Dick, and Harry in this country." Billy was so angry that Matti was afraid he was going to throttle him the way he'd grabbed Karl the other day. Then Billy stopped. "I'm sorry, Matti. I know you mean well." Billy paused. "I told you how I met Clara, didn't I?"

Matti nodded.

"I really thought things were going well between us." Billy stood silent for a moment. "I haven't been to St. Paul in a long time. Just maybe I should give it a try."

For the next week Matti was up two hours before dawn to carry wood and water before he left to tend the store. Matti was proud that Billy trusted him to run things, but the supposedly slow time turned out to be busier than ever. On his first day alone two gold prospectors stopped by on their way to Rainy Lake City and bought a month's provisions. And several homesteaders chose the same day to stock their larders. By the time Matti had swept the floor and straightened the shelves at the end of the day, he had to ski home in the moonlight.

Billy returned from his trip alone. All he said was, "Clara's folks weren't gracious but they weren't mean neither."

The following afternoon Matti was bent over the woodpile, filling his arms, when a voice behind him said, "Do you need some help?" The English was so heavily accented that he could barely understand the words, but the voice was familiar.

Matti turned. "Father! Since when do you speak English?"

"I've been practicing since Christmas. There's only one other Finn in our camp, and he's half-deaf and toothless, so I got tired of talking to myself." Father paused and switched back to Finnish. "The truth is, you and your uncle were right. If we're going to live in America, we'd better learn to talk American. But never in the sauna, of course."

"Of course," Matti said.

As Father bent to help Matti with a load of wood, he admired the woodpile. "It sure is a relief for me to know that Mother and the girls have a good man to look out for them."

"So what brings you home so soon?" Matti asked.

"We've caught up on our contracts," Father said, "and the boss gave me a few days off to catch up on my own logging."

"What logging?" Matti asked.

"The logging we need to do to get our house built. If we fell the cabin logs when the ground is still frozen, they'll skid easy. Then you can get them peeled while I'm finishing up at the lumber camp, and we'll have the walls up before planting time."

Matti shook his head. Father was ever the optimist.

For the next three days they were up at dawn and felling pine trees. The morning after Father returned to his logging camp, Matti began skidding the logs. Hurrying in case a warm spell turned the trails to mud, he worked as fast as Maude and Katie's strength would allow.

Since the mules were out of shape from the winter, they

needed to rest more often than usual. But Matti could tell that they were excited to be in the harness. Whenever he stopped to let them "blow" and catch their breath, Katie pawed the ground and looked over her shoulder as if to ask, "Isn't it time to get back to work?"

"Don't you worry, Miss Katie," Matti called, "you'll have lots of chances to pay us back for all that hay you've eaten this winter." Though Matti had often teased Father for talking to his mules, he found himself carrying on long one-sided conversations in the solitude of the woods. The mules seemed to perk up and listen as if they understood every single word he was saying.

Once the logs were landed up the hill from the sauna, Matti began peeling them. The bark sheared off the balsam in long sheets, but the red pine was more stubborn.

Mother was so anxious to have a proper house that she insisted on helping. Matti was impressed with how easily she handled the drawknife. However, when Anna and Kari tried to peel a log, they could barely make a scratch. Finally by standing on opposite sides of the log and pulling the drawknife together, they peeled off a small strip of bark. "Look, Matti," Kari and Anna said, "we're logging."

"You certainly are," he said. Matti then took a chisel and cut the girls' initials into the log. "Now you can find your special log after we put our house together."

Matti's whole body ached when he lay down to sleep that night. He would rather haul milk pails all the way to Soudan than have to pull on that drawknife another day.

CHAPTER 32

As the days passed, Matti searched for a way to cheer up Billy, but nothing seemed to work. At times Billy joked with his favorite customers and seemed to return to his old self, but as soon as the store emptied of people, his glumness returned. One afternoon Matti took a chance. He sat down with a pen and paper. After looking up a half dozen words in his dictionary and trying several different beginnings, he decided to be direct.

Dear Mrs. McKenzie,

I hope you are not angry at me for writing, but I wanted to tell you how much Billy misses you. Though the folks may seem hard at times in these parts, they are

*good people. And I am sure that Billy and I are not the
only ones who miss you. For what will Black Jack do
without his licorice and chewing tobacco deliveries?*

*You really should see the springtime up here. The first
flowers are just beginning to blossom. Billy told me
about the time he met you and how beautiful the moon
was on that steamboat ride across Big Bay.*

*The moon will soon be turning full again. I wish you
were here to share it with Billy.*

*Your friend,
Matti Ojala*

On the way to the depot to mail the letter, Matti thought
about turning back. Maybe it was none of his business. He was
probably just wasting a penny buying a stamp. Mr. Saari helped
him fill out the front of the envelope:

MRS. CLARA HUGHES MCKENZIE

SUMMIT AVENUE

ST. PAUL, MINNESOTA

"St. Paul is a mighty big place," Mr. Saari said. "I don't
know if this address will get your letter to the right house."

"I owe it to Billy to try," Matti said.

"Good morning, brother."

Matti turned. It was Timo, grinning broadly.

"What are you doing up so early? Or haven't you been
to bed?"

"I really have given up on those saloons." His eyes were
clear and bright.

"What about your wagon driving job?" Matti asked.

"I'm off until the roads dry out." He slapped Matti on
the back. "Let's go!" They talked the whole way to the cabin.

Mother and the girls gave Timo a big hug, and then everyone sat down for coffee to hear about his sleigh driving.

When Timo pushed back his stool, he said, "We'd better finish peeling those logs, Matti. I'm sure Mother wants her house done in time for the wedding." Matti was so impressed that Timo had called him Matti, rather than little brother, that at first he didn't notice the word *wedding*. Then Matti remembered the nice girl Timo had brought to the store.

"Wedding?" Mother said. "What wedding?"

"Why, didn't I tell you?" Timo said with a sly grin. "I'm getting married in June."

Mother jumped up and squealed like a little girl. She and the twins asked a million questions as Timo explained that his wife-to-be, Ida, was the daughter of a man named Arne Koski, who worked at the Pioneer mine in Ely. Mother was relieved to hear that the girl was both a Finn and a Lutheran. Since the Koskis had grown up in Soudan, the wedding would be at the Lutheran church there.

Bored by the wedding talk, Matti finally stood up.

"I better help, Matti," Timo said. He looked glad to have an excuse to escape the house.

Matti was impressed by Timo's new attitude. He was twice the worker he'd been last fall. When Timo noticed Matti's back was hurting, he was careful to make sure that Matti didn't strain himself with any heavy lifting.

They finished peeling the logs three days later. Matti and Timo put down their drawknives and stepped back to admire their work. Timo said, "We did good—"

"Look." Matti cut him off. Together they turned toward the lake.

Timo said, "The ice is gone!"

Waves were rippling across the silver water. "I can't believe I missed it," Matti moaned. For the last week the ice had been darkening to a honeycombed sheet, and Matti had promised himself that he would see it go out. This morning there had been a big raft of ice in the middle of the lake, yet it had suddenly vanished.

They walked to the shore. "It sounds like summer again," Timo said. Matti nodded. After listening to the mournful winds of winter, the lapping of the waves was heaven-sent music.

Just then Matti heard a shout. "Hey there, *Kapteeni.*"

It was Father. "For a minute I thought squatters had taken over my homestead claim." He stepped forward and crushed Matti in a big hug, but when Timo reached out to shake his hand, Father turned cold. "What brings you to the woods?" he asked. "Have you come out here to have your little brother teach you how to work? He's been a godsend since I had to go off to the lumber camp." Matti couldn't believe his ears. For once his hard work had not gone unnoticed.

"I know I let you down," Timo said. "But it won't happen again."

Father looked Timo in the eye for a long time. Finally he extended his hand. "Put her there," he said in English. "I'm learning American talk from the men in camp."

As the two men shook hands, Matti asked, "Are you done for the season, Father?"

"Not quite. I've been chomping at the bit ever since the bottom fell out of the ice roads, but I got stuck doing a heap of end-of-the-season repairs."

The minute Father walked inside, Mother said, "Timo's getting married."

"What?" Father turned to Timo. When Timo nodded,

Father grinned slowly. "If you're set on making me into a grandpa, I'll have to start looking for a rocking chair."

"You don't have a long enough beard to be a grandpa," Kari said, and everyone laughed.

Mother added, "I think your father's a bit too frisky for a rocking chair just yet." Matti added, "Unless we can find one with wheels and a steam engine."

At dawn the following morning, the men were hauling their tools down from the barn to start work on the cabin when Black Jack hollered from the shore. "Anybody home?" he said. "I thought you'd have the walls half done by now." Maude trotted down to say hello.

"What a voice!" Timo said, shaking his head. "I'd forgotten all about your neighbor."

Father nodded. "I figured he might stop over to help, but I didn't expect him this early."

"This isn't so early for Black Jack." Matti recalled last spring when Black Jack had often rousted him out of his blankets.

Anna and Kari ran out the door when they heard the commotion. "It's Mr. Black Jack," Kari shouted.

"You've got that right," he called. "How about if you little ladies help this old lumberjack tie up his boat?"

Kari looped his stern rope over the dock post while Anna tied the front of his boat to a tree on shore. Using his axe handle for a cane, Black Jack planted his stump on the dock and climbed out of his boat. "That's good, girls," he said; then he reached in his pocket and handed them each a shiny penny.

"I don't hear any chopping," Black Jack called as his peg leg thumped on the dock. "Is that slugabed Matti up yet?"

"Morning, Jack," Father said, grinning because Black Jack could see that Matti was standing right beside him.

Only a few minutes later Eino Saari and Taipio walked down the driveway, carrying axes. As Father shook Eino's hand, Matti said, "Good morning, Taipio," in English, and Taipio said "Good morning" back to Matti.

"Talk Finn, so a man can understand you," Black Jack scolded.

"Times change, Jack," Father said. "I've been thinking about asking Matti to give me English lessons, too."

"That'd be a waste of time if you ask me," Black Jack said. Then he turned to Eino. "Your boy looks a mite runty to heft an axe."

"He may be little," Eino countered, "but he's a hard worker."

Timo picked up a shovel and turned to Matti. "You ready to hit her hard, brother?"

Once the cornerstones were set, they divided into three crews. Father and Black Jack notched and fit the logs on one side, while Timo and Eino Saari took the opposite side. Matti and Taipio did the skidding.

As soon as Matti hitched up Maude and Katie and dragged the first log to the building site, the wood chips began to fly. The men worked so fast that by the time Taipio and Matti got a log positioned on one side, the fellows were calling for a log on the other side. Taipio got along with Katie, who took an instant liking to him, and with Black Jack, who decided that Taipio had "big *sisu* for a little guy." As usual Black Jack whistled as he chopped, but this time his song had new parts to it.

Mother's cooking helped keep everyone happy. Black Jack couldn't get enough of the fresh baked *pulla* that Mother offered during the midmorning coffee break. Just before noon

Mrs. Saari arrived with some *piirakka,* a delicious rye-crust pie filled with meat and potatoes and carrots, to go along with Mother's soup.

When Black Jack raved about the food, Father said, "What do you know about fine cooking, Jack? You'd like anything that hadn't sat in your stewpot for a month."

"Stew ain't eatable until it's aged a bit."

Only a week later Matti and Timo nailed the last roof board in place on their cabin. Though Mr. Saari had to work at the depot that day, Taipio stopped by to help them celebrate. After Matti hammered down the final nail, Father hung a birch bough on the gable for good luck. Then just as Timo tossed his hammer to the ground, Matti heard a loud caw.

He looked up and saw a crow sitting on the peak of the sauna roof. It tipped its head one way and then the other, then flew straight toward the new cabin. Just when it looked as if the bird were going to land at Matti's feet, it flapped its wings and arced upward. As the crow passed overhead, it let out a sharp caw and rolled over twice in midair.

"I've never seen a crow do that," Taipio said.

Father looked at Matti and smiled. Father's eyes asked the same question that was turning in Matti's mind, but Matti decided that he would never know the answer for sure.

While they picked up the tools, Black Jack walked over to the rowan tree. "This little beauty sure is growing fine," he said.

Matti hadn't looked at the rowan in a long time, and he was amazed to see tiny leaves opening on the branches.

"I thought those caterpillars had chewed it dead," Father said.

"Can we decorate it for the wedding, Mother?" Anna asked.

"Wedding?" Black Jack said.

Father nodded. "Timo's getting married in June."

Black Jack's eyes lit up. "I'll make sure that I have my fiddle tuned and ready."

CHAPTER 33

The next morning Timo needed to return to town. Before he said goodbye, he turned to Mother and Father. "Ida and I have been talking," he said, "and we were wondering if you'd mind if we filed a homestead claim next to yours."

"Mind?" Father said. "We'd be proud to have you as neighbors. And that way we could pass our section on to Matti one day—he surely deserves it."

"What did you say?" Matti stared at Father.

"Is there something wrong with your ears? I said one day this farm will be yours." He paused and smiled at Matti. "You earned it."

"I'll take a trip to the courthouse this week." Timo waved and started down the path, then stopped. "I almost forgot. Ida's parents would like you to come to dinner next Sunday."

As Timo walked away, Father clapped Matti on the shoulder and said, "Your mother and I have been talking about how we could make things right by you. This will at least be a start."

Matti stared at the cabin and the fields beyond. It took a long time for Father's words to sink in. Could this land really be his someday? All Matti had ever wanted was Father's respect. But having his own farm would be more than he'd ever dreamed.

Before the family could move their things from the sauna to the new cabin, Father and Matti had to tarpaper the roof. When they finished, Father climbed down and stepped inside the cabin. Though it was dark as a cave, Father paced the length of the room. "Our kitchen will go there," he said, waving his hands, "and we'll cut out a nice window overlooking the lake there. Then—"

"Anybody in here?" Mother poked her head into the room. "Why are you two standing in the dark? I'll get the lamp."

As she left, Father winked and said, "I think a saw would be a better idea. Don't you?"

By the time Mother returned, Father had stepped outside and drawn pencil marks for a window, and Matti had fetched the brace and bit and a saw.

Father drilled a row of parallel holes and slid in the saw blade. Then as Matti cut down one vertical line, Father drilled starter holes on the other side. When both cuts were done, Father handed Matti the sledgehammer and said, "Would you do the honors? You've put a whole lot more labor into these logs than I have."

Stepping into the cabin, which was lit only by sunlight from the rough-cut doorway and the flickering of Mother's lamp, Matti thought back to his long shifts in the Soudan mine. As he hefted the hammer, he recalled the candle smoke and the ore dust and the constant powder smell of his steel-drilling days. If only Uncle Wilho could be here to share this moment!

Matti took a swing at the middle log. The wall just shivered. "Harder, Matti," Kari yelled from the other side.

"Stand back," Matti yelled, swinging with all his might. He hit the wall once and then again. The third blow brought a loud crack, and the girls yelled, "Hooray!" as the logs tumbled onto the ground. Dust rose into the air, and golden light poured through the opening. "How's the view?" Father asked.

"Perfect!"

Anna and Kari ran to the doorway and hopped inside. "It's as big as a castle," Kari cried, extending her arms and twirling like a dancer in the middle of the floor.

"That makes us twin princesses," Anna said.

Mother and the girls gave the cabin a good sweeping. Then Matti helped Mother carry in her dishes and her carved wooden trunk while the girls lugged the bedding and blankets. Mother opened her trunk. She picked up her porcelain bellpull with its braided velvet cord. Light flashed off the gilt rim and blue flowers. She held it in the corner. "How would it look here?" she asked.

"Perfect," Matti said.

Anna and Kari were about to go outside when Matti asked, "Aren't you forgetting something?"

They both thought for a moment, then they turned to each other. "Our special log," they said, squeezing Matti's hands. The girls searched every wall, but they couldn't find their initials.

"Did you turn the log wrong-side out?" Kari asked.

Matti shook his head.

After the girls looked around the room one more time, Matti said, "Do you give up?"

They both nodded. "I'll show you," he said. Matti picked them both up. Turning slowly, he faced each wall in turn, saying, "It's not there or there or there." The girls looked confused. "But we're getting very warm."

Finally he tipped back their heads so that they could scan the long tie beam that ran down the middle of the cabin. The letters *A.O.* and *K.O.* were carved side by side along with the date, May 15, 1901. Matti had added it this morning.

"That's the prettiest log in the whole house," Kari said.

"No," Anna said, "it's the prettiest log in America."

CHAPTER 34

The rest of the month was a mad rush for Mother to pre-pare for Timo's wedding and for Matti and Father to ready the fields for planting. Luckily Father's Christmas dynamite made their plowing much easier than last year. They seeded twice the ground and Father was confident that they would have extra grain and potatoes to sell in the fall.

Mother and Father had been all smiles since they returned from their dinner at the Koskis'. Mother called Mrs. Koski and Ida "dears," and Father was convinced that he'd found another sauna partner in Mr. Koski. They also brought back a milk cow. Father said that it made sense to spend the money because they could sell enough cream and butter in a year to pay for it.

The girls were excited that they would have their very

own cow, but when Father noticed Matti's silence, he said, "What's wrong? I thought you'd be happiest of the lot, now that you won't have to lug those milk pails from the Saaris'."

"I was just thinking ahead."

"To what?"

"To the cow barn we're going to have to build," Matti said.

Father slapped him on the back. "You're beginning to understand how the world works."

On the day before Timo's wedding, Maude started *eeoow*ing loudly up at the barn. Matti looked out on the lake and was surprised to see Black Jack rowing across with a passenger. Matti thought he might be out fishing with someone, but he kept pulling straight for their shore. Matti walked down to the end of the dock.

"My lady friend and I thought we'd come for a little visit," Black Jack called.

The lady was Mrs. Winston. She smiled at Black Jack's joke and waved. As Matti helped her out of the boat, she said, "Mr. Mattson was kind enough to escort me."

Mother and the girls met the visitors halfway between the shore and the house. The girls trailed behind the ladies, whispering in awe about Mrs. Winston's beautiful white hat and green gingham dress. Mother invited Mrs. Winston into the house for coffee while Matti took Black Jack to the barn to see Father.

After the visitors left, Matti and Father walked into the cabin and found Mother sitting at the table dabbing her eyes with a hanky. Her right hand was clenched in a tight fist.

"What's wrong?" Matti asked.

Mother tried to speak, but her voice caught. Finally she opened her palm and said, "Look."

It was Grandmother's brooch.

"What in the devil?" Father whispered.

Mother stood and gave Matti a big hug. "She insisted that I take it because of you, Matti. She said you'd been such a big help to her and to Billy"—Mother stopped and swallowed—"that she wanted to show her appreciation."

With her blue dress and ruby brooch Mother nearly out-shone the bride on Timo's wedding day. The one hard part of the wedding for Matti was returning to the Lutheran church in Soudan. He thought back to the bitterly cold night they arrived at the train depot. He tasted the dust of the rockfall on the day of Wilho's accident. He saw the broken brim of Wilho's helmet, Aunt Hilda's black veil, and the nickel casket plate that read "At Rest" all over again.

Through the reciting of the vows and the exchange of the rings, Matti could hear the cable hoist and the crusher up at the mine. He kept thinking about the hundreds of miners who were still working underground. They toiled in the cold and the dark, knowing that it was only a matter of time before a ledge of rock released without warning. Even as the minister gave his final blessing and the bell rang out the marriage of Timo and his bride, Matti knew that on another day the bell above their heads would be tolling the same dark message that had shattered Aunt Hilda's heart.

Black Jack was the star of the wedding dance at the Finn Hall in Soudan. Though Ida's relatives had wanted an accordion player to furnish the music, once they heard Black Jack's fiddling they were impressed.

"I thought I'd seen everything," Ida's father, Arne, said, "but a one-legged man who can play the fiddle and dance at the same time is one for the record books. I would have driven all the way from Ishpeming to see that man."

Mother also invited a new family, the Lamppas, who had just moved in south of the depot. Two surprise guests were Billy and Clara Winston, who came by wagon from the store.

By good fortune the weather stayed clear and warm, and Mother and Mrs. Saari were able to set the food and drinks on tables outside. Father and Matti also built a small bonfire where people could visit.

Arne Koski discovered that Black Jack had lived in Oulu, the town where Arne had grown up. The moment Arne saw the scars on Black Jack's hands, he grinned and said, "You knew the tar makers?"

Matti complimented the Saari boys on being so sociable. They spent a good part of the evening practicing their English with one of Ida's nieces. When Black Jack played a foot-tapping tune that he called the "Rovaniemi Chicken Dance," Taipio even took a short turn on the dance floor with both Anna and Kari. Matti got a dancing lesson of his own from Mrs. Winston. She glided across the rough floor of the hall as if she were waltzing in a marble ballroom. When they were done, she curtsied and said, "Thank you for the dance, sir."

Matti bowed proudly as Clara Winston continued, "I'll be forever grateful for that letter you wrote. I'd just gotten back from a dull afternoon tea when the mail arrived. Your words about Billy and the moonlight on Vermilion made me realize how pale and dreary the city is compared to the north. The winters may be cold, but the warmth of these people"—she cast her eye toward Billy, who winked from across the room—"more than makes up for it."

*   *   *

After the last guests left, the Saaris stayed to help clear the tables. They didn't finish until after midnight. By that time Anna and Kari had fallen asleep in the back of the wagon.

Though Ida's parents had offered to put the family up for the night, Father had declined. Pointing to the full moon and the clear, star-flecked sky, he said, "Our road will be well lit for traveling."

But by the time they'd loaded the dishes in the wagon, Father was yawning. He turned to Matti and asked, "Can you handle the driving?"

When Matti nodded, Father patted him on the back and said, "Good man." Only minutes later Father was stretched out in the wagon bed between a box of dishes and the twins, snoring loudly.

Mr. Saari chuckled and said, "Since you've got a full wagon, Black Jack can ride with us." Mother waved goodbye and thanked everyone one last time for coming.

Matti grinned at being called a good man. He picked up the reins and started the mules down the road. Suddenly Maude planted her feet and refused to move. Though Katie was normally the "bad" mule, Maude was holding back this time. Matti flicked the reins and said, "Let's go, Maude. Pull like your sister Katie." Katie's ears perked up, but Maude refused to budge. Matti felt Mr. Saari and Black Jack staring at him from the other wagon. What could he do now?

Uncle Wilho had always told him that if a man wasn't smarter than a mule, he deserved to walk. Matti suddenly thought of a trick. "Rest if you want, Miss Maudie," he said, letting the reins go slack, "but Black Jack will beat us home."

The moment Maude heard Black Jack's name, she turned

208

her head and looked at the wagon beside them. "Mutti's right," Black Jack called to Maude, "and I just might steal all your hay."

At the word *hay*, Maude finally started forward. Though she sighed loudly at having to pull a heavy load long past her bedtime, she and Katie made good time on their way back to the homestead.

Soon everyone was tucked in bed. But Matti still felt restless.

"Aren't you coming to bed?" Mother asked.

"I want to walk down to the lake for a minute," he said.

The weathered planks of the dock creaked as Matti stepped toward the end. The black water was still and dappled with starlight. The wings of a nighthawk whistled overhead.

Matti thought of Uncle Wilho. If only Wilho could have seen this day. He loved a good bonfire and a dance. But he loved the company of fine people most of all. He would have liked everyone at the wedding.

For the first time since Matti had arrived in America, he felt that he was part of a family that extended beyond the borders of their farm. He looked back at the homestead, the homestead that would be his someday. Moonlight reflected off the window of the main cabin and washed the rocks and trees with a soft, silver white. The hillside that had been a maze of stumps and brush only a year ago was now a neatly tilled field. Down the bay Matti could picture the home that Timo and Ida would soon be building.

When a fish splashed out in the deep, Matti turned. A perfect moon hung above the pine ridge where Matti had watched his pet crow disappear last fall. A loon called from the far shore, and he caught the faint scent of water lilies. Then it was quiet.

Across the lake Matti could see a yellow point of light

glowing in Black Jack's window. As Matti turned to head back to the cabin, he heard music. He stopped and listened harder.

There it was again—a violin. Though Black Jack had played lively folk tunes all through the wedding dance, this music was totally different. Yet it sounded familiar. Matti suddenly smiled: The melody was the same one that Black Jack so often whistled. This was Black Jack's very own song.

The notes rose and fell with a slow, sliding rhythm. Sounding deep and still, they reminded him of an ice-locked lake or a lone pine growing out of cold, black rock. Then just when the tones couldn't get more mournful, the pace picked up. The sounds were suddenly sharp and quick, skipping over the lake like a leaf caught in a cataract. Black Jack played faster and faster. Matti imagined that this was how the tar makers of Oulu felt hurtling down their spring flood rapids. Matti saw the dark men, fists raised and cheering, as they flew under the bridges of their town. All at once the music was a storm, striking white fire across the sky. Then it stopped.

Matti waited for the violin to start up again, but it was quiet. What he heard next wasn't pretty, yet it made him smile. For drifting across the still waters of Sampo Lake was the sound of Black Jack laughing loud and long.

Afterword

The story of Matti's family is typical of the quarter of a million Finnish immigrants who arrived in America during the first two decades of the twentieth century. Some of these immigrants left their homeland to avoid being drafted into the Russian army. Others sought freedom from the far-reaching powers of Finland's National Lutheran Church. But most Finns were motivated by simple economics—they were poor. Wealthy families owned large tracts of land in Finland, forcing most men to work as tenant farmers or itinerant laborers. Those who did own small farms often had to earn a living from only ten or fifteen acres. When America's Homestead Act offered 160 acres to anyone willing to start a farm, the Finns saw this as a grand opportunity.

However, the reality of American life seldom matched its promise. Though Finland had a 98 percent rate of literacy—the highest of any European country—Finnish immigrants had so much difficulty learning English that they often ended up at the bottom of the economic ladder, working as lumberjacks, miners, farmhands, and domestic servants. Many Finns homesteaded by choice, but others were pushed into farming when they were blacklisted by the mining companies during the strikes of 1907 and 1916. Since Finns were outspoken advocates for social justice, they were often targeted by company spies who reported their activities to the bosses. Miners were often fired for discussing unions, attending Industrial Workers of the World (IWW) meetings, or even reading socialist newspapers.

The Finns who left the mines and started homesteads slowly began to realize their dreams. Small farming communities sprang up across the iron ranges of Minnesota, Wisconsin, and Michigan, as Finns worked hard to grow crops on rocky, cutover timberland that no one else wanted. Despite a harsh climate that offered only a three-month growing season, their *sisu* allowed them to found member-owned cooperative stores, creameries, and seed plants; they built town halls, churches, and schools.

In the end, a lifetime of hard labor often left a Finnish family with nothing more than the clear title to a small tract of rock-strewn land. Yet in the process these homesteaders had achieved something they valued much more than money—an independent lifestyle and the freedom to speak their minds.

Acknowledgments

Special thanks to my agent, Barbara Markowitz, and to my many Finnish American friends in Minnesota, Wisconsin, and Michigan, who have been so willing to share stories of their heritage.

For help with my research I would like to thank James M. Kurtti, editor of *The Finnish American Reporter;* Outi Vuorikari, director of the Kuopio Church Registry, Kuopio, Finland; Ritva Rönkkö of the Kuopio Museum; Heikki Viitala, secretary for international affairs of Kuopio, Finland; Annikki and Matti Ojala of Lehtimaki, Finland; Dr. Michael Karni, director of Sampo Publishing; Harry Lamppa and Betty Birnstihl of the Virginia Historical Society; Richard Fields of Minnesota's Tower-Soudan State Park; John Korpi, Andy Larson, Marcella Nelson, and Pete and Nancy Yapel of Tower; Dolly Nevala of Embarrass, Minnesota; Ed Nelson and Deb Fena of the Iron World Research Library; Joel Wurl, Halyna Myroniuk, and Daniel Necas of the Immigration History Research Center at the University of Minnesota; and the staffs of the University of Minnesota's Duluth, Hibbing, and Virginia libraries.

Finally, I would like to extend my gratitude to my family, Barbara, Jessica, and Reid, for all their support.

Glossary of Finnish Words

The Finnish language is unique in that it has no close associations within the European family of languages. This makes Finnish extremely difficult for nonnative speakers to master, and it also explains why Finnish immigrants to America had so much difficulty in learning English.

Finnish uses the same Roman alphabet as English, but it has only nineteen letters (no *b, c, d, q, x, w,* or *z,* except in foreign words)

ANTEESKI - Excuse me.

HAUKI - the northern pike.

HYVÄÄ HUOMENTA - Good morning.

JOULUPUKKI - Santa Claus.

JUHANUS DAY - Midsummer's Eve. A celebration of the longest day of the year and the feast of St. John, held on the Saturday closest to June 24.

KAKSI - two.

KALAKEITTO - a fish and potato soup.

KALAKUKKO - a rye-crust pie filled with pork and fish.

KALEVALA - the Finnish national epic poem, a series of ancient songs preserved by rune singers from remote villages and collected and published in 1835 by Elias Lönnrot.

KAPTEENI - captain.

KIUAS - a sauna stove.

KOLME - three.

KUPPARIMUMMU - a cupping woman, one who bled the sick by making a small incision with a razor and using suction cups made from the tips of cow horns.

LAESTADIANS - followers of the preacher Lars Laestadius, who was opposed to drinking, gambling, and exhibitions of personal vanity.

LOUHI - an evil witch in the *Kalevala*.

LUUKO - a small gable door used to let the smoke out of a *savu sauna*.

NISSU NASSU - gingerbread cookies in the shape of little pigs.

PIIRAKKAA - a rye-crust pie filled with meat, potatoes, and carrots.

PTRUI - a command, meaning "Halt."

PULLA - a cardamom-flavored sweet bread.

PUUKKO - a knife.

PUUKKOJUNKKARIT - knife wielders.

RUUSUNUKKE - a rose doll. A disparaging term applied to a girl who is pretty but doesn't work hard.

SAMPO - the magical mill in the *Kalevala* that could generate equal amounts of gold, grain, and salt.

SAUNA - pronounced *SOW-na*. A Finnish steambath.

SAVU SAUNA - a traditional-style smoke sauna with an open fireplace.

SISU - strength, courage, tenacity, and integrity all wrapped into one. The will to succeed no matter how impossible the task.

TÄYDELLINEN - perfect.

VÄINÄMÖINEN OR VÄINÖ - the hero of the *Kalevala*, who sought the magic *sampo*.

VAPPU - May Day celebration.

VIHTAS - a sauna whisk, generally a bundle of birch branches and leaves, used to lightly beat the skin to increase circulation.

VIILI - yogurt.

YKSI - one.

About the Author

William Durbin was born in Minneapolis and lives on Lake Vermilion at the edge of the Boundary Waters Canoe Area Wilderness in northeastern Minnesota. He is on leave from teaching English at a small rural high school and composition at a community college and has supervised writing research projects for the National Council of Teachers of English, the Bingham Trust for Charity, and Middlebury College. His wife, Barbara, is also a teacher, and they have two grown children.

William Durbin has published biographies of Tiger Woods and Arnold Palmer and books in the My Name Is America series. His first novel, *The Broken Blade,* won the Great Lakes Book Award for Children's Books and the Minnesota Book Award for Young Adult Fiction.

You can visit William Durbin at his Web site: www.williamdurbin.com.

BACKYARD VEGETABLE GARDENING

Hugh Wiberg

Galahad Books • New York City

Dedicated to the memory of my late father-in-law, George Willie Jackson, a fine gardener, but more important, a good friend.

Contents

A. House
B. Picnic Table
C. Maples
D. Grape Arbor
E. Plums, Standard
F. Flower Garden
G. Pecan Nuts
H. Filbert Nuts
I. Apples, Standard
J. Blueberries
K. Vegetable Garden
L. Fruit Trees, Dwarf
M. Cherry, Standard
N. Chinese Chestnuts
O. English Walnuts
P. Arbor Vitae—30'

PLOT LAYOUT

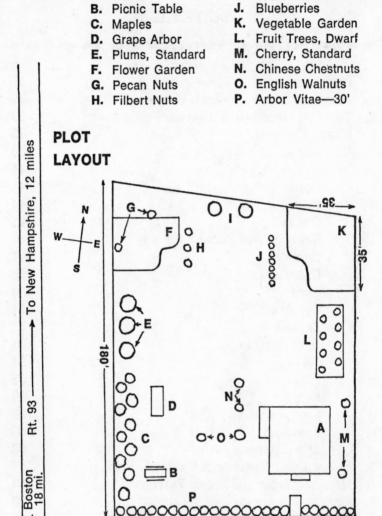

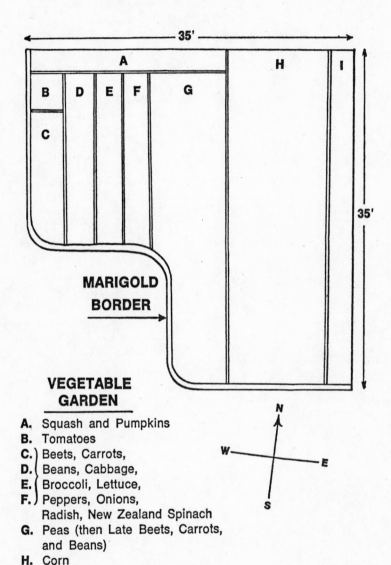

35'

A

B D E F G H I

C

MARIGOLD BORDER →

35'

VEGETABLE GARDEN

A. Squash and Pumpkins
B. Tomatoes
C.⎱ Beets, Carrots,
D.⎰ Beans, Cabbage,
E.⎱ Broccoli, Lettuce,
F.⎰ Peppers, Onions,
   Radish, New Zealand Spinach
G. Peas (then Late Beets, Carrots,
   and Beans)
H. Corn
I. Asparagus

N
W — E
S

Introduction

It is my belief, after discussing vegetable gardening with many practicing and would-be backyard gardeners, that there exists a need for additional simple, practical, "how-to-do-it" literature on the subject.

When I moved from an apartment in Cambridge to Wilmington, Massachusetts (eighteen miles northwest of Boston), ten years ago, I could not wait to get that first vegetable garden planted. Thoughts of harvesting my own fresh peas and corn led me to the local library that first winter to read up on the intricacies of backyard farming. I was surprised that there was so little information available prepared with the beginner in mind.

Thus I proceeded, largely by trial and error, to teach myself. I encountered all of the usual problems one would anticipate, including poor soil, insects, drought, rabbits, chucks, fertilizer questions, early and late frosts, and so on. All these difficulties, which appeared insurmountable at first, were, if not licked, at least understood and controlled.

(One conclusion I have reached is that there is no way to prevent some damage and loss to insects. But they can be controlled.)

Four years ago I was transferred by my company to a position which takes me away from home for four consecutive days two or three times a month. Out of necessity I discovered that if a few simple techniques are utilized, the garden can remain untended for a full week. These techniques are not new, but they are not generally known.

In other words, having a successful vegetable garden does not demand constant back-breaking work. In the spring there is a week or two, including evenings and weekends, of fairly constant activity, and again perhaps a few Saturdays of additional chores in the fall.

The rewards more than compensate for the effort expended. The difference in taste and texture between "store-bought" and "home-grown" produce is highest on the list of benefits, and the moderate exercise involved is something most of us need and would not otherwise get. From the economic point of view, if you eventually become enthusiastic enough to maintain a garden approximately 2,000 square feet in size (about 40 feet by 50 feet), you can expect to save, with the aid of a standard-size freezer, three or four hundred dollars a year. Beyond these tangible advantages, there are certain psychological factors which are, in the final analysis, probably most important of all. It is difficult to express in words the special thrill, undiminished each year, of seeing the first corn shoots poking through the ground five or six days after planting. How can one express in words the sense of accomplishment one feels when the pea vines are hanging heavy with pods before the Fourth of July? And what a special treat to see young eyes light up when the first corn is picked and fifteen minutes later is steaming on the table!

Finally, and certainly not least in importance, the medical profession is becoming increasingly aware of the health benefits to be gained from the regular consumption, several times a week, of garden-fresh vegetables. A well-respectd nutritionist of a generation ago, Dr. Victor Lindlahr, observed that "you are what you eat." Since you and I have no way of knowing what quantities of chemicals and highly toxic insecticides have been used to grow and process "store-bought" vegetables, and what long-range injurious effects these chemicals may have on our systems, the desirability of growing your own vegetables, as close to naturally as possible, becomes increasingly evident.

I do not consider myself an authority on the subject. Every day of the gardening season I learn something new. The reader will likewise not be an expert upon completing this book. This much I am sure of, though: by applying the suggestions and ideas put forth here, you should, barring unpredictable acts of God, increase measurably the output from your garden, while reducing your physical effort.

In the interest of continuity, the contents are arranged in chronological order, starting with planning your vegetable garden and ending with a brief chapter of afterthoughts. Included in the major section dealing with individual vegetables I have included the varieties which, for my soil and climate conditions, have performed most consistently. It goes without saying that these selections are only one individual's choices; undoubtedly other varieties should be experimented with to satisfy your own soil and climate conditions and taste preferences.

In the concluding chapter, I mention briefly those directly observable health benefits which fresh and frozen vegetables have had in my family of five.

This book is a summation of a decade of personal experience, and its information is intended for the inexperienced.

Seasoned vegetable growers may find some new helpful hints. Essentially, though, this effort is designed to help the beginner and that person who has entertained vague notions of some day having a fling at growing vegetables, but could never quite get over the idea that it is simply too much trouble for what you get out of it. It is not necessarily so!

CHAPTER 1

Planning the Vegetable Garden

I suspect that one of the important reasons for vegetable gardening failure is overambition. Tackling too much the first time, and then experiencing a gradual loss of zeal and ambition as too many small chores get further and further behind, has ruined many a good start. And this is too bad, because once a person has had an unsuccessful experience with any undertaking, a mental block is established, and it takes a lot of motivating to initiate the second attempt.

If you are weighing for the first time the question of whether or not to try a few vegetables, give way to the impulse; you'll never regret it, as long as you sincerely resolve to give the project consistently the little time and effort it requires. Anything in life that is worth doing at all requires a certain amount of work.

If you have tried it before and were dissatisfied with the results, perhaps one reason was that you attempted to prepare and plant too large an area. Then, when the problems of weeding, thinning, insects, watering, and so forth, set in, it just became too much of a burden. Well then, let's start over in a small way, so that the mistakes will be of lesser import and the little victories will encourage gradual expansion later on.

Another thing: make a family project out of it. Children over eight years of age can help out and usually enjoy doing so if the effort is approached in a "fun" rather than a "work" sense. You ask, "How do you make gardening fun for a nine- or a ten-year-old?" Try this approach: buy eight or ten packets of seeds (include radishes, carrots, beets, corn, New Zealand spinach, cucumbers or squash, lettuce, and string-beans) and make a seed chart with them. Glue or tape plain white paper to some heavy under surface like poster board or corrugated cardboard. Then, using white glue, attach a dozen or so of each type seed, in groups, to the paper. Don't identify them. Then make a game out of identifying the different shapes of seeds. Finally, when everyone has made his or her guesses, write the name under each group and see who did best. If you can get this far, it should be simple to discuss the "miracle" of nature, which transforms these dried-up, insignificant bits of matter into plants hundreds of times larger and produces food delicious to eat.

I don't think my children were too different from most, and after the "seed chart game" they were interested enough to want to plant seeds.

LOCATION

An important requirement for a successful garden is a location which gets at least five hours of direct sunlight a day. Eight to ten hours is ideal, but you can get away with less if necessary. Study your property with this in mind.

A south or southeast exposure is preferable to permit maximum exposure to sunlight.

If possible, have the vegetable garden within 150 feet of the house, because you may find it becoming burdensome to walk a longer distance and back when something needs doing. The usual spot is off to the side in back of the house, or in a back corner. So that you might perhaps gain an idea or two for use on your own property, I am including a diagram of my own half-acre plot. You will see that the side which faces the house is shaped (not completely by accident) to form the letter W. This border, planted with dwarf or hedge-type marigolds, makes a most attractive display in July, August, and September. More on this in Chapter 5, "Making the Vegetable Garden Attractive."

The garden should be at least 40 feet away from such shallow-rooted trees as maples, elms, and poplars; otherwise, beside the obvious shading problem, you will have trees competing with the vegetables for available moisture and nutrients.

SIZE

The size of the plot to be planted depends on a combination of the availability of space, the size of your family, whether or not you plan to do some freezing, and your own ambition.

What one person might consider a small vegetable garden another will consider medium-sized, and vice versa. It depends on your orientation. A man with several acres and eight children might consider a garden of 50 by 100 feet to be medium in size. Compared to a vegetable farm or a truck garden, this could be considered small. However, to the man on a 6,000-square-foot plot near the city, this 5,000-square-foot garden would certainly be described as large.

Somewhat arbitrarily, then, I would consider a vegetable garden to be small if less than 450 square feet (about 15 by 30 feet), medium from 450 square feet up to 1,000 square feet (about 30 by 35 feet), and large if over 1,000 square feet.

The beginner would be wise to start off with something in the small range, say, 10 feet by 20 feet, or 15 feet by 25 feet. Do not necessarily restrict yourself to the traditional rectangular shape. At the very least, give one or two sides a curved edge. Remember, and we will pursue this again in Chapter 5, a vegetable garden should not, and does not have to, be an eyesore.

How much can a plot this size produce? Since the answer to this question varies so much, depending on condition of the soil, availability of sunlight and moisture, length of growing season, distance of vegetables between each other and between rows, and so on, it would be senseless to estimate yields. The first year or two, the emphasis should not be on quantity. Consider *anything* you harvest the first year as a bonus beyond the knowledge and experience you have gained. It takes two or three years to correctly gauge the amounts of vegetables a particular plot will yield. You will soon find the optimum size for your family, which can be "worked" comfortably and efficiently.

PLANTING PLAN

A simple chart should be drawn, to decide beforehand *what* will go *where*. Since the sun travels from east to west, and always at a slight angle from the south section of the sky (rather than from directly overhead), follow these two basic guidelines:

1. Plant tallest vegetables on the east (or northeast) side of the garden, and then roughly in descending order, down to the smallest-sized plants on the west (or southwest) side.

2. Run rows in north-to-south lines, or at least not exactly east to west.

By observing these rules, you will obtain maximum sun exposure. If circumstances do not allow strict observance of both suggestions, do not worry about it. Your vegetables will grow anyway, with perhaps a slightly longer maturing time. The important thing is to be sure that the corn (if you plant corn) is situated on the very east or northeast edge of the plot.

Included is a plan which I have used with minor variations from year to year. You might notice that I have not observed rule 1 above in the case of the asparagus. I have these along the easterly side because this crop is harvested in May and June, well before it would be shaded by the corn, which directly adjoins. The few asparagus stalks which are left to feed the root systems (via photosynthesis) manage to find sunlight enough to do their job.

In the final chapter ("Afterthoughts") we will touch on the matter of varying the locations of vegetables in the garden after two or three years in the the same spot.

CHAPTER 2

The Soil and Spring Preparation

PREPARING THE SOIL

You can read, in a hundred different articles and books, about a wide variety of soil preparation techniques. Anyone who has given this subject his or her attention has a slightly different variation on the same theme. Yet, when you examine them for the least common denominator, the objective is to work toward a deep, well-drained, organically rich garden soil.

Let's take a minute on each of these requirements:

Depth You can grow vegetables in 6 inches of soil, underneath which may be hard-packed clay or even rock. But do not expect much in the way of productivity. Most vegetable roots will naturally penetrate to a depth of 18 to 24 inches or more, seeking moisture and nutrition.

If you are not familiar with just exactly what-all lies beneath the surface of the plot you intend to cultivate, get your spade out and dig a hole to a depth of two feet. If you are fortunate enough to see good brown topsoil down to that depth, you are starting out well ahead of the game. More likely you will find, in an area not previously gardened, perhaps 2 to 6 inches of topsoil, underneath which will be varying consistencies of sand, clay, and shale.

Shortly, we will discuss two methods of achieving the desired vegetable garden depth.

Drainage   Drainage ties in closely with depth. The term "drainage" simply refers to the garden's ability (or lack of it) to pass water easily into the subsoil, thus preventing waterlogging. Root systems do not develop properly where they are forced to exist for long periods in heavy mud.

Good drainage encourages quicker soil warm-up in the spring, prevents erosion of topsoil in heavy downpours, and provides the right conditions for bacteria to convert organic matter into readily available nutrients.

Usually, preparing the soil to a depth of 18 to 24 inches will also provide adequate drainage. In that rare instance where you find yourself on top of completely nonporous clay or rock, you must consider one of these alternatives:

a. Check your property for a more congenial subsoil,
b. Remove enough topsoil to enable you to "open up" the hardpan with a pick, or
c. Install tile or drainage pipes, about 4 inches in diameter, at a depth of 2 to 3 feet, to carry off excess water.

Alternative "c" is admittedly a lot of work and should not, I would guess, be necessary 98 percent of the time.

Organically Rich   This, my friend, is "where it's at." The primary objective of every vegetable gardener, truly "organic" or otherwise, should be to obtain and apply as much organic material (leaves, manures, grasses, peat moss, bone meal, garbage, and so on) as he can beg, borrow, or steal. Many gardeners attempt to get by on bagged commercial fertilizers, with little thought to proper soil conditioning. I have not used chemical fertilizers for six or seven years because I am convinced, through personal observations, that they are unnecessary. With my simple system of soil enrichment, detailed shortly, powdered fertilizers would be superfluous, if not in fact dangerous. I say "dangerous" in this sense: most people do not pay strict attention to directions. Too often the reasoning proceeds something like this: if 5 pounds of (let's say) 5-10-5 fertilizer per 100 square feet will do the job, then twice or three times as much wil produce twice or three times the results. Not so, of course, since too heavy a concentration of powdered granular fertilizer will usually burn tender root systems. Further, controlled experiments seem to indicate that commercial fertilizers repel earthworms, another of the Creator's free gifts to the gardener. Worms not only add rich organic matter to the soil by way of their leavings, but they also act to aerate the soil.

In the final chapter, I'll have one or two additional comments on the continuing organic versus chemical fertilizer controversy.

OBTAINING PROPER DEPTH

Let's first assume an extreme situation, wherein you are going to prepare an area either never previously tilled or else known to be shallow as to topsoil. The best—not necessarily the easiest—approach would be to consider double-spading, also known as "trenching." Several agricultural stations have made extensive tests with double-spading, and the results are consistent: noticeably improved yields. The consensus is that proper root development is severely impeded when hard-packed layers are encountered beginning 6 inches or so below the surface. Poor roots, poor vegetables.

Simply stated, double-spading is digging the soil two spade depths down instead of one, which means to a depth of at least 18 inches.

Before starting, accumulate whatever organic materials you have access to. A most important part of this operation is the addition of such matter to the soil. If your location precludes access to manure, leaves, grass, and the like, and if your budget can afford it, purchase a couple of bags each of peat moss, processed cow manure, and bone meal. Bone meal, incidentally, is simply ground-up bones obtained from slaughterhouses. It is a terrific source of phosphorous, one of the three basic elements required by all plants for good growth. Bone meal also contains much smaller quantities of nitrogen. Your organic materials supply the necessary amounts of the third element, potash.

Begin spading at one end of your plot by removing a full spadeful of topsoil along a 6- or 8-foot strip. Try to get a good 8 or 9 inches down on this first excavation. Pile this top layer on the other side of the trench, along the opening. Now you are down to the subsoil, that most important layer 9 to 18 inches below the surface.

Next, in this same trench and without actually removing more soil, spade down into this subsoil as deeply as your spade permits, mixing in quantities of your organic materials. There are no inflexible rules on just how much to use. Be as generous as possible, keeping in mind that you want to divide what matter you have available about equally into the area you plan to dig. It is difficult, if not impossible, to use too much organic material. If you are using bone meal, mix in about 4 cupfuls per 6-foot strip, as a rough guide. Yes, you *can* use bone meal along with manure, leaves, grass, and so on; the problem is that it tends to be expensive. Price it in 20- or 40-pound bags, though; you will be surprised how much less costly it is per pound in larger quantities.

Now remove a second 6- to 8-foot strip of topsoil from the plot, directly beside your first opening. As you remove this layer, place it on top of the first section you have finished "working." Repeat the deep spading in this second strip as above, adding and mixing in the organic material as you go. Then you simply back up a foot, and continue repeating this cycle.

When you reach the other end, the topsoil you removed from the first strip is transported back and fills your last strip. Rake smooth, and you are ready to plant.

You say you are worn out just reading about it? Okay. Then the way to approach it is to either enlist some manpower from inside or outside the family, or else spread the chore over two weekends, working several half-hour hitches. Based on my own trenching, I would guess that there are about four to six hours of moderate effort involved in double-spading a plot roughly 16 by 24 feet. And you have to do it only once.

One thing I am convinced of is that you will be well satisfied with the results of going to this extra effort by the end of your first growing season. Still not convinced that it's worth the trouble? Try this: select a corner of your garden area, perhaps a section about 4 feet by 10 feet, and double-spade this much, loading in the organic fodder as suggested. Then select another area of the same size which will *not* be double-dug, and plant short rows of the same vegetables in each. Prepare this second, or "control," plot as described in the next paragraph. Let the results of this experiment dictate your further consideration of this system.

I mentioned earlier that we would consider two approaches to achieving good depth and drainage. The second requires less work but presupposes that you will be gardening an area which has been previously tilled or is at least known to consist of average loose soil. A supply of organic materials is again most desirable. Here, though, spread a mixture of whatever you have fairly evenly over the entire garden surface. Then spade it all under as deeply as you are able, mixing some, as you proceed. You are ready to plant, after smoothing with a rake.

ACIDITY—ALKALINITY (pH)

A few nontechnical words are in order at this point concerning soil pH.

I have seen vegetable gardeners dumping crushed limestone into their gardens year after year, and not really having any idea why they were doing it. Habit, I suppose, is the answer, probably prompted by a vague notion that limestone is "good" for vegetable gardens. It *is* beneficial, when it is required. Otherwise, it can do more harm than good.

"pH," by definition, is the degree of acidity (sour) or alkalinity (bitter) of a given soil. The extent of one or the other is predetermined by the chemical nature of the rock from which the soil has partially resulted. Most soils in this country are slightly acid, in the range of 5.5 to 7 on the chemist's pH scale, which starts at 0 (ultra acid) and goes to 14 (ultra alkaline). Notable exceptions are areas in the West bordering the alkali deserts, and lands that are relatively near salt marshes.

Vegetables do best on soils with a pH of 6.5 to 7.0, just a shade on the acid side. The microscopic organisms in the soil which transform decomposing plant and animal substances into usable plant nutrients thrive at a pH at or just under neutral (7.0).

Chances are your soil is within the safe range (6.0 to 7.5) and does not require limestone. I have read in several sources that soil heavily laced with organic matter tends to stabilize around a pH of 7.0. I have not added limestone to my soil for several years, and it holds steady right around that point.

It is a simple matter to check this out. Most garden supply outlets and nurseries sell inexpensive soil test kits which come with easy-to-follow directions. Or you can write to your state university, in care of Agriculture Extension, to ask the procedure for mailing or delivering soil samples for test, at a nominal fee.

The quick and rather inexact method for getting an idea of how your soil pH shapes up is to purchase a small packet of litmus paper at the local drugstore. Litmus paper is used immediately after a rain, while the soil is moist. Simply press a piece into the soil and watch for a color change. A change to blue indicates alkalinity; pink (light red) shows acidity. No color change? You are in luck: your soil is neutral. The drawback with litmus paper is that, although you can determine in which direction your soil lies, it is hard to decide the degree of the problem.

Should you determine that your soil is acid, the solution is to add crushed limestone, which, fortunately, is about the least expensive item at the garden or farm supply center. From what I have been able to research, the accepted rate of application is 1 ton per acre to raise the pH one point on the scale. Since you and I are probably not about to cultivate one acre, this divides down to 20 pounds per 440 square feet. Or 50 pounds per 1,100 square feet, which is a plot about 30 by 35 feet. Slight errors either way will not do any harm. The time to apply is in the spring, and the application can be accomplished when you are spading in your organic materials. Do not simply spread it on the surface and hope it leaches in. Most of it will run off with the first good shower. Besides, limestone moves very reluctantly through the soil; thus, it should be mixed into the subsoil. An application will last two or three years.

Should you encounter an alkaline soil, a good shot of manure and other organic materials will go a long way toward lowering the pH level. This is so because, as organic matter decomposes in the soil, acids form which gradually neutralize the excess alkali.

YEAR-TO-YEAR SOIL MAINTENANCE

Like a car or a house, the vegetable garden requires, to continue producing at maximum efficiency, a certain amount of regular maintenance. Here is how I have been caring for my 1,200 square feet of vegetable area:

Each fall, we go on a leaf hunting expedition. I am fortunate in having almost unlimited maple trees in the area. Since kids seems to instinctively love playing in piles of new-fallen leaves, there is plenty of willing child power available. Large plastic trash-barrel bags are great for hauling leaves. You can get six to eight of them, each weighing 30 to 40 pounds when stuffed full, into the trunk of your car, unless you drive a compact. (The custodian at the town dump, although he might scratch his head and look at you a little strangely, won't mind if you haul away some of the bagged leaves which generally show up during October.)

The leaves are roughly spread out over the garden, resulting in a layer 1/2 to 2 inches deep, depending on available time and ambition. To keep them from blowing away, we throw sticks and boards on them. Any other organic matter you have around, such as old hay, plant residue from this year's garden, and so on, can also be added to the soil surface, along with leaves. If you have or can borrow or rent a shredder, put it to work. The smaller the size of your materials, the quicker they decompose and make humus and fertilizer for next year's crops. I leave all of this on top over the winter. One annual spading is all that is necessary. This whole fall operation takes about eight hours of my time, split half and half on two Saturdays. This is, of course, with some help from the neighborhood small fry.

Phase two begins about April 5 to April 10 here in Massachussetts. Again, we need only a half of two Saturdays to accomplish this next task—and bear in mind that my garden is fairly large, at 35 by 35 feet. This next step simply adds additional organic matter on top of the leaves prior to spading it all under.

Your locality will determine whether or not animal manures are available to you. The local stables are usually only too happy to donate the results of their spring housecleaning. Horse and cow manure can be used fresh, but use chicken manure very sparingly, unless it is five or six months old. I have been spreading roughly an inch of horse manure over the bed of leaves put down the previous fall. If fresh stable manure is not available, processed bagged cow manure is fine. Again, the larger the bag, the lower the cost per pound. If your soil test indicates a need for limestone, apply it now.

Finally—and do not necessarily try to do this all at one time (or all by yourself)—spade this one- to three-inch layer of materials as deeply into the soil as you are able. I have tried using a Rototiller to accomplish this task, with little success. The rotating tines just scratch the surface and clog up quickly because of the bulk of the materials involved. If your garden is larger than, say, 30 by 40 feet, it would probably pay you to hire a small tractor operator. Most towns and villages have someone who advertises in the spring to plow your garden for, depending on size, from $8 to $15. For a smaller plot, there is still no substitute for a good spade shovel.

Once you have your garden "turned over" and raked smooth, you are ready to plant.

Composting   No book on vegetable gardening would be complete without some discussion of composting.

According to Webster, compost is "a mixture of decomposing vegetation, manure, etc., for fertilizing soil." I have personally never utilized a compost heap as such, since my present system of fall and spring soil conditioning precludes the need for it. In a sense, my garden plot itself is a compost heap, since there are always quantities of organic materials throughout the top 24 to 30 inches in various stages of decomposition.

For those who are reluctant to handle fresh or partially

rotted manures, composting offers an alternative. You need a little patience, however, since the complete composting cycle normally takes from two to six months, depending on which materials are used and what time of the year you start. During the winter months the activity of the organisms (bacteria) breaking down the material is slowed way down, unless you have a heap which is several feet thick. Your compost is "done" when you have a rich, brown, nearly odorless humus. The soil-conditioning and moisture-holding properties of finished compost cannot be overemphasized.

You can go to great lengths in constructing a compost bin, or you can be very informal. There is considerable literature available on this subject, and the gardening section of your local newspaper may touch on various methods of composting. Whatever the mechanics of making a compost pile, here, basically, is what you do:

Find an out-of-the-way corner of your yard where you can spare anywhere from 3 by 5 to 8 by 12 feet. If you do not want the somewhat unkempt appearance of an open pile, contruct a simple bin, using rigid posts in the four corners, and any kind of fencing material you have available or can purchase. Use whatever organic materials you can find, with a large percentage of either fresh or bagged manure as your main ingredient. Manure is not absolutely essential, but it surely helps. In 4- to 8-inch layers, load into a deep pile (a couple of feet deep, at least) whatever it is that you have gathered. Bear in mind that there are no set formulas or percentages of ingredients involved here; whatever material you use will eventually produce pretty much the same end product. Water the layers every 6 inches.

In roughly their order of availability, here is a list of items which are commonly used in compost piles: manure,

leaves, grass clippings, hay (fresh or spoiled), garden residues (stalks, vines, corncobs, and the like), weeds, garbage,
sewage sludge, brewery and slaughterhouse wastes, sawdust,
leather dust, pine needles, nutshells, and tobacco stems. As
you proceed, and depending on your ability to obtain them,
sprinkle in bone meal, an inch or two of earth, a little limestone, wood ashes, and phosphate rock or granite dust. These
all add to the mineral content of the heap.

At the top of the pile, fashion a depression to catch rain.
Then, once every four to six weeks, mix the whole mass with
a pitchfork. Do not pack down the heap, for considerable
oxygen is necessary to allow the slow "burn" process to take
place. In the heart of a working compost pile, the temperature will quickly reach 120 to 150 degrees. Some gardeners
have two piles working, started several months apart, so as
to have a supply in the spring for spading into the garden
and more ready in the fall for winter protection of peren-
nials, roses, and shrubs.

Chapter 3

Insect Control

A recent issue of *Agricultural Research* had an article concerned with work being done at several state agricultural extensions on the breeding of insect-resistant vegetables. What encouraging news this is to the backyard vegetable gardener, who annually struggles with the problem of whether or not to use insecticides! At the last count, the agricultural scientists came up with twenty-five vegetables reportedly able to resist the onslaughts of no less than thirty-five species of insects. Your yearly seed catalogues will (it is hoped) soon be making these varieties available. Until they do, though, we must give some thought to protecting the fruits of our labors from corn borers, cutworms, bean beetles, vine borers, aphids, and on and on, which are inevitably lying in wait.

Perhaps fifteen years overdue, the government is finally taking steps to control, if not completely prohibit, the sale of DDT and the other highly toxic and long-lasting fluorinated hydrocarbons. It is pretty generally conceded that several species of wild life are on the brink of extinction because of the indiscriminate use of these insidious killers during the fifties and sixties. If you should come across a garden supply center still selling DDT-based insecticides, give some thought to suggesting to the management, in a friendly way, that they should be withdrawn from the shelves.

I tried for two years to harvest vegetables without any spraying or dusting whatsoever. I wanted to provide the family with totally chemical-free vegetables if at all possible. I harvested about 75 percent of what I planted; the bugs got the rest. And what was salvaged was often inferior in size as a result of weakening of the plants by insect attack. So, reluctantly, I decided it was time to fight back. My philosophy has always been "Live and let live," but I begin drawing the line when a good share of the corn and bean plantings stand to be wiped out by the borers and bean beetles.

Until two years ago, I used rotenone dust pretty exclusively. This contact and stomach poison, also sometime called "derris," is nontoxic and safe to use on all vegetables. Its major disadvantage is that it does not discourage all insect pests all of the time. Rotenone is also available as a wettable powder, but it is not really water-soluble, so that it requires constant agitation in the sprayer.

A fairly recent and significant insect control development is Sevin (carbaryl). Extensively tested by its originator, and well recommended by several state agricultural stations, this insect control agent comes pretty close to answering a gardener's prayers. I am well pleased with my experience with Sevin, and it is convenient to use, since it is available in a wettable powder.

ADVANTAGES OF SEVIN

1. It is an all-purpose control, highly effective for protection against just about all common vegetable insect pests.
2. It is relatively low in toxicity and dissipates entirely after six or seven days.
3. It is not absorbed into the fibers of the plant it is used to protect, thereby assuring against the ingestion by humans of toxic residues.
4. It is available in both dust and wettable-powder form.

DISADVANTAGES OF SEVIN

1. It can, IF DIRECTIONS ARE NOT FOLLOWED CAREFULLY, be harmful to bees and other beneficial insects.
2. It has a rather short life, necessitating once-a-week spraying.

A compressed air sprayer is ideal for applying Sevin. Here is the program I have used, with near-perfect results: Friday or Saturday evenings, depending on weather conditions, I mix in the pump sprayer two gallons of solution, using the wettable Sevin powder and being careful to follow the directions to the letter. Then, after the sun has gone down (this is important, since by then the bees have all returned to their hives) I walk up and down the rows, applying the spray LIGHTLY while trying to get total coverage on all parts of the plant. It is not necessary to saturate each plant; a very fine mist assures maximum protection. If the wind is blowing rather hard, or if it is showering, I wait until the next night. The important thing is to get into the habit of doing this small chore on a regular weekly schedule. The entire operation takes me fifteen minutes a week—five minutes to mix and ten to spray.

When the bees do become active again the next day, they simply avoid contact with the vegetables, as do all other insects.

As mentioned in the section on pumpkins and squash (Chapter 4), do not dust or spray these plants during that one month flowering period which is usually over by the end of June or early July. You do not want to interfere with the very important pollination process which takes place then.

I feel it is just a matter of time until a totally effective, completely organic insect spray will be discovered. Until that time we must decide for ourselves how best to protect the vegetables. For those among us who will insist on abstaining from the use of chemical deterrents (and I say, more power to you!), rotenone provides fairly good plant protection. Personally—and there appears to be a lot of corroborative evidence coming from seedsmen and state agricultural extensions—I am reasonably satisfied that Sevin, USED AS DIRECTED, is a safe and highly effective insect control agent.

CHAPTER 4

Vegetables

Before getting into the culture of the individual vegetables, it might be well to discuss a couple of matters which are common to all garden crops: weed control and adequate moisture. (Insect control has been treated separately; other usually less troublesome problems, including early and late frosts and rabbit and woodchuck troubles, are mentioned in the final chapter.)

Weed control. In a word, mulch. Weed seeds have a tough time germinating through two or three inches of grass clippings, hay, peat moss, pine needles, or whatever organic materials you can locate. I generally lay on the mulch when the young plants are an inch or two out of the ground. You can mulch just after planting if you allow a narrow opening for the vegetable seeds to germinate through. Side benefits of mulching include:

1. The addition of gradually decomposing vegetable matter to the soil;
2. Maintenance, as an insulator, of fairly constant soil

temperature, a condition which greatly benefits proper plant development;
3. A retainer of moisture, cutting down on watering by as much as 75 percent.

If you are going to be stubborn and insist that your garden looks better without a mulch, then the alternative is either hand weeding or hoeing. A garden larger than 300 or 400 square feet presents quite a weeding problem if left unmulched. If you have not already done so, pick up a copy of Ruth Stout's book entitled "How to Have a Green Thumb Without an Aching Back," one of the pioneer efforts on the benefits to be derived from the liberal use of mulches. Check your local library if you cannot locate it at the bookstore.

Moisture. As mentioned just previously, a 2-inch (at least) layer of mulch will cut down on your watering by a very significant factor. During the one or two inevitable drought periods each summer, you will have to soak the garden every two or three days if you have an exposed soil situation. With my mostly grass-clipping mulch, I do not have to use the sprinkler more often than once in seven to ten days. During periods of normal rainfall you may even be able to put the hose away for a month or more. With water becoming an increasingly scarce commodity in many communities (to say nothing of the *price* of water), this is one good way to conserve the supply.

One deep soaking is far better for the vegetables than several shallow sprinkles. To determine how much water your hose or sprinkler is dispensing, place an empty tin can in the garden and check it periodically. I have found that an inch of water will penetrate to a depth of 7 to 10 inches, depending on the amount of organic matter contained in a given section. Once every three or four weeks, if rainfall has been light, I like to put down 2 to 3 inches of water to ensure that the deepest roots are occasionally getting a drink. If you have a normal water-table situation, this may not be necessary due to the capillary movement of water from below. When in doubt about the moisture situation of your garden, select a typical spot, spade down 18 inches or so, and proceed according to what you find.

ASPARAGUS

I have often felt that the best $5 I ever spent was for fifty 1-year-old asparagus roots, purchased a few years ago. If you have priced canned asparagus in the market recently, you are aware that this is one of the higest-priced vegetables in the store. Yet every home gardener who can permanently spare a 4-foot strip along one edge of his garden can harvest fresh asparagus spears year after year. A well-planted bed can be expected to produce for twenty-five years or so. The beauty of this vegetable is that, once planted, you can pretty much forget it; like peonys, the same roots produce new spears each spring.

This last summer, their third full year in the garden, we cut about 250 spears from these fifty roots. This was enough for eight meals for our family of five. I am giving some thought to doubling this planting eventually, so as to have some for the freezer.

You can start this vegetable from seed, although by doing so you are delaying your first harvest by at least one year. To do so, simply plant the seeds in rows 8 inches apart, allow three or four seedlings to develop per foot, then transplant the roots to their permanent location very early the following spring.

If possible, obtain one- or two-year-old roots from your garden supply center. If they do not sell them, they can probably tell you who does. (Some of the large mail-order seed companies still sell one-year roots.) Decide first how much space you can afford, allowing about 18 inches per root and leaving a minimum of 2 feet (3 feet is better) between rows. My bed along the east side of the garden measures 35 feet long by 4 feet wide. This area contains two parallel rows, and each row contains twenty-five roots spaced just under 18 inches apart.

When to Plant   As early in the spring as the soil can be worked (March 10 to April 20, depending on the locality).

How to Plant   Remove the top 10 or 12 inches of soil along the length of the first row, to a width of about 1 foot. Dig into the subsoil, down to 18 inches if possible, whatever compost or rotted or dry processed manure you have available. If you can afford it, mix in a cupful of bone meal for each root you plant. Next, shovel back 3 inches of the topsoil you removed. Now plant the roots 16 to 18 inches apart, spreading the root sections with your fingers. Cover the roots with more soil, so that the "crown" is about 2 inches below the surface. Tamp this down *gently* to fill air holes and make the soil firm. Your trench will probably not be filled to its original level at this point, and that's good. Asparagus do best starting out with only a shallow layer of soil over them. This depression will also act to catch and hold rain water. At the end of the first growing season, you can level off to the surrounding surface. If you are going to plant two or more rows, be sure to allow an absolute minimum of 2 feet between rows. Deep-soak each row, as finished.

Do not cut anything the first or second year. The third year, you can take about half of the spears sent up from each root. Thereafter, cut all but two or three spears per root, since the plant does require some top growth to ensure proper continuing plant development.

To control weeds and conserve moisture, keep a constant 2- to 4-inch layer of mulch on the bed. Grass or hay (or compost and peat moss) is excellent. After the spears have stopped appearing, apply an inch of top dressing of manure and a scattering of bone meal. Your weekly insect control procedure (Chapter 3) will keep the asparagus beetle under control.

Recommended Variety: Mary Washington.

BEANS

Most gardeners plant the so-called "bush" beans, green- or yellow-podded, rather than the tall-growing "pole" beans. The bush beans are highly productive, considering the space they take, and are very easy to grow. If you are going to start cautiously with only a half-dozen different vegetables, be sure to include a row or two of bush beans.

When to Plant   After the last spring frost, about May 5 in central New Jersey, May 20 in northern Massachusetts.

How to Grow   Plant seeds 2 inches apart in 2-inch-deep furrows. Space the rows about 15 inches apart, and plant no more than four rows to a section, which will allow you to tend two rows from each foot path. When the young plants are 3 inches high, thin to 4 inches apart.

Beans are a fast-maturing vegetable—50 to 60 days, depending on the variety. Succession plantings are wise, two weeks apart, to ensure a continuous supply. Make your last planting a heavy one to load up the freezer. As you will note in the section on peas (if you decide to plant peas), some of the space freed by the removal of the pea vines can be used to plant and harvest your freezer crop of beans. I generally make the final planting around July 10 and harvest this planting by September 10 or so.

Suggested Varieties:

1. Tendercrop—Harris (green)
2. Burpee's Tenderpod (green)
3. Eastern Butterwax—Harris (yellow)

BEETS

I look on beets as a two-in-one vegetable, since the greens are equally edible. Roots and tops are excellent sources of iron, plus vitamins, A, B_1 and C. This is another of those easy-to-raise vegetables which should be included in every vegetable garden.

When to Plant   As early in spring as the soil can be worked.

How to Grow   Plant the seeds ½ inch deep, 1 inch apart, in rows not closer than 1 foot apart. As with beans, carrots, onions, and other thrifty-sized vegetables, I have found it convenient to plant four rows to a section, in order to reach two rows from each path.

The beet seed is unique in that each may produce several individual sprouts. This means that hand thinning will be required after the plants are an inch tall. Allow the small plants to develop fairly close together, since later thinnings, when the beets are about the size of a quarter, are especially tasty. Allow 3 to 4 inches between those that remain to mature.

Plant several times, two weeks apart, to provide a continuing harvest. Since beets will continue to grow after a couple of light frosts, you can plant, in the north, right up until the middle of July. From planting to harvest is 60 to 80 days, depending on type. In Chapter 7 we will discuss winter storage.

Suggested Varieties:

1. Burpee's Red Ball
2. Pacemaker—Harris
3. Detroit Dark Red

BROCCOLI

This vegetable is a favorite with us for several reasons: without exception everyone in the family likes it, the plant continues to produce smaller side "heads" after the main one is cut, and it freezes well, retaining almost all of the original taste and texture. Try at least a dozen plants.

When to Plant   For a very early crop, start inside or in the cold frame in March or April; otherwise, outside when ground can be worked.

How to Grow　　If started early, set the young plants into the garden about 18 inches apart, 2 feet apart, if you have plenty of room. Allow 2 feet between rows.

If planting seed directly into the garden, plant them ½ inch deep, 6 inches apart, in rows 2 feet apart. When several inches tall, thin to one plant every 18 to 24 inches in the row.

The tightly-packed green "head" which forms is actually a mass of yellow flowers in the bud stage. The trick is to cut the head just before these buds begin to open. Cut well down the stem (4 to 5 inches), but leave sufficient center stalk for the development of side heads.

The green cabbage worm will give you fits unless you spray or dust weekly, as suggested in Chapter 3.

Plant more in midsummer for the freezer. Broccoli will take a couple of light frosts. Time for maturity is 55 to 75 days.

Suggested Varieties:

1. Green Comet—Harris, Burpee, and others
2. Waltham 29—Harris

CABBAGE AND BRUSSELS SPROUTS

These two are closely related; thus, their requirements are similar. Both are heavy feeders, and a deep, rich soil is a necessity. Brussels sprouts is another vegetable which loses very little flavor and texture after six months in the freezer.

When to Plant　　March or April in the cold frame, April to June in the garden.

How to Grow Seeds are planted ¼ to ½ inch deep and are later thinned to one plant every 18 inches, rows 2 feet apart. Both are long-growing vegetables, requiring 80 to 100 days, depending on the variety.

The Brussels sprouts form in a thick cluster along the central stem. They are harvested from the bottom up after they attain golf-ball size. Break off the lower eight or ten leaves late in September when the first sprouts are maturing and continue to remove three or four more leaves, still working up from the bottom, each week. This allows room for the sprouts to fully form and directs most of the plants' energies into the vegetable rather than the leaves. Do not worry about frosts; some gardeners insist that a couple of good hard frosts improve the flavor. We have cut Brussels sprouts as late as early November.

Suggested Varieties:

Cabbage: 1. Harris Danish Resistant
            2. Burpee's Surehead

Brussels sprouts: 1. Jade Cross Hybrid—Several seed
                    companies

CARROTS

One of the events we look forward to each year is that time when the first carrots are about 3 inches long. Cooked until you can just barely push a fork through them (perhaps ten minutes) and then buttered and salted to taste, this is one of those *extra*-special taste treats. Try it, and see if you don't agree.

When to Plant When the soil is workable, right through mid-July.

How to Grow Plant seeds thinly (three or four to the inch) ½ inch deep, in rows about 1 foot apart. I plant four or five rows to a section in rows 12 to 15 feet long. Do not plant all at once: I would suggest a row or two every two weeks until midsummer. Make your last planting a generous one, to provide a supply through the winter. Although carrots do not freeze well, there is a simple way to store them for use right through the winter. See Chapter 7.

I break all the rules on spacing, when it comes to carrots. They grow well as close as ½ inch apart, until they reach 2 or 3 inches in length. At that point you can begin thinning to 2 inches apart, harvesting these baby carrots for an early meal or two. They are a wonderful source of Vitamin A. Carrots are hardy, and will continue to grow through several frosts. They take 60 to 75 days to reach maturity.

Suggested Varieties:

1. Pioneer—Harris (superior in all respects)
2. Nantes Half Long—Burpee

CAULIFLOWER

Not found in the majority of backyard gardens, cauliflower is one of those vegetables you should plant at least once, so that you can say you tried. Its culture is a little more involved than the culture of other garden crops, and some folks just do not want to take the little extra effort they require. We have had fair success with them.

When to Plant   Start in the cold frame in April, or plant seed in the garden after last frost.

How to Grow   The special requirements mentioned above are:

1. Extra nitrogen is required. Since cauliflower is a very heavy feeder, it helps to have a soil well "innoculated" with manure or, better, dried blood. Dried animal blood, available now in bags at most garden supply outlets, has a 12 percent-by-weight content of readily available nitrogen.
2. Cauliflower will not tolerate even partially dry soil. I have had good luck with fashioning a depression of 1 or 2 inches in the soil around the plant to catch and hold water.
3. The large upper leaves should be flopped over the developing heads and tied loosely in place, to keep the sun from causing the whiteness to discolor.

Cauliflower does best if not subjected to the severe heat of midsummer. It is best grown as a spring crop, with seeds started in early April in the cold frame and then transferred outside after the danger of frost is past, or else started about June to mature in the fall.

The plants should be allowed to develop not closer together than 1½ feet, in rows about 2 feet apart.

Cut the head when it measures 5 or 6 inches across, while the "curds" are still hard.

Suggested Varieties:

1. Burpeeana—Burpee
2. Snowball Imperial—Harris

CORN

I try to give that section of the garden planted to sweet corn a little extra "shot" of decaying leaves and manure about every other year. Corn requires a high nitrogen-content soil to produce fully developed ears. Even if your garden is extra small, give over a section on the east side to several short rows. If you can afford the space, plant two or three varieties with different maturing times, or else plant the same favorite variety three or four times, two weeks apart. Planted all at once, you'll have more than you can handle for a one-week period.

Eating the very first ears of early spring corn, about the middle of July in Massachusetts, is a pleasure second only (for us) to sampling the first peas a week or two earlier.

When to Plant   After the soil is well warmed up, which is usually about May 15 in this area, and up to early July.

How to Grow   Two "systems" are used, "hill" planting (a misnomer really, since no actual hilling is done) and row planting. Both have their defenders; I like rows, for no special reason. In hills, five seeds are spaced, 2 inches deep, into a block about 15 inches square (usually a kernel at each corner and one in the middle of the block). When the plants are about 3 inches up, thin to leave the three strongest ones in each hill to mature. These hills should be no closer than 2½ feet in the row.

For row planting, seed should be sown every 6 inches. When well started, say 3 or 4 inches tall, thin to one per foot. For midseason or late varieties, allow at least 2 feet between rows: for the smaller, faster-maturing early varieties, your rows can be as close together as 15 inches. In either case, do not allow the stalks to develop closer than 12 inches from each other in the row.

Be sure *not* to plant corn in single, or even double, rows. To assure total pollination from tassels to silk, corn should be grown either in blocks of hills or in sections containing at least four rows. We have been planting six rows at a time in sections about ten feet long. By succession-planting this much at a time, we harvest four or five dozen ears several times each summer. Ears are ready to pick within a day or two of the tassels and silk turning brown.

If you happen to be in an area where crows have been known to steal seed corn shortly after sowing, plant your kernels 4 inches deep instead of 2. Mr. Crow will not go that deep, and the corn will come along just as well.

Most important! For top quality, eat corn within an hour of picking, before the sugars begin turning to starch.

Your weekly spraying is critical with corn. If you fail to spray once a week, you can expect the worst from borers in the stalks and earworms in the kernels.

Suggested Varieties:

1. Wonderful—Harris (80 days)
2. Honeycross—Burpee (85 days)
3. Spring Gold—Harris (65 days). Best of the earlies.

CUCUMBERS

Cucumbers are best grown in spacious gardens. You can get away with a couple of plants in a small garden by allowing the vines to ramble off toward an unused corner.

If you are especially partial to cukes and want an early crop, start seeds in milk cartons early in April, for setting out after the danger of frost has passed.

When to Plant   Outside, seed or plants, after last frost or about the same time that tomatoes are set out in your area.

How to Plant   This is one vegetable which, like squash and pumpkins, should be grown along the edge of the garden to allow for the trailing vines. It is a simple matter to direct the runners in whatever direction you wish them to go.

On a well-manured or composted seed bed, plant six to 8 seeds 1 inch deep, in groups 3 or 4 feet apart each way. Later, thin to the four strongest plants. Cucumbers require two months from planting to harvest. Cukes can be picked and eaten at any size after they reach three inches or so.

Your regular weekly dusting (or spraying) will prevent excessive damage by the striped or spotted cucumber beetle.

Suggested Varieties:

1. Burpeeana Hybrid—Burpee
2. Challenger—Harris

LETTUCE

Like cauliflower, lettuce does not take kindly to the heat of midsummer. If you have a shady corner in the vegetable garden, you might try a dozen or so plants there. Many varieties of "heading" and "loose leaf" lettuce are available; experiment with several to find which do best in your circumstances.

When to Plant   Start seeds in the cold frame (or a window box) in April, or plant seed outside after the last frost.

How to Grow   If setting out early-started plants, place them about 6 inches apart if the loose-leaf type, and 1 foot to 15 inches apart if the heading type. Allow 18 inches between rows.

From seed, plant ¼ inch deep, and try to sow very thinly, one or two per inch if possible. When the seedlings are well on the way, thin to the distances suggested in the previous paragraph. As with carrots and beets, quarter- to half-size plants are extra delicious. A fall crop can be had by starting seeds in the garden in mid-July.

Lettuce requires more than average moisture, so be sure to water regularly if rain is inadequate. A grass or hay mulch is, of course, highly desirable.

Suggested Varieties:

1. Great Lakes (heading)—Harris, Burpee, and others
2. Salad Bowl (loose-leaf)—Burpee

NEW ZEALAND SPINACH

All gardeners have their special little prejudices, I suppose. One of mine is that, considering its simplicity of culture, productivity, nutritional value, and good taste, this vegetable is not grown nearly enough. If you or your children have the usual aversion to spinach, give New Zealand spinach a try. Most people claim the taste resembles regular spinach, but we feel it is much superior. It is not, in fact, a true spinach. This "green" thrives in hot, dry weather and, as you pinch off the stem ends, it continues to produce leaves over a long growing season.

When to Plant   Since young plants cannot take transplanting, sow seeds in the garden after the last frost.

How to Grow   Soak the very hard seeds for a full day prior to planting. Plant 1 inch deep, two or three seeds per foot, in rows 18 inches apart. Keep the soil very moist until the seedlings show through. When plants are several inches tall, thin to stand 1 foot apart. If it turns out that you do like this vegetable, keep in mind that it freezes well, a fact which might warrant a second planting in midsummer.

Each plant will produce good quantities of thick green leaves without letup, until stopped by the first frost. Stems are edible also, but the best part of this vegetable is the outer 3 or 4 inches of the newly formed shoots.

Suggested Varieties:

New Zealand Spinach (Same name, all seed companies)

ONIONS

A deep and well-fertilized bed is a must for the production of quality onions. Trenching (double digging), with the incorporation of a liberal quantity of manure or compost into the subsoil, will pay off in large, well-formed specimens early in the fall.

When to Plant   Plant seeds or sets just as early as garden soil can be worked.

How to Grow   Plant seed ½ inch deep, 1 inch apart, in rows 10 or 12 inches apart. After eight to ten weeks, thin to 2 inches apart, using these tiny onions, stems and all, in salads. From then (about mid-June) through the summer, you can harvest the partially grown onions for eating fresh or, best of all, boiled, then buttered and salted to taste. We prefer them, for boiling, about the size of a half-dollar. To obtain full-sized onions, those left in the garden should eventually stand 4 or 5 inches apart. Do not be concerned when the tops flop over and break off. This is normal, and means that the onions are about ready for harvest.

From Sets. Sets are simply baby onions, about the size of a dime, which the growers have harvested the previous fall and stored over the winter. They are relatively inexpensive and are sold in plastic bags of 1 to 5 pounds. Their advantage over seeds is obvious: they provide edible-sized onions much earlier in the season.

Plant sets 2 inches apart, about 2 inches deep. Rows can be fairly close; mine are usually only 8 inches apart. After eight weeks, they will be just the right size for baby boiled onions. Pull every other one and allow the rest to go to maturity. Thus you have two crops: one in midsummer for boiling or eating as scallions, a second late in the summer as full-sized, all-purpose onions.

Weed control is important with onions. Either hand-pull or lay down a 2- to 3-inch mulch.

Suggested Varieties:

1. White Ebenezer
2. Yellow Ebenezer

Peas

I admit that I find it hard to speak and write dispassionately about peas. This is simply because they are my very favorite vegetable. I experience great sorrow (only slightly exaggerated) when I reflect that the first twenty-five years of my life had slipped by before I first tasted FRESH garden peas. What a waste! However, what's done is over, and at least I am making up for lost time, now.

The vast majority—perhaps 80 percent or more—of the population have never eaten freshly harvested peas. At the mention of the word, people envision the nearly tasteless mush which is available in cans on the grocer's shelves. Although techniques of processing and canning vegetables have improved markedly over the last ten years or so, you are still comparing "apples" and "oranges" when you try to relate the taste, texture, and appearance of home-grown and store-bought peas. Garden peas, picked at their prime and cooked for five to seven minutes (within an hour or two of harvest, if possible), have a distinctive sweet taste and a consistency not unlike that of fresh corn. Add just a trace of butter and salt, and you will discover the reason for all this enthusiasm!

When to Plant   As early as soil can be tilled, but NOT if a heavy mud condition still exists. This normally means the first or second Saturday in April, here in Massachusetts. Peas cannot take midsummer heat; they should be in and out by the Fourth of July.

How to Grow   Peas thrive in a variety of soils but do best when grown on loamy, organically rich beds. The pea, as a legume, does not require a heavy concentration of nitrogen. (Legumes, unique among vegetable classes, "fix" nitrogen from the air by means of bacterial action in and around the roots.) This crop does best in an alkaline soil, at a pH of 7.0 to 8.5. You may have to apply a little extra crushed limestone to this section of the garden.

The one critical extra step required in pea growing is the supplying of some kind of support to get the vines up and off the ground. The usual procedure is to provide brush or twigs along the rows. I've tried this and found it to be inefficient, as well as an eyesore.

Here is my system, and I recommend it purely on the basis of consistently heavy harvests:

Plant double rows, 8 inches apart. These double rows should be 3 to 4 feet from the next pair of rows, to allow for a foot path. By hoe or trowel, make the rows 2 inches deep, and plant the seed 1 inch apart. Young plants will not need to be thinned. Firm the soil, then deep-soak the area with the hose or sprinkler. You can eliminate the need for this last step by soaking the seeds in a pail overnight.

Sometime between germination and a growth of 2 or 3 inches, drive stakes into the ground at each end of the rows, centered between the double rows. Purchase a roll of 3-foot chicken-wire fence. As I recall, this cost me $3 or so, and is a once-every-ten-years investment. One 50-foot roll will thus accommodate two 25-foot double rows of peas. Fasten the fencing securely to each pole, after stretching it tight. Every 8 feet along the row, drive in a pole or stake for added support. Tie the fence to the pole with string or, better, feed the pole down through the holes in the fence first, then drive it into the earth. I have read that it is dangerous to use wire fencing for pea support because of the possibility of burning the tendrils on hot, sunny days. Don't believe it; it just is not so.

Through trial and error, I have learned that peas grow better and set more pods if the roots are heavily mulched. I have used pine needles or grass clippings, whichever was most plentiful at the time. Peas apparently do not take kindly, especially at the roots, to severe fluctuations in temperature. This mulching also serves to keep weeding down and retains moisture in the soil.

You will quickly learn, through opening a few pods prematurely, when the peas are ready. They reach a certain fullness which the eye will recognize with a little practice. Do not allow the pods to hang even two or three days too long; as in corn, the sugars will turn to starch if the peas are left on the vine.

When the last of the peas are in the freezer and the wire fence is rolled up and put away (about July 4), it is time to plant more beans, beets, carrots, and whatever else will mature within 70 days. This is another fringe benefit with peas: that piece of garden can be "double-cropped" each year.

There is one sure way to find out if, for you, peas are or are not worth the extra step or two. Plant 5 or 6 feet of single or double rows following the above suggestions, and decide for yourself if the rewards justify the labors.

For some reason, pea growing is quite popular in our town, to the extent that the editor of the local newspaper annually awards a "mythical silver pea spoon" to the first gardener who harvests enough peas for a meal. This occurs about June 15.

Suggested Varieties:

1. Burpeeana Early—Burpee
2. Lincoln—Harris and others

PEPPERS

Because of their very long growing season, sweet peppers are most often purchased by the backyard gardener as started plants, along with his tomatoes. Since a dozen plants will set you back only a dollar or so, this is probably the best way to proceed. For the average family, six to twelve plants are plenty, unless you want extra to give away or you plan to stock the freezer. We have taken peppers out of the freezer eighteen months after they were put in and found them perfectly edible.

When to Plant   From seed in the cold frame by mid-April; from started plants, after the last frost is past.

How to Grow   Peppers are not especially heavy feeders. Very average garden soil will probably support them. Set plants into the row about 1½ feet apart, with rows no closer than 2 feet.

If you have had good luck with tomatoes, chances are you will have no problems growing peppers. Their culture is quite similar.

Suggested Varieties:

1. Calwonder—Several seed companies
2. Fordhook—Burpee

SQUASH AND PUMPKINS

To obtain the maximum in size, quantity, and quality, follow the detailed directions outlined in Chapter 6. If you do not care to go to quite that much trouble for your squash, follow the guidelines for planting and harvesting cucumbers.

Squash fall into two categories, summer and winter. Summer squash are the comparatively soft-skinned varieties which will not store for long periods. These include yellow crookneck and straight-neck types, zucchini, and cocozelle.

Winter squash, with hard shells which allow fall and early-winter storage, include butternut, acorn, blue hubbard, and buttercup.

One variety which the small-scale gardener should consider is Burpee's Bush Table Queen Acorn. The squash develop close to the central stem on a practically runnerless plant. These can be planted 2 feet apart in rows, without fear of a jungle of vines developing. Each plant will produce five to eight full-sized acorn squash.

Suggested Varieties:

1. Seneca Prolific—Harris (summer)
2. Butternut—Most seed companies (winter)
3. Burpee's Bush Acorn—Burpee (winter)

TOMATOES

The new hybrid tomato varieties are, for the most part, highly resistant to fungus diseases (also called "wilts"), which were only a few years ago the bane of backyard gardeners. The beauty of tomatoes is that, when all else fails, you will probably still succeed with this most popular garden plant.

When to Plant   Start seed in window boxes in March or in the cold frame in April. Set plants outside after all chance of frost is past.

How to Grow   Tomatoes do not *have* to have an especially deep or rich soil. However, they will produce more
fruit for a longer period if grown in a seed bed that is well
prepared (with aged manures or compost). Everyone you
talk to will have a different "never fail" system for growing
tomatoes. Not to be outdone, here is mine:

Although I have raised tomatoes from seed, it seems to
be more practical to buy a dozen or eighteen started plants.
A dozen plants provide our family of five with all we can
use, with plenty left over for non-gardening friends. About
Memorial Day, since we had a killing frost as late as June 3
one year, we set in twelve plants. These are spaced every
2 feet, in two rows 4 feet apart. About 6 inches away from
the young plant, a sturdy pole is driven into the soil, so as
to stand about 5 feet tall. Since space in my garden is at a
premium, I train the main stem up this pole, pinching off
all lateral shoots. This creates a tall but still very productive
plant. Twine or tape can be used to attach the vine loosely
to the pole.

If you have plenty of room and do not want to bother
with stakes, set your young plants at least 3 feet apart in
each direction, and allow them to develop naturally. To
prevent spoilage of those tomatoes which may come into
contact with the soil, provide a generous grass or hay mulch
all around. This will also resolve the problems of weeding
and retaining moisture. See Chapter 3 on insect control.

At the end of the growing season, be alert to first-frost
warnings. Most of the green tomatoes still remaining on
the plants in September will ripen in the cellar, at temperatures between 60 and 75 degrees.

Suggested Varieties:

1. Burpee's Big Boy—Burpee
2. Moreton Hybrid—Harris
3. Burpee's V F Tomato—Burpee

MISCELLANEOUS

A few words on ten other less generally grown vegetables:

Celery   Requires extra-fertile soil and an extremely
long growing season—more than 150 days from seed. Cannot
be harvested in the north unless started inside by early
April for transplanting after last frost. Set young plants at
least 6 inches apart in rows. Stalks of mature plants will
be green at harvest, although white stalks can be attained
by providing shade, usually by propping up foot-wide
boards along the rows. Care must be taken to shade only
the stems, not the greens. Another method of blanching
the stalks is to mound up soil around the stems as they
develop. Actually, color is unimportant as far as taste is
concerned.

Eggplant   This is one of those vegetables you should
try when looking for something a little different. A marvel-
ous variety of tasty dishes can be prepared from eggplant.
They require an early start in peat pots or a window box,
for transplanting outside well after danger of frost is past.
(The cold frame does not provide the consistent heat required to get this plant well started.) Allow 2 feet between
plants in the garden, and harvest fruits when about grape-

fruit size, or when they attain a high gloss. Keep the fruits picked, and the plants will continue to produce up to frost.

Kohlrabi   Often grown as a spring or fall crop, kohlrabi requires (or, at least, does best in) a deep, well-manured loam. This assures fast maturity and a more tender, better-tasting end product. Plant in rows 1½ feet apart; thin to 4 to 6 inches apart. Harvest when about tennis-ball size. They will naturally get much larger than this, but they quickly deteriorate in texture and taste if allowed to continue growing. Kohlrabi is a hardy vegetable; you might plant a row or two in July where radishes or peas have been harvested, to provide another early-fall vegetable. Kohlrabi can be winter-stored the same as carrots and beets; see Chapter 7.

Lima Beans   Strictly a warm-weather crop, lima beans prefer a rather loamy soil, perhaps shading toward sandy. Plant late (mid-June in Massachusetts) in rows at least 1 foot apart, and spaced 6 inches in the rows. More than average moisture is required to produce well-filled pods, so provide a mulch if possible. While they come available in bush and pole varieties, I would suggest you try the bush types for reasons of convenience. Burpee's Fordhook is especially tasty and a dependable grower.

Muskmelon (cantaloupe).   Although more fruit than vegetable, cantaloupe is usually grown in a corner of the vegetable garden, where the vines can trail. Best started indoors or in the cold frame, their culture is the same as for cucumbers. I have had good luck with Fredonia's Supermarket variety. The melon is ready to pick when it separates easily from the stem.

Parsnip   A very long-season plant. Seed of parsnip can be planted outside the same time as beets and carrots, which is any time after the soil can be worked. Plant the seed thinly, and only ¼ inch deep. Allow 1 foot between rows and thin to one plant every 4 or 5 inches when plants are well on the way. Since parsnips are so slow to germinate and make early growth, some gardeners interplant radishes between the rows. Radishes are in and out in 30 days, before the parsnips require more space. Parsnips can take several frosts and winter-store the same as the other root crops.

Potatoes   Only the gardener with lots of space will attempt potatoes, especially since this vegetable is always available at a reasonable price at the market. Potatoes do well in cool climates, which explains why the states of Maine and Idaho produce this crop in abundance. Potatoes need an acid soil (pH of 5.0 to 6.5 is best) and should never be planted in heavily manured soil. Plant chunks of seed potato, each containing one to three "eyes," about 3 inches deep, and space them 1½ feet apart. Provide a deep soaking once every ten days or so, and keep weeds down with several inches of straw or hay. Harvest time has arrived when most of the top growth has become withered. A weekly application of Sevin or rotenone will keep insect pests to a minimum.

Radishes   Quick and foolproof—that's the radish. If you like them, they are great for filling in bare spots during the growing season. Do not sow several long rows all at once; it is better to plant a 6-foot row every other week for a continuing supply. Plant the seed ½ inch deep in rows as close as 5 or 6 inches; thin to 1½ or 2 inches apart.

Champion, Cherry Belle, and Comet are all excellent varieties.

Swiss Chard   This is actually a variety or close cousin of the beet, especially grown for its leaves. Not universally well loved (at least, in my house), its cultivation is identical to that of the beet.

Turnips (and Rutabaga). A hardy root crop, turnips do best if not subjected to the heat of midsummer. Plant a row or two in mid-July for harvesting in October. Like beets, they will survive (and possibly be the better for) several frosts. Turnips store well, as described in Chapter 7.

CHAPTER 5

Making the Vegetable Garden Attractive

I am afraid that the words "vegetable garden" too often conjure up a picture of an unattractive, off-in-a-corner area of the yard which somehow has to be apologized for. Some gardeners go so far as to hide the vegetables behind rows of hedges, shrubs, blueberry bushes, or what have you. Maybe the reason for this is the idea that the vegetable patch suffers somewhat when compared with the flower bed. Or perhaps it is because subconsciously the gardener half expects that, by mid-August, he will again have a drought-stricken, weed-choked mess on his hands.

Well, I have both flowers and vegetables, and in my yard it is the vegetable garden which gets the most attention from visitors—largely, I think, because there is order and symmetry about it. Consider trying one or more of the following suggestions:

Utilize a Shape Other Than the Traditional Rectangle

The shape I chose allows me to create a huge (yellow) flowering initial (W) which stands out from the surrounding greens and browns. So immediately there is something distinctive and unique and, thus, of some conversational value.

Many other letters of the alphabet can be created as a border pattern, if that idea appeals to you. You might even run rows of your border flower into the vegetable garden proper, to create the desired effect.

The possibilities for varying shapes are limited only by the boundaries of your imagination. If your property is quite small and therefore restrictive of what you can do, at least use gentle curves instead of straight lines on one or two sides.

Border Some or All of the Vegetable Garden with a Low-Growing Annual, Preferably Marigolds

I read an article a couple of years ago (I have forgotten exactly where) which claimed that something in the roots of the marigold repels root nematodes. Nematodes are almost microscopic-size, eel-shaped organisms (plant parasites) which infest a great many soils. A severe infestation of them can cause stunted and malformed plants which, as a result of damaged root systems, produce inferior vegetables. This article rang a bell in my mind, because I had observed, without previously making the connection, that the vegetable plants growing within 4 to 6 feet of the marigold border I have always used were noticeably more vigorous and productive than those further away. In an effort to corroborate this admittedly circumstantial evidence, I wrote to the University of Massachusetts' Department of Agriculture. Dr. R. A. Rohde, the head of the Department of Plant Pathology (and a recognized authority in the field of nematology), replied, in part, "When actively growing, marigolds secrete a sulphur-containing compound which is released into the soil and actually kills nematodes living there. The beneficial effects tend to build up from year to year; thus it does have possibilities for the home gardener." Dr. Rohde went on to mention that the "marigold effect" was first discovered by Dutch bulb growers, who found that bulbs grew better when interplanted with marigolds. Apparently it took them several years to convince scientists that this was not an old wives' tale.

I start about a hundred seeds of semi-dwarf (18 inches at maturity) marigold either in the cold frame about mid-April or in rough wooden flats a week or two earlier. Remember that you need about 4 inches of soil in a flat to bring the plants along to about 3 or 4 inches in height. They get transplanted to the border at about the same weekend we put the tomatoes and peppers out. By starting the seeds early, we have a flowering border from late June through mid-September, when the first frost hits. By covering them with light plastic sheeting, we are able to keep them going well into October.

If money is no object, or if you would rather not bother with starting the flowers from seeds, you have the alternative of picking up several dozen started marigold plants from your local nursery or garden center. Planted 1 foot apart in the border, they create an unbroken hedge of color throughout the summer.

Incidentally, another aid toward controlling root nematodes, other than disinfecting or fumigating the soil with chemicals, is crop rotation. More on this in the final chapter.

PLANT ARROW-STRAIGHT, PARALLEL ROWS

In Chapter 4, on specific vegetables, we discussed distances between rows and plants.

Besides utilizing available garden space most efficiently, a vegetable garden having perfectly straight rows is, somehow, more pleasurable to observe than the garden with meandering rows. I suspect some will question the necessity of going to this extra trouble for a vegetable garden. I would counter that argument with (a) it is not that much extra work, and (b) it is time we got over the notion that the vegetable garden is strictly a drab, utilitarian operation, to be silently endured and esthetically ignored.

For very short rows, use a yardstick to depress a straight groove into the soil.

For medium-length rows, say 6 to 15 feet, obtain a narrow piece of wood, as straight as you can find, with which to mark the rows. Pressed into the soil at the sharp edge, you have a ready-made seed depression.

For rows longer than 15 feet, push short sticks into the soil at both ends of the row, attach string an inch above the surface, and pull taut. With a hoe edge, you can then trench out a shallow, reasonably straight row. In place of a hoe, I have found it just as convenient to use my long piece of wood, using the tightly pulled string as a guide.

Where you have several rows side by side in a section, keep a ruler or yardstick handy to keep the rows as close to parallel as possible.

Does that sound like a lot of unnecessary bother? My only further comment would be that your little extra effort will reward you generously later on, every time you are just out walking around to see how things look.

Use Mulch, If Possible

The *organic* benefits of mulching are pretty generally known. Briefly, as the mulch material breaks down, it acts to replenish the soil with those elements and minerals consumed by the vegetables. Other functional benefits of mulching are:

1. A water saver. A mulch greatly retards water loss, thus conserving a commodity which is rapidly becoming scarce in many communities.

2. A temperature stabilizer. Experiments have demonstrated that vegetables not subjected to extremes of heat and cold grow stronger, are generally healthier, and are better formed.

3. A weed preventative. Weed seeds have a tough time germinating under a 3- or 4-inch blanket of mulch. Weeds, besides being unsightly, compete for water and food with the vegetables.

The point of consideration here is the *visual* value of a mulch between plants and rows. Some people prefer the appearance of the bare earth, but most folks who experiment with mulches gradually appreciate the fact that with the use of mulches weeds are scarcer than before. Where weeds are growing in profusion, an atmosphere of chaos seems to grow also.

What to use? I am fortunate in having nearly a half-acre of lawn. Going a little longer between mowings, I have a steady supply of grass clippings, especially in May and June, when growth is at its fastest. If I need more than I can obtain from my own yard, there are usually non-gardening friends with lawns who are happy to donate grass clippings.

In the absence of sufficient grass, most any available organic material will do. Other substances to be used are shredded leaves, straw, salt marsh hay, ground corncobs, peat moss, shredded bark, pine needles, and dry, processed cow manure. Sawdust can be utilized, but since it is nitrogen-deficient, it should be supplemented with cottonseed or soybean meal.

Placed at an even height between rows, after the plants are 1 or 2 inches up, the well-mulched vegetable garden presents an ordered, cared-for appearance.

CHAPTER 6

How to Grow 100-pound Pumpkins

The question "Why grow giant pumpkins?" might well be raised right at the start. A good question, and certainly everyone will not be interested in attempting to do so.

However, I have had a lot of fun raising really large pumpkins, and I offer the following reasons for considering such a project:

If you have children (or if not your own, then neighborhood children), they will take great pleasure in having the largest jack-o'-lantern in the area for Halloween. (A 100-pound pumpkin measures about 65 inches around.)

I have found growing giant pumpkins to be the best way to interest children in vegetable gardening. As they watch the very noticeable day-to-day growth of the pumpkins during the heat of the summer, their curiosity is aroused and they soon want to experiment for themselves.

There is a ready market for unusually large pumpkins. The two weeks before Halloween, you will have little trouble selling them for (in my locality, at least) between $4 and $6 each, depending on their size and shape.

Once you start producing these giants, it is easy to generate contests between neighbors or within a whole town, to see who can grow the largest one. (I have an unofficial contest going within the company I work for, with manufacturing plants in three states.)

You will have all the pies you and your whole neighborhood can consume.

To summarize, then, here is why you might consider growing extra-large pumpkins:

1. So your children will have the biggest jack-o'-lantern on the block,
2. To stimulate interest among youngsters toward vegetable gardening,
3. As a money-making possibility,
4. To promote contests for heaviest and best-shaped speciments, and
5. For pies.

If you have decided to proceed, here we go:

What seeds do we use, and where do we get them? The only variety of pumpkin I know of which has the potential to produce greater than 100-pound specimens is *Big Max*, sold originally by Burpee but now available through other seed companies as well. I am sure you can find them at most seed bars featuring Burpee seeds. There are certain crossbreed squash which will produce giant fruit, but these do not have the true pumpkin color or shape.

When and how are the seeds planted? Let's start out with the knowledge that we are going to try to provide 150 days—five full months—for the pumpkin plants. If you are south of the Mason-Dixon line (roughly speaking), you have no problem. North of this line, it becomes necessary to assist Mother Nature in providing a long enough frost-free growing season. Here in northern Massachusetts, our growing season averages 120 days but varies from 100 to 140 days. Thus, we start the seeds inside, usually between March 20 and April 10. The date of the first fall frost here will average September 20.

An ideal container for starting pumpkin seeds is the bottom half of a wax-coated milk carton; the half-gallon size is good, but the gallon container is best, since it provides more than ample room for root growth. Fill this container to within 1 inch of the top with plain garden loam. If you have any well-rotted manure available, mix it in at a ratio of three parts soil to one part manure.

Place *two* seeds near the center of the container, about 1 inch apart, then cover with ½ to ¾ inch of additional soil. Firm the soil over the seeds. Next, add a cup of water to the container by pouring it in at the sides. If you squeeze the carton slightly, you will create a small opening at the sides for water intake. Let the last few drops soak down through the top surface, to moisten the seeds. Now, to prevent moisture loss, place wax paper or, better, clear plastic film, such as is available in tear-off boxes, over the container and secure it in place with string or a rubber band. This covering of the container is not absolutely necessary, but I have found that with it a higher percentage of seeds germinate, and a day or two sooner, than if the container is left uncovered. Further, covering the boxes as suggested eliminates the need for additional watering until after the seeds have sprouted.

Finally, place the containers any place where they will receive constant 70-degrees-plus temperature but not more than 80 degrees. If they are subjected to higher than 80-degree heat, they will germinate too quickly and grow tall and spindly. Your seeds will (or should) germinate in seven to twelve days. I have seen a few real slowpokes take as long as eighteen days, so do not despair too soon. Sunlight is *not* necessary to *start* the seeds.

I have found that, when I plant twenty containers as described, I will usually get at least one of the two seeds to germinate in fifteen or sixteen boxes. Do not expect 100 percent germination—it just does not happen. In those cases where both seeds come through, let them both grow for a week, then select the weaker, smaller one and gently pull it out. One plant per box, no more. Incidentally, always start a couple more containers than you can use; your neighbor will want to try his luck, also.

Now that the seeds are sprouted, what next? At the first sign of germination, remove the wax paper or plastic film cover. Within a day or two after the young plants have broken through, we must begin to provide direct sunlight. Most people, myself included, are not fortunate enough to have a greenhouse. So we do the next best thing: we select a window or two on the south or west side of the house. If the sill is not wide enough to accommodate the containers, you may have to call in your carpenter in residence to fashion a simple sill extension. Somehow, try to see that the containers are sitting in the sun for a minimum of four hours a day. Five to six hours is ideal.

This cluttering up of the window sills is a little awkward,

but it is, I think, a small inconvenience. If you have toddlers
in the house, you will have to put your thinking cap on to
ensure against the obvious.

I have found that, by adding 1 to 1½ cupfuls of water
to each container every other day, I can keep the soil damp,
but not wet. You do not want water standing at the bottom
of the box. If you get good, strong sunlight for five or six
hours straight, you will find that the plants will require
additional watering. A little common sense is in order here;
a lot depends on the heat and humidity inside the house
and the amount of available sunlight.

This next step is optional; my "organic" friends will
frown on this, but I have had excellent luck with the
following feeding program, prior to setting the plants outside. Purchase a box of water-soluble, highly concentrated
plant food. You have probably seen these (usually green)
containers in garden supply outlets. There are two or three
brands available, all good. *Following the directions exactly,*
water with this plant food every ten days to two weeks.
Do not succumb to the temptation of adding "one for the
pot" as though you were brewing a cup of tea. The manu-
facturer spent a lot of time and money figuring out the
optimum solution before he put the product on the market.
The usual amount is 2 level tablespoonfuls per gallon of
water; but, again, read and follow the label.

After about four weeks, you can set the containers outside, thus adding the benefits of additional sunshine and
fresh air. This also starts the "hardening off" process. Keep
an eye on the weather forecast, though, and early in the
evening bring the plants back inside at the slightest possibility of frost.

What about preparation of the garden area into which

we will transplant the young pumpkin plants? A week or so before the actual transplanting takes place, we want to do certain things by way of preparing the "pumpkin patch" soil. We might refer to this process as "stacking the deck."

As to location: your pumpkin area should be a specially prepared site either off to one side or to the far side of the vegetable garden, so that the vines can ramble. Keep in mind the fact that the vines can trail as far as 30 or 40 feet. If you take the trouble to "curl" the runners, the plants can be kept in a smaller area.

Depending on how ambitious you are, and whether you have some willing helpers available, the extent of your efforts at this stage will determine the ultimate size of your pumpkins. We are about to load up the pumpkin patch site with as much organic fertilizer as we can lay our hands on. Here's how I proceed.

In my main vegetable garden, I leave a 4-foot-wide strip along the north edge for pumpkins (and a few squash). This strip is about 35 feet long, and I will eventually set the individual pumpkin plants in about 4 feet apart.

Here's how we stack the deck. Trench out the topsoil with a spade to a depth of 18 or so inches (2 feet is better) and to a width of about 2 to 2½ feet. Sounds like a lot of work, but the exercise, at a moderate rate, will do you good. If you are only going to try three or four plants, you can handle this chore within an hour. Try just a few the first year; if you think the effort is worth it, you can always expand next time around.

If you have access to a dairy farm or a stable, avail yourself of nature's best fertilizer. Most places will give manure away in the spring, and some will make a small charge.

Chicken manure is great, but do not use it unless it is three or four months old. Hen manure is considerably more potent than horse and cow manure and will, if used too fresh, "burn out" your plants. I prefer horse or cow manure, since it is impossible to use too much of it, even fresh, for pumpkins and squash.

Should you fail to locate a source of manure, invest a couple of dollars in a bag or two of dehydrated, bagged cow manure. This form is practically odorless and very easy to handle. If you have any rotting leaves or compost available, now is the time to put that to use, also.

Into your trenched-out area dump 6 or 8 inches of manure, leaves, and so forth (if you want to go all the way, add and stir in a pound or two of powdered bone meal and a handful of regular lawn and garden lime, also). Next, shovel back a few inches of the soil you removed. Now load in another 6 inches of your organic material, more soil, additional bone meal and lime, and so on, packing down each layer firmly with your foot, until you are back to within a few inches of completely refilling the trench. Be sure to tamp the layers down; otherwise, you will leave a lot of air spaces, which will later result in too much settling. Let the top 6 inches, into which the pumpkin plant roots will start their growth, be plain topsoil.

Now that you are back near the top, fashion out a rough saucer with your hands, the purpose of which will be to catch and contain rainfall. Now we are ready to transplant.

When and how do we set the young pumpkin plants out? The plants can be set out after reasonable danger of a late frost has gone by. This is the same time you would normally put out pepper and tomato plants in your locality. For my section of the country, this means Memorial Day, May 30. If things have really warmed up by May 20, though, and we are faithful in watching for forecasts of a late frost, we will usually transplant well before Memorial Day. I have found that my vines are so long by May 15 or so that I almost have to move them into their permanent beds by mid-May. Just keep something handy (bushel baskets, plastic sheeting, or newspapers) to do a cover-up job should the need arise. These coverings, should they be needed, must be anchored in two or three places with stones or sticks to keep them from blowing away.

Always transplant on a cloudy or rainy day, or, at the least, after the sun has gone down. If the weather forecast for the next day is for an unusually hot, sunny day, wait a day or two.

Now we set the young plants in. First, add 1 or 2 cupfuls of water to the container, to thoroughly saturate the soil. Next, gently tear away the sides of the paper-board container (if you have used milk cartons), trying to keep the whole root ball intact. Do this right down where the plant will be set into the ground. When the container is completely removed, set the plant carefully into a shallow, hollowed-out area and work the surrounding earth in around it. For extra support, finish up with the plant an inch deeper than it was in its starter box.

If you have used a wood or metal container to start the plants, first water the container thoroughly. Now, invert the plant and tap the container firmly, easing the whole root ball out. Then set in as above.

Finally, allow a slowly running hose to thoroughly soak the soil under and around each plant. If too far away to use the hose, pour several gallons of water into each "saucer" from a pail. There is no doubt that plenty of water immediately after transplanting is most important in getting the young pumpkins to "take."

How about insects? There is only one serious pest which can spell disaster if left uncontrolled. I lost one whole year's effort to this pest, the squash vine borer. For the last couple of years, though, I have had no problem.

When I first encountered the borer, I did not immediately recognize the source of the trouble. My plants were wilting and dying for no apparent reason. Eventually I discovered small holes, about ⅛ inch in diameter, in the vines. Slitting open one such vine at the hole and working my way along, I soon found a white grub burrowing it way through the stem. This is the larval, and most destructive, stage of the squash vine borer. If allowed to remain unchecked, this larva would burrow into the soil before winter, pupate, and emerge in the spring as a clear-winged, wasp-shaped moth. This moth lays its eggs on the plant leaf, at the point where leaf meets stem. The tiny young hatchlings eat their way down the stem and on into the main vine, all the while sapping the strength of the plant and causing stunted growth.

I should mention that some areas are relatively free of this pest. Avoid spraying or dusting unless you have actually seen the borers in your vines. The situation finally became so bad in my garden (they seem to multiply geometrically each year if unchecked) that I decided to avoid planting pumpkins and squash for one whole season, in an effort to break the cycle. I enlisted the cooperation of my immediate neighbors on this, figuring that if there were no plants around for the moths to lay their eggs on, we would benefit accordingly the following year. It worked. Although not completely eliminated, they were at least controllable.

To Control: Do *not* spray or dust while the plants are flowering, just prior to forming the tiny pumpkins. If you do, you will get no cooperation from the bees, which are necessary for proper pollination. After each plant has set two or three pumpkins, you can begin a control program. Incidentally, always spray or dust after sunset, when the bees have returned to their hives.

Since I have fruit trees, I also have a compressed air (hand pump) sprayer. The past year or two I have had excellent success using wettable SEVIN (carbaryl) and the pump sprayer, applying it once a week for eight weeks from about late June and through August. The beauty of this particular chemical is that it completely disintegrates and disappears after six or seven days, leaving no harmful residue. From all I have been able to gather, SEVIN is one of the very safest chemicals available for use in the home garden. Directions for mixing, to be followed to the letter, are on the package. Whatever else you may use for control, stay away from DDT and all other chlorinated hydrocarbons.

For you strictly organic gardeners, rotenone can be used, with perhaps less success than with wettable SEVIN. Rotenone is a contact and stomach poison, derived from the roots of certain tropical plants, and is of very low toxicity to man and animals. Apply rotenone dust to the leaf axils and stems of the plants at eight- to ten-day intervals and immediately after a good, heavy rain. A small hand duster, available at hardware and garden supply centers, is the most efficient way to evenly distribute dusts.

Remember, when using sprays or dusts, GO EASY; err on

the conservative side when applying. Look on them as necessary evils, to be used only after you have actually observed insect pests in action.

How many pumpkins do we allow to form on each plant? If you want to attain maximum-sized pumpkins, pinch off all but one pumpkin from each plant. Wait until three or four have formed; then choose what seems to be the roundest and best-looking fruit. Remove all the others. They will snap off easily when bent backward. Continue to remove newly formed pumpkins while the runners continue to "set" them. You are thus allowing the root and leaf system to channel all available plant food, moisture, and sunlight into a single pumpkin. Of course, if you want a lot of medium-sized pumpkins (40- to 60-pounders), you can allow four or five fruits to come along, per plant. Try it both ways on different plants, and make your own evaluations of the results.

Any additional fertilizing required? With adequate moisture (which means at least one deep soaking a week either naturally or by sprinkler), you will reap the benefits all summer long of your earlier soil preparations. However, if you have bet a week's wages that your largest pumpkin will be the heaviest one in town, try this:

Organic Feeding: Get a large wood or metal barrel and fill it one quarter full of chicken manure (a little less if very fresh). Fill the barrel the rest of the way with water, and stir. Allow to set a day or two; then once a week pour a couple of gallons of the "tea" into each plant saucer (depression). If poultry manure is not available, use horse or cow manure and *half*-fill the barrel; then proceed as above.

Chemical Feeding: Use the concentrated water-soluble plant food. The larger the container, the more economical, of course. Apply two gallons per plant, every two weeks, right through the growing season. Again, follow the directions on the package to the letter.

Good luck! My biggest one so far? A modest 115 pounds, which measured 70 inches in circumference. I have had several others well over 100 pounds. I have seen and heard of Big Max attaining 135 pounds each, though, so this gives us something to shoot for.

CHAPTER 7

Cooking, Freezing and Storing

Since this is not a cookbook and I am not a cook, my observations on preparing vegetables for the table will be limited to technique.

COOKING

If we have invested a considerable portion of time, thought, and effort on our vegetable garden, if we have nourished the soil with generous amounts of nitrogen, phosphorous, potash, and trace elements by regularly adding organic materials to it, if we have watered it, weeded it, mulched it, protected it, and even talked to it from time to time, then the chances are excellent that we shall harvest food which is loaded with all of the elements, vitamins, minerals, calcium, iron, and carbohydrates which our bodies require for good health. Assuming that we have done most or all of these things and are thus in a position to reap the nutritional rewards which well-grown vegetables afford, it follows that we should not pour most of our efforts down the sink just before dinner. And yet this is just what is allowed to happen in too many cases. By boiling fresh vegetables too long, a very high percentage of their vitamins and minerals escape into the water. Estimates of these losses run as high as fifty percent or more. No, I am not about to suggest that we eat all of our vegetables raw. However, we should give serious thought to preparing vegetables for the table so as to preserve as much of their health-giving benefits as possible. Here are a few suggestions for minimizing vitamin and mineral loss:

When possible, *harvest your vegetables as close to mealtime as possible*. Should this be impractical, cold-wash, dry, and store immediately in the refrigerator.

Unless their skins are very tough and unattractive, *do not peel* vegetables before cooking. A high percentage of their minerals are wasted when the skins are discarded, and the insides of a peeled vegetable are just that much more vulnerable to vitamin loss.

Use a pressure cooker. Very little water comes into contact with the vegetables, and what little there is can be served with the food or used to make gravy.

Bake or broil vegetables occasionally. Either method is better than boiling in water.

When cooking in water is unavoidable *place the vegetable into rapidly boiling water and return to a boil quickly. Cook until barely tender, and remove from the water at once*. Try to find a use for this vegetable water. Gravy is one possibility. At the risk of sounding like a health food "nut" (which is not necessarily bad), I would suggest you consider chilling this cooking water in the refrigerator, flavoring it to taste, and drinking it cold.

Have the whole family eat raw vegetables whenever pos-

sible. Your body is absorbing 100 percent of the nutritional value when no heat and water processing are involved.

FREEZING

When all of a crop cannot be consumed immediately, freezing is the best method of preserving vegetables. The exception to this rule concerns the root crops, which we will consider in the next section, "Storing." Modern freezers also allow the family to enjoy home-grown vegetables through the winter.

Most cookbooks have directions for freezing vegetables. The important points to remember are:

1. Harvest the vegetables as close to freezing time as possible. If you can get them into the freezer within an hour of picking, so much the better.

2. Freeze vegetables when they are at their prime, not after they have become old and unpalatable! Freezing does nothing to improve the flavor or texture of inferior vegetables.

3. Do not over-blanch. Blanching—the quick-boiling process which stops the growth enzymes in the vegetable—is a necessary evil in freezing, since some of the vitamins are lost even in the short space of one to three minutes.

4. Have two sinks available for cooling. The first will have ordinary cold tap water, the second ice water with plenty of ice cubes. Immerse the blanched vegetable in the water in the first sink for about a minute; then transfer to the ice water for two minutes. Pack immediately into airtight containers and place in the freezer. Replace the cold tap water in the first sink after each "batch," and add ice to the second as required.

5. Freeze in not larger than 1-pint containers, in order to quick-freeze the whole package in the shortest time possible. We have found plastic sandwich bags, especially the lock-fold type, very practical as to size and efficient utilization of freezer space. To insure an airtight package, we use two plastic bags per package, reversing the direction of the second.

When freezing sweet corn, it is best to remove the kernels from the cob. Corn on the cob comes out of the freezer with considerably less than the quality it went in with. To freeze winter squash, especially butternut, cook as though you were preparing it for the table, puree, cool in the refrigerator for an hour or so, place in airtight containers, and place in the freezer.

I have suggested that root crops do not freeze well. This has been my experience, but some people freeze beets and carrots and claim reasonable success. My efforts to freeze them, tried with varying blanching times, have always resulted in noticeably poorer quality as to taste and consistency.

STORING

Root crops, which include beets, carrots, parsnips, turnips, and potatoes, do not have to be removed from the garden until well after everything else is harvested. They can take several frosts and can, in milder climates, be left in the ground right through the winter if kept covered with a 1-foot-thick hay or straw mulch. In the more severe northern areas, they must be removed and afforded protection.

Several years ago, I began storing beets and carrots in a

wooden barrel, sunk into the ground behind the house. Here is what is involved:

Locate a sturdy wood barrel, of 20- to 30-gallon capacity. (I have a 20-gallon pickle barrel, obtained from the local submarine sandwich shop.) In some convenient spot close to the house, dig a hole 1 foot deeper than the height of the barrel and about 6 inches wider. Gather a bushel or two of leaves and/or hay. Before the ground freezes solid, remove the beets, carrots, turnips, and so forth. Do not wash them— they go into the barrel as is. Before layering in the vegetables, drill a hole in the bottom of the barrel to allow for drainage.

At the bottom of the hole, lay down three or four inches of hay or leaves, then place the barrel into the pit. Stuff leaves and hay all around the sides of the barrel, to a thickness of several inches. Put a couple inches of your layering material into the barrel, then a layer of vegetables. Try not to place vegetables on top of or in direct contact with other vegetables. If the hay or leaves you are using are very dry, sprinkle a little moisture on each layer. To store successfully for three or four months, the vegetables require a temperature between 33 and 40 degrees and humidity of around 80 to 90 percent.

When the barrel is about full, top it off with a thick layer of whatever material you are using, up to the surrounding surface. At the very top, place several inches of newspaper (with a rock to hold them in place), to keep out the rain and severe cold.

Check the barrel weekly to prevent rodent damage or drying out. We have eaten beets and carrots stored in this manner as late as early March.

What about winter squash? Butternut, acorn, and blue

hubbard squash need higher temperatures to store well than are afforded by a barrel sunk into the ground. A dry location with a temperature around 50 degrees is best. This is a problem for most folks, since the temperature in the average cellar is closer to 65 or 70 degrees. We store our squash in the coolest corner of the cellar, using them as required. At the first signs of deterioration, usually after six or eight weeks, we cook up what is left, puree it, and place it in the freezer. Butternut squash frozen in December still tastes quite good when cooked and eaten the following May or June.

CHAPTER 8

The Cold Frame

I have intentionally held this chapter toward the end of the book. The reason for this is that a cold frame is not a necessity: you can have a successful garden without one. There are, however, two good reasons for considering a cold frame:

a. It will enable you to harvest several vegetables (including lettuce, tomatoes, peppers, squash, and pumpkins) four to six weeks earlier than you would otherwise, also eliminating the expense of buying started plants.
b. A cold frame provides an opportunity to scratch that terrible "itch" to get started, a problem which usually sets in about the end of March or early April here in northern Massachusetts.

What is a cold frame? A cold frame is nothing more than a miniature, very compact, early outdoor garden, the construction and use of which allow for the protection of young vegetable plants from killing spring frosts. From the cold frame the six- to eight-week-old plants are carefully moved to their permanent locations in the vegetable garden after the chance of a late spring frost is pretty well gone. This will be when you can put out tomatoes in your area, which is May 25 to May 30 in northern Massachusetts.

Where on the property should the cold frame be located? Try, if at all possible, to find an out-of-the-way location, preferably with a southwest exposure, somewhere along the property edge or in a corner, which will afford:

a. At least six hours of direct sun each day,
b. Reasonable distance from traffic, human and animal, and
c. A location away from the low spot in the surrounding area, since cold and frost, like water, will seek out the lowest levels.

How big should it be, and how is it constructed? On size, there are no limitations either way. Mine measures 42 inches wide by 5 feet long, and this size was simply predetermined by the size of an unused storm window sash I was able to beg. (The storm window, obviously, is what protects the plants from frosts, when resting on top of the frame at night.) Although storm windows are ideal, several other coverings can be used, among them plastic sheeting, an old tarpaulin, or an old, lightweight blanket. These latter coverings, when spread over the frame at night, should be anchored with rocks or boards to ensure against their being blown off.

A storm sash containing glass is definitely preferable,

since you can leave it in place on top of the wood frame at all times, being careful to prop it open with blocks or stones at two corners on sunny days. By opening it up 1 or 2 inches during the direct sunlight hours, you will prevent a too severe buildup of heat, which would kill the young plants. An inexpensive thermometer will guide you, placed in a shady corner of the frame. Interior temperatures should not be allowed to exceed 80 degrees. Temperature is controlled by adjusting the opening of the sash. If you want to go to the trouble, you can hinge the sash to the wood frame along one side.

As to construction, how is this for simplicity: go down to your local lumber yard and order as much 2 by 8 second-grade wood as you will need to enclose your cold-frame area. For instance, for my 3½ by 5-foot frame, I bought a 7-foot piece and a 10-foot piece and sawed them in half. (As I recall, this set me back about $2.50 three or four years ago.)

You do not have to be a professional carpenter to nail these four pieces securely together. Before doing so, you should:

a. Using a yardstick or measuring tape, plot out your rectangle. Drive four small sticks into the ground at the corners and connect all four around the outside with a string, an inch or so off the ground, and pull taut.

b. With your spade, completely remove the top 6 inches of soil inside the string-enclosed area. Be careful to make straight sides so that your 2 by 8's will fit in snugly.

c. Place your four pieces of wood into the scooped-out

area so as to form the rectangle, and butt the ends
together at right angles. Properly positioned, the top
of this wood frame will be about 2 inches above the
surrounding ground area. Take care at this point to
ensure that the wood is positioned as level as possible,
so that the window sash will lay on evenly all around.

d. Nail it together solidly, using at least 3-inch-long
nails.

That's all there is to it. Using halfway decent wood, the
frame should last eight to ten years before needing replace-
ment. A good coating of creosote may double this span.

With 6 inches of soil removed from the enclosure, plus
the 2 inches the wood extends above ground level, your
young plants have 8 inches in which to develop. I have
found this to be more than enough. (In a pinch, I am sure
you could use 2 by 6 boards, in which case you would remove only 4 inches of soil.)

What about the soil itself, in the cold frame? I have had
good luck with just plain old topsoil. Be sure to have a
minimum of 8 inches of relatively stone-free soil, spading
first the whole enclosed area to a depth of 12 to 15 inches
to assure adequate drainage. This cold frame topsoil need
not be fertilized. All we are doing here is starting the plants.
There is adequate food in the topsoil to get the plants well
started. Heavily fertilized cold-frame soil might tend to
force faster growth than nature intended and could, in fact,
burn out the tender root systems altogether. Later on, out
in the properly prepared main garden, these vegetables will
receive all the nourishment they can handle. (This is discussed in Chapter 2.)

When are the seeds actually planted in the cold frame?

Count back six or seven weeks before the date of the average last spring frost in your area. Since our last frost AVERAGES May 20 here in Wilmington, I usually plant the cold frame about April 1 to April 10, depending on weather conditions. As a rough guide, use this rule of thumb: add six days to the date of May 20 for every 100 miles north or subtract six days from it for every hundred miles south of Boston, Massachusetts, as your average last frost. (Of course, if you live within three or four miles of the ocean, your last spring frost will be anywhere from a week to three weeks earlier than otherwise.) Using this guide in central New Jersey, say, the New Brunswick region, which is about 220 miles south of Boston, the gardener might plant his frame around March 25, since the last-frost date will average May 2 to May 6 in this area.

Are there certain vegetables which do not lend themselves to the cold frame? Yes, especially the root crops, such as beets, carrots, and radishes. I generally start a row each of cabbage, broccoli, Brussels sprouts, lettuce, tomatoes, peppers, cucumbers, squash, and pumpkins. Do not try to start corn, peas, green beans, or New Zealand spinach in the frame, since, even when extreme care is used in transplanting, they just do not take kindly to being disturbed.

What is "damping off," and how do you control it? This is a term given to a wilting and dying of the young vegetable (or flower) plants shortly after they germinate. It is a fungus which is encouraged by very high humidity and poor ventilation. The "damping off" microorganisms are found almost universally and are a major source of discouragement to gardeners.

I have used this method to sterilize my cold-frame soil with a great deal of success: After the soil is smoothed and otherwise ready for planting, pour 4 or 5 gallons of boiling water, using a sprinkling can if possible, directly over the soil. This effectively kills any "damping off" fungi which may be present. You must wait a day or two for the soil to return to normal temperature and texture. The frame must be covered during this waiting period, to prevent reinfection by wind from surrounding soil. Finally, wash your hands before handling seeds.

Now that we are prepared to plant, how deep do the seeds go and how far apart? With my 3-foot-wide frame, I have found a yardstick a most handy tool for planting. Holding the yardstick at each end, depress the thin edge about ⅛ inch into the soil. Do not feel that you need a draftsman's caliper to measure the depth; if you vary slightly either way, there is no problem. No yardstick available? Use a small stick to furrow out a shallow depression, or even your index finger. I further favor the yardstick because there is something rather attractive about the arrow-straight rows of young plants coming along. Make your rows 3 or 4 inches apart for small seeds such as lettuce, tomato, and pepper and 5 to 6 inches apart for the large ones like cucumbers, squash, and pumpkins.

Using thumb and index finger, space in the small seeds two or three to the inch. Later, when the seedlings are well started (about ten days after they break the surface), thin to one to the inch. The large seeds, like pumpkin, squash, and cucumbers, can be individually planted about 3 inches apart. Gently cover the seeds and firm the soil over them. Here, again, the flat of the yardstick is excellent for firming in the soil over the seeds.

How and when do you water the cold frame? The first watering should be immediately after planting. Use either a fine spray off your garden hose, or a sprinkling can. The point here is not to disturb the seeds by laying on too heavy droplets of water. Do not be afraid to wet it down well; assuming you have provided good drainage, you cannot drown the seeds. Water thereafter every third or fourth day (depending on drying conditions) unless you receive adequate rainfall. Remove the sash completely on rainy days, provided it is not a heavy downpour.

Remember to prop the sash open in the morning, just before the direct rays of the sun get to the frame. Then get into the habit of closing it tightly each night, even if you are sure there is no chance of frost. If the day is completely devoid of sunlight, open the window an inch anyway, just to keep the air circulating.

What does "hardening off" mean? This term refers to the brief period, just before transplanting into the main garden, during which the plants are toughened to ensure survival outside of their incubator. About ten days before transplanting, begin leaving the window sash up at night, provided no outright frost warnings are given. During the day either remove completely or prop up the window to allow direct exposure of the plants to sun and wind. We want to begin simulating actual garden conditions, BUT NOT ALL AT ONCE! Go slowly. Err on the side of conservatism. You can also ease up on the watering during this ten-day period. The roots are now 4 or 5 inches into the soil and can go several days without a soaking, UNLESS you experience unusual temperatures in the high 80's or low 90's.

How is the actual transplant accomplished? I have had good luck with first wetting down the frame before removing any plants. By so doing, you can lift the entire moist root ball, without exposing any of the tender root system to the air. The single plants can be gently placed in any available box or tray for transport to the main garden. (See Chapter 4 for distances needed between plants in the rows.) Tender loving care is called for here; you are trying to deliver the individual plants to their second homes in a condition as close to that in their cold frame as possible.

Place the young plant into the soil to the same depth it came out of in the frame. Firm the soil around it, but take care, again, not to disturb the root system.

Finally, when the section is complete, put a fine spray on the area for a half-hour or so. Thereafter, regular waterings are in order, with the desired goal to be one deep soaking a week, either naturally or by sprinkler.

This is important: Transplant either in the evening or on a cloudy day. If you try to move the plants in the heat of the day, you are in trouble! Even with the most meticulous care, there will be some root shock in transplanting, and immediate direct sunlight could be fatal.

CHAPTER 9

Afterthoughts

In the introduction, I mentioned that the purely nutritional aspect of vegetable gardening was high up on my personal list of answers to the question, "Why raise vegetables?"

I don't think anyone will seriously argue the observation that the condition of our bodies depends, not exclusively but in large measure, on the quality of the food we eat. This tends to be borne out by insurance company statistics, which demonstrate that farm folk not only enjoy a longer life expectancy than city dwellers, but are freer from sickness and certain physical disabilities as well. (Certainly there are several other significant factors which directly influence these circumstances, including air, water and noise pollution, overcrowding, and all of the stresses which accompany the "rat race" of living and working in the city.) Farm people, in comparison with city people, tend to eat far greater quantities of fresh vegetables. And fresh vegetables have not had most of the nutritional "goodness" processed out of them on the way to the dinner table. Just recently an article appeared in the papers revealing that over a hundred different chemicals are used in the commercial preparation of some foods for the market. No doubt most of these are harmless to our systems but I wonder if, in the long run (and I am thinking here of generations yet unborn), they *all* are.

The observable (and admittedly circumstantial) results in my immediate family of a higher than average intake of fresh vegetables are, I think, worth noting. Over the last ten years, my three youngsters have each averaged *two* days a year out of school, due to illness. This includes colds and flu. During that same period, I have missed a total of *one* day of work, for health reasons. The average number of days absent for school children is eight to ten days a year. I simply offer this as another reason why I shall continue to raise the largest share of the vegetables we consume. There is no longer any doubt in my mind about the very important part which fresh vegetables play in creating and maintaining sound bodies.

The following are some of the most frequently asked questions relating to food raising:

1. *What do you think of the continuing organic versus chemical controversy?*

Answer: I don't think it is necessary to take sides on this issue. What I do think is that a little more open mindedness is in order here. I have found that, among gardeners, a discussion of this subject (like religion) too often generates more heat than light.

The organic point of view is simple enough: absolute avoidance of all chemicals, including powdered fertilizers and toxic sprays in the garden. This can be accomplished by the liberal use of organic additives to the soil, along with adequate sunshine, moisture and the use of biological controls whenever possible.

I find that, with no particular ax to grind either way, I have "evolved" to a position about 90 percent on the side of the organic philosophy.

The other 10 percent is probably more an effort to stay aware of recent technology in this area than anything else. I feel that the insecticide Sevin is a worthwhile step forward on the chemical side. Yet, in the hands of the careless, it must be stressed that lack of attention to directions for use can be dangerous. (See Chapter 3.)

Very few issues in life are either "black" or "white." Consider all the evidence, experiment, then make your own judgment.

2. *How much money do you save in a year with a medium-sized vegetable garden?*

Answer: I mentioned earlier a figure of three to four hundred dollars a year. However, this purely dollars-and-cents answer is misleading and incomplete. Added to it must be the money saved due to fewer medical and dental bills as well as less frequent trips to the marketplace.

This dollar savings will vary widely according to the condition of your soil, how efficiently you space plants and rows, and whether or not you "double crop."

3. *Are there any hard and fast rules concerning spacing of plants?*

Answer: Certainly not. The suggestions offered in the sections on individual vegetables are guidelines. The beginner should err on the side of caution and allow a little *more* space than recommended. As experience and soil condition improve, you can bring the rows and plants closer together. On this matter there is no substitute for trial and experiment. .

4. *How does one cope with an overabundance of rabbits and woodchucks?*

Answer: I suppose this depends a lot on your willingness to use a rifle. I have no compunctions along these lines, since I feel that too much of any animal in an environment is not good. Since man has pretty well eliminated (at least in the suburbs) the natural enemies of rabbits and chucks, it follows that man must take over as the controlling agent. If one or two neighbors and I did not thin the bunny population each spring, it would be very difficult to grow a garden. Even so we lose a little, but this is normal.

The only alternative to open warfare would be to enclose your garden with a three- to four-foot wire or picket fence. If you live in a rather densely populated area, this may be the wiser choice.

5. *What other strictly biological controls are available for control of insects?*

Answer: Several come to mind. One is to encourage a healthy bird population in the neighborhood. Birds consume a phenomenal quantity of insects. Set up feeder stations in winter and be faithful in keeping them well stocked. In the spring and summer continue to feed, perhaps once a week, to provide the birds with an incentive to stay in *your* area.

We see more and more ads which allow for the purchase by mail of ladybugs and praying mantis egg cases. These carnivorous insects destroy a wide variety of harmful garden pests and should be protected wherever found. Each year we see a half dozen or so of the mantes in our garden, often a full three inches in length. The children love to watch them.

6. *What about plant diseases, such as "wilts," mildews, and fungus?*

Answer: I have been fortunate in having had very little trouble with plant disease. I would like to think that this is due to a combination of excellent soil conditions (which promote vigorous growth), an ideal open location, and the use of newer disease-resistant vegetable seeds whenever possible. Well grown vegetables, like healthy humans, are better equipped to ward off diseases than would otherwise be the case.

Where diseases are noted, destroy infected plants by adding them to the compost heap, or removing completely from the area. When buying seeds, select disease-resistant varieties.

7. *What is the best way to handle late spring and early fall frosts?*

Answer: I became interested in this problem the hard way. Several years ago my entire tomato, pepper, squash, pumpkin and cuke plantings were wiped out by a frost which hit on *June 6*. Even though this is perhaps a once-in-a-decade occurrence, forewarned is forearmed.

Lightweight plastic sheeting (drop cloths) are very handy for frost protection. For a week or so after setting out the tomatoes, keep an ear tuned to the early evening weather report. If possible frosts are forecast, cover the plants with whatever you have available. Other than plastic, newspapers are good, taped together to cover a larger area.

We are able to keep the more tender vegetables (and marigolds and other flowers) "going" right through October by using the light plastic sheeting. If your garden center does not carry plastic, you should be able to obtain it through your hardware or paint store. Plastic is being substituted more and more in the painting trade for the more cumbersome canvas drop cloths.

8. *Is it really necessary to rotate the vegetables in the garden each year?*

Answer: I have seen gardeners grow the exact same vegetable in the same spot year after year. I have done so myself in the case of corn and peas. However, there appears to be evidence to support the claim that many insect and disease pests will accumulate in an area if the host vegetable appears in the same place each year. Also, since the different "families" of vegetables have different needs as to feeding requirements, it would seem to make sense to do some occasional rotation. By "families" is meant the heavy feeders, including cabbage, squash, corn and tomatoes; the light feeders, which covers all the root crops; and the legumes, which are the peas and beans.

I would recommend not more than three years for a vegetable in the same location.

9. *Are there any good publications available dealing strictly with vegetable gardening?*

Answer: If you are not already getting it, I'd suggest a trial subscription to "Organic Gardening and Farming." Write to Subscription Department, Emmaus, Penna.

10. *What can one do to maintain enthusiasm toward growing vegetables year after year?*

Answer: This will not be much of a problem if you have resolved in the beginning to give the garden the care it does require. Success with vegetables is like success in anything—enthusiasm tends to be perpetuated by positive results.

Don't take anyone's word as gospel (including mine) for what is the best variety of a vegetable. Chances are that every one of the available types is *somebody's* favorite.

Each year try one or two of the more unusual vegetables not grown in your garden before. This will provide something new to look forward to and hold your enthusiasm.

One final suggestion: keep a notebook. Without keeping a written record, it is just about impossible to carry over to the next year all you have learned from the current growing season. No matter how faithfully you follow directions and suggestions in this and other gardening books, there are bound to be a few disappointments, even for the well-seasoned gardener. If you have made a record of the problem, with your assessment of the cause and cure, you will be that much less likely to encounter the same difficulty twice. Note also dates of last spring frost, first fall frost, planting and harvesting dates of each vegetable, and whatever else you feel will aid you later on.

Good luck, and good gardening!

NOTES

NOTES

NOTES

NOTES

NOTES

NOTES

NOTES

NOTES

NOTES

NOTES

NOTES

NOTES

NOTES

NOTES

NOTES

NOTES

NOTES